Wayne Wetherill
from Peggy and Ernest
Christmas - 1948.

CHINATOWN FAMILY

BOOKS BY LIN YUTANG
Published by The John Day Company

MY COUNTRY AND MY PEOPLE

THE IMPORTANCE OF LIVING

MOMENT IN PEKING

WITH LOVE AND IRONY

A LEAF IN THE STORM

BETWEEN TEARS AND LAUGHTER

THE VIGIL OF A NATION

THE GAY GENIUS: THE LIFE AND TIMES OF SU TUNGPO

CHINATOWN FAMILY

CHINATOWN FAMILY

a novel by

LIN YUTANG

The John Day Company

NEW YORK

CHINATOWN FAMILY

Chapter 1

ꞏꙄꞏꙄꞏꙄꞏꙄꞏꙄꞏꙄꞏꙄꞏꙄ

I

TOM LAY IN BED, HIS LIMBS TIRED AND all the muscles of his body sweetly relaxed, ready to fall asleep on this memorable first night after his arrival in America. His mother had just clicked off the switch triumphantly, and the light of the globe hanging over the middle of the bed had gone out, leaving for a second a streak of liver red that danced across his eyes. His toes hurt slightly, pleasantly, a new sensation for Tom. He did not often have new shoes, whether leather or cloth, and his father had bought him that day a new pair that cost three dollars and twenty-five cents and had insisted on his putting them on. The nerves across his arches tingled, and his ankles felt stiff, but from the middle of his heel came a sensation that really hurt.

He was drowsy, as a boy of thirteen can be healthily drowsy after a day of excitement. He wanted to sleep. His sister Eva, one year younger, was lying beside him. As he turned on his mattress and let his fingers fall curled on the edge of the bed, he saw the moon above the jagged, square, unfamiliar roofs of the houses across the avenue. For a time, his bed seemed to rock as if he were still on the ship which had docked that morning. He had not been seasick, as Eva had been, but the swaying motion of his bed continued. The moon seemed to swing in the sky, but when he opened his eyes wide, it stood still over the rooftops. Then he knew he was on land in a strange city in a strange country.

He had eaten too much that day, a Chinese lunch followed by a Chinese dinner, after being starved on the freighter for forty-five days. His mind was dim and a little giddy, and only the recollection remained of the swallowing of mouthfuls of inexhaustible rice, oiled by rich gravy and voluptuous hunks of bean curd fried in fat. The sleepy feeling crept over him, dark, sweet, and tender.

But Eva was awake.

"Are you asleep?" she whispered.

"Yes, I am."

"No, you are not."

Eva moved to rise from the bed. The mattress rolled and rocked again.

"What are you doing?" Tom asked.

He saw Eva's shape tiptoe across the room.

Click, click! Click, click! The light over his head went on and off three times.

"Oh, Eva!"

Giggling and triumphant, Eva jumped into bed again and pulled the sheet over her.

From across the room came the old father's voice. "Children, stop playing with the light. It is electricity!" The Cantonese word, *tin,* had a heavy thumping tone—*"Hai tinnn!"*

It was electricity! Momentous word in Tom's mind, symbolic of all that was new and marvelous in this new world of miracles. The brother and sister had been playing with the switch in the afternoon. Tom had scrutinized the crisscross pattern of the filaments; he had known electric light in Canton and on the ship, but they had not had it at home and the wonder never ceased. He knew he was going to explore that incomprehensible marvel someday; just now he only wanted to understand that nice, neat infallible click. Tom was very im-

4

pressionable; he liked to puzzle things out for himself, things that didn't puzzle Eva. His father had said, "It is electricity," pronouncing the word with great respect. Electricity was lightning, and he had lightning over his bed. The thought was tremendously exciting.

Out of the silence of the night there had come at regular intervals a mad rushing sound that boomed and rumbled past the bedroom window and rocketed into the dark distance. As the sound approached, the rails wailed like demons in the night, the windowpanes shook, and he saw a succession of bizarre lighted train windows rush by in orderly procession, and then he heard the wheels of the Third Avenue El train screech to a halt at the Eighty-fourth Street station.

A train flying in midair before his window! Tom was fully awake now. The noise did not surprise him. He had had a few notions about America before he came to this country. America was a country made all of machines, and machines were of course noisy, and, Tom reasoned, America should be noisy and full of that rushing motion, speeding motion, going somewhere—click—stopping—click—progress—click, click! What puzzled him was something else, something that left him no rest. He got up and peered down from the window. It was unbelievable. How could a flying demon with carloads of people be supported on such thin steel pillars? That was the miracle for Tom. A flying train whizzing in mid-air supported on matchsticks. Tom scratched his head. He wanted so much to know.

As he looked up, he saw men and women in their nightclothes, men with bald heads and women with almost bare bosoms, leaning on cushions and pillows out of the windows across the street.

He went back to bed. It was hot, noisy, strange, and all tremendous and wonderful. Eva was asleep already. His head was heavy, and his stomach was full.

The next thing he knew it was already morning.

5

"What do you think of Father?" whispered Eva, at the first movement Tom made in his bed. Tom was still in slumber. She shook him. "What do you think of Father?"

"What?" Tom rubbed his eyes. Without thinking, he knew that something good, something wonderful and exciting had happened to him. Then the realization that he was in the United States of America, in famous, fabulous New York, darted into his consciousness. He jumped up. "I am in New York! I am in New York!" It was like saying he was in Wonderland.

"Do you like Father?" asked Eva again.

"I like him," said Tom. "Isn't it strange to have a father?"

"It is not strange. He is our father," protested Eva.

"But it is strange to have a father."

"Don't you like the feeling of it?" Eva always greatly respected Tom's opinions.

"Yes, the feeling is nice. It's like having a double roof. You've got a roof already, and you get another roof. It's nice."

"He works so hard for us," said Eva. "We didn't know."

Of the two, Tom was a little whiter and more slender. Eva, though still a child, had a more prominent jaw and cheekbones and a rather flat bony forehead above her little shining eyes. Her simple, direct smile and her queue made her look like a doll.

Tom had not seen his father since infancy, and Eva had not seen him since she was born. The "father" in their minds was a dream, a legend, a reality so remote that it was unreal.

In good years and bad, the father had sent them money. Family legends told that he had come to the United States with the Alaska gold rush. San Francisco was known to all Cantonese back home as Old Gold Mountain, and to the overseas Chinese in America as the Great Port. Their father had sent home what were called "gold dollars." What Cantonese villager on the south coast—in Toishan, Sunwei, Fanyu—had not heard of the gold country? The plain fact was that villagers whose sons were in America received remittances, had savings and could buy farms, and those who did not could not. Some had built "foreign houses" in Canton.

Twice had Tom Fong, Sr., gone home to China, to stay for little more than a year, and then had returned to America to earn more foreign gold.

But ever since the children had known anything, their father had been in New York. The fact that New York was not Old Gold Mountain did not make any difference—across the fabled Pacific, the two points merged in the distance. There were village legends that the Chinese were mobbed, robbed, killed, and many were driven out of the West Coast, and it was a family legend that their father, Tom Fong, Sr., had escaped to the East Coast after some thrilling adventures. But that was long ago; these stories always sounded like pirate tales. The fact remained that Tom Fong, Sr., survived, and that, year after year, he and the other villagers' sons continued to send gold dollars home to support parents, brothers, and wives and to send their nephews to school. It was a story of survival; it was success; it was struggle triumphant.

On and on the villagers' sons came, and the immigration officials were merely obstacles Heaven placed in the path of men determined to achieve success with patience and persistence. The immigration difficulties were nothing to laugh at, but you laugh at them when you have nothing to lose.

Look at Tom's second elder brother, Yiko. He had come as a seaman at the age of sixteen and jumped ship, and now he was Frederick A. T. Fong, Insurance Agent, representative of Cornelius United States Underwriters! The Department of Justice didn't know. Why it should be the business of the Department of Justice, Washington, D.C., to know his whereabouts, Frederick A. T. Fong never quite figured out. Frederick A. T. Fong always added Washington, D.C., when he mentioned the Department of Justice. He was friendly to everybody, and when he met an American, he always said, "I am Frederick A. T. Fong," without waiting to be introduced.

So while Tom and Eva grew up in their village in Sunwei, their eldest brother Daiko and the second brother Yiko were living with their father in New York. The family was neatly divided into two halves, one earning and the other spending. The mother was one roof, a perfect roof, for Tom and his sister, and the father provided the other roof. Now the two halves were united, and the two roofs overlapped.

To the younger children, the father had been a mystical entity. From all the evidences—the family letters that arrived about once in six months, sometimes at longer intervals; the drafts that usually came with them, especially when the New Year was drawing near; and the trips Tom sometimes made to town with his mother when the letters arrived and the amazing fact that the bank gave them real money when presented with that not too elaborate piece of paper—from all these evidences Tom was willing to conclude that the mystical entity existed, as Christians conclude from the rain and snow and birds and flowers that God exists. His father's letters were always brief and not very communicative. It was either times were good or times were bad, and "enclosed you will find a draft for——."

There were other evidences of the existence of the father. In the first place, the mother believed in him. In the second place, her own brother, Tom's Uncle Chan, was in New York, too. Uncle Chan did not live on Olympian heights, hidden in the clouds; he made his presence felt in their home across the seas; his letters were more frequent and more chatty, even loquacious; real things were happening in New York. It was from one of Uncle Chan's letters that the people at home learned of the dramatic marriage of the eldest son Daiko to an Italian girl named Flora. Tom's father had not thought the fact even worth mentioning. In the third place, there was another old man, also by the name of Fong, now over sixty, who had comfortably settled down in their home village after a lifetime in America and who told Tom, the inquisitive child, about things and customs in the United States, on which the old man was the unquestioned authority.

One of the unforgettable stories old Fong told was that in America there are restaurants without waiters where you put a nickel in a slot and, click, a whole chicken, roasted and brown, sprang into view. Nobody of course questioned such an authority. He would be offended if anybody did. He made a tremendous impression on Tom.

"And turkey?"

"Yes, and turkey. A whole big turkey."

Tom's mouth watered.

"You see what you want through a glass and put in the nickel, and out it jumps. Yes, Amelicans are clever. You go to Amelica when you grow up."

Tom, of course, had wanted to come to "Amelica." He wanted very much to. All the ancient stories about the killings and muggings of the railroad men could not scare him. All the tales about the big bugaboo, the Yiminkeok (Immigration Bureau), and its quiet, absurd tactics stimulated the boy's imagination. What was this Yiminkeok but a lot of officials? By the universally accepted dictum in China officials were a pest to the people anyway. They were no different from the Chinese officials he knew. Why should they be? So long as you have a relative in America you don't have to worry. An official may be an official, but a relative is a relative.

Tom Fong, Sr., had wanted his family to come. For ten long years he had been wanting them. But it was not easy. If his family should come across the continent by railroad, the traveling expenses of three people would come close to a thousand dollars. When was he going to earn and save so much money from his laundry? Some years ago, when he thought he had saved enough to send for his family, his bank had failed. Business was bad; fewer people sent their laundry. Those who remained his customers no longer sent their underwear, those who sent shirts seemed to change their shirts once instead of twice a week, and there was much work and little money in sheets. He lowered his prices; he worked long hours (heaven be thanked that there was no law against that!); he stood on his legs and sweated until eleven in the night; and he put all his money in a little cloth parcel inside a steel cabinet locked and hidden in a lower drawer. He had lost faith in all banks. He once prayed for delivery to come from fan-tan and was rewarded with the vision of winning two hundred dollars and then, in the hope of achieving all of his ambition, lost it all again. Thereafter he played moderately, but as a relaxation, not as a means of bringing his family over. But he continued to spend ten dollars systematically every year to take chances on the Irish sweepstakes.

A stroke of good fortune came in the person of his second son, who was beginning to do well as an insurance agent. Generous soul that he was, he handed over one day a check for five hundred dollars, his first savings, and said to his father, "Here, take this and send for Mother and the young children. Tell them Yiko sent the money. I know you want Mother here. It is all in the family."

Something stirred very deep in Tom senior's heart when he heard his son's offer, so deep that it took a long time for his feeling to come to the surface. The armor of patience and strength that he had worn for years had been pierced, and all his muscles relaxed. Slowly a contracted smile found its way to his face, and beads of moisture formed in his eyes. He was so touched that he could not say a word. He merely wiped his eyes. They seemed to say, "I appreciate it, my son. I have wanted very much to have your mother come."

With the money kept severely untouched in the bank, Tom's mother planned to go. For herself, she would rather have remained in China. The arrangement of living as the head of the family back home had been perfect for Mother Fong, and going at her age to America, where the language and customs were so strange, was hardly a pleasant prospect. But she wanted it for Tom and Eva, and there was unanimity of opinion in the family and great excitement among the children. They were not able to go until after the grandmother died. How long this was going to be nobody could tell. Leaving her alone would of course be outrageous, and they were willing to wait. But it could not be very long; Grandmother was in her eighties. Tom secretly wished it would happen soon and then blushed at the thought. But when Tom was thirteen, his grandmother died and was properly buried, and so they came.

No, it was not easy. There were those immigration officials, and there were immigration laws, laws made, it seemed, especially to keep Chinese out of America, or to let in as few as possible. But Chinese are used to officials and know of old that there are ways to get around laws. Yiko's way had been to jump ship. But a mother and her children could not do that. Neither could they be floated ashore in barrels on the California coast or smuggled across the Mexican border. A laundry-man certainly could not bring his family into the country legally. But a merchant could if the children were not yet twenty-one years old. And Uncle Chan was a merchant, with a fine busy grocery store in Chinatown. Uncle Chan was glad to help to bring his sister and her children over.

So the legal procedures were taken to make Tom Fong joint owner of the grocery store with Uncle Chan. Thus in the somewhat blinking eyes of the law, Tom Fong became a merchant. Both he and Uncle Chan knew that this was a temporary expedient, to satisfy the law. It was irregular. But the thing was done.

Tom senior's eyes had come to have a softer look in the last months. His hair, clipped evenly at the back, was already whitish gray. But when you looked at his face, there was not a record to tell what he had gone through, and only a few deep wrinkles across the corners of his mouth told of a healthy maturing old age. He had high cheekbones, narrow eyes, and a long upper lip drawn sharply downward at the sides, so that it was sometimes hard to judge whether he was serious, or displeased, or about to smile, or just being contented. That downward-curved upper lip concealed a whole load of emotions seldom expressed. It also expressed patience and endurance as if it was saying, "We shall see who has the last laugh." He had always been a silent man with a good strong constitution. The few words he spoke to his eldest son, whom he called Loy, were about business details. Some days late in the afternoon, to Loy's surprise, he would say in his throaty voice, "Le's go Chatam Squay." Then Loy knew they were going to have a good dinner at a restaurant in a basement in Chinatown and come back to work until eleven or twelve.

Father and son ironed and ironed and ironed deep into the night, silently and contentedly, in the room and a half in the basement of the house in a crosstown street in the Eighties. Outside was a red sign marked in big white characters, TOM FONG HAND LAUNDRY. There was not such a thing as a "hand laundry" any more, but the tradition persisted and was properly conformed to. The short stocky figure of the father, with its powerful shoulders, and the thinner taller figure of the young man moved about under the white glow of hundred-watt lamps like silent robots.

It was a good little world, safe and peaceful and without problems, except that once in a while old Fong would ask Loy discreetly, "When am I going to have a grandchild?"

"Don't know."

"What's the matter with Flora?"

There the conversation always ended.

The problems of the laundry were simple. They were making an honest living. They had enough customers and everybody paid his bills. Their one purpose was to deliver clean laundry, quick laundry, and get paid in return. There were no employee problems, no union. Every minute they spent at the large ironing board meant more nickels. It was just like picking up nickels from the street. There was no limit to what they could earn except sheer physical exhaustion. The father at almost sixty was stronger than the young man. Often he would tell his son, "Loy, you go to bed," and go on working himself. When Flora was there, helping with the packing and the accounts, he always asked them to go to bed early. He had his own idea about heredity—a strong grandchild could not come from a weakened mother.

So it was a simple world. Nobody could do anything to them. In the final analysis that was why Tom Fong called "Amelica" a good country. It was a wonderful thing, peace. They wanted to be left alone, and they were left alone. The Chinese government did nothing to him, and he did nothing to the Chinese government. The United States government did nothing to him, and he did nothing to the United States government. The New York police had nothing to do with him, and he had nothing to do with the police. He loved China as one loves one's own parents, but to him China was a community of people rather than a state—a community of people bound by common beliefs and customs.

Around him lived Czechs, Greeks, Italians, Jews, Germans, Austrians. He did not understand the arrogant sovereignties of nations. All of these were people intent on making a living for their families. More by necessity than by conviction, the Chinese since Manchu days learned that every son of China abroad had to look out for himself, almost like people traveling on Nansen passports. You would be surprised how you could get along without a thing called the state if you are a peaceful citizen. If you are a thug or a gangster, your home government can't do anything to protect you anyway. So on this pattern of free-lancing and self-governing individualism, Tom Fong had drifted to New York as hundreds of thousands of his brothers had penetrated Arkansas and Illinois and Lima and Cape Town and Dresden and Marseille. In 1847 a Chinese traveler recorded meetings with his compatriots on the island of St. Helena. It was conclusively proved that government protection was unnecessary.

But individuals were different. Flora, for instance. When Flora wanted to marry Loy and Loy wanted to marry Flora, the father said in characteristic American fashion, "Okay," which meant he couldn't do a thing about it, for Flora was a woman and one woman was like another. Chinese girls were scarce in New York; why should his son not marry a woman? Flora was foreign, but she had pretty eyelashes and a small mouth with very even teeth. Her breasts were good, which is an important test for maternity. So the old father said "okay." He knew how badly he himself needed Loy's mother, though he never gave anyone an inkling of his sacrifice in exile until that day when his second son gave him the check and saw how deeply he had missed the mother.

Flora, being an American woman, was demonstrative. When an American woman was happy, she had to be demonstratively happy, and when an American woman was thankful, she had to be demonstratively thankful. When an American woman was in love, she was terribly demonstratively in love. There was strength in reserve and danger in demonstrativeness. How does a reservoir become a reservoir except by being dammed up? The father put down many of Flora's ways as Americanisms. But when Flora, in the full view and presence of the austere father, kissed his son while at work, it was one of those things you would expect to happen but refuse to expect to happen, but which had now happened. Loy was annoyingly undemonstrative when Flora kissed him. But looking at his son, the father felt that he could not be sure Flora would continue to love Loy, but Loy would continue to love Flora always.

Flora was only twenty-two, and she had dark passionate eyes, with long lashes such as only a white woman could have. Her skin was not as good as a Chinese woman's, and her forearms were covered with visible hair. Thin and slim, her face was set off by beautiful dark tresses, which made it all very womanly as far as the father's judgment of womanliness was concerned. Some one had told the father about the deeply passionate Italian women. A deeply passionate woman may be interpreted as one with many husbands or one with many children. Father Fong hoped it was the latter. Her love for his son was shown in many ways, in her good cheer and willingness to help in the shop, in her trying as far as she could to like Chinese ways, and above all, her sharing and liking their Chinese food. On this last important point there was luckily no conflict, and the bedrock of international democracy seemed, in the present instance, to be secure. More international marriages have been wrecked on badly done lamb chops than on differences of a strictly national character.

4

When Tom and Eva saw the Statue of Liberty as the small Panama-registered freighter pulled into New York harbor, the sight of that goddess and of the skyscrapers was not new to them. They had seen these structures on post cards and the screen many times, but now they were in the round. You felt you could reach your fingers behind them, which was not the case with a post-card picture. Yet some of that picture effect still remained. It is like seeing a movie actress in person. She seems to have stepped down bodily from the screen, but she still talks as she does on the screen, and you still don't think her quite real. Eva looked and looked at the skyscrapers, afraid that the dream picture might at any time dissolve and vanish. She turned round several times and looked again, and each time the skyscrapers were still there.

On the wharf to receive them were Father Fong, Daiko and his wife Flora, Yiko (Frederick A. T. Fong), and Uncle Chan. Yiko was the prominent one, in a handsome bright-blue suit with a carnation in his lapel. He was not only the tallest and biggest of them all, he was responsible for producing the cash that brought the family over and was consequently in every sense a "big brother." He had seen the younger brother and sister only seven or eight years ago, whereas Daiko hadn't. He was happy that he was somebody in Chinatown. Out of respect for this great occasion, he had put on a black bow tie.

Without the knowledge of Daiko and his father, Frederick A. T. Fong did something that upset and embarrassed the mother greatly. He had brought a photographer. When the mother walked down the plank, followed by the young children, he went up and planted a kiss on her, while embracing her affectionately. There was a flash. Mother Fong could have swooned.

After the exciting exclamations and bewildering questions and mutual wonderment when the two halves of the family were united after a separation of twelve years, Yiko wanted a group photograph taken of this memorable occasion. The father and mother really should sit down, but there were no chairs on the wharf. Flora, standing beside Daiko on one side, put on a brave smile, but she was still inwardly shy. Uncle Chan, as one of the three elders, was also in the center. He was in his forties. He had put on his best Sunday suit, which was black alpaca, very shiny from use. The surface of his protruded, fat-filled, tensely rounded belly, the most important portion of his anatomy, gleamed like the identical part of a seal. His dark round head, his few thin whiskers, his shining skin, and his swaying motion all contributed to the impression of a seal. Yiko, standing at the other end behind Tom and Eva, putting his hands widespread on the two children's shoulders, with the carnation and his forward-looking smile, seemed to protect his younger brother and sister under his invisible wings.

The mother, a woman of fifty, with a strong, square face, had not yet recovered from the filial but highly unclassical embrace.

"Ah-Tong, whatever you took that picture for?" she said in Cantonese to Frederick, revealing thus the name for which A. T. was the mysterious symbol and which the owner scarcely would care to have discussed. He was Freddy on the amiable social level, Frederick on the legal, professional, check-signing level, and Ah-Tong to his parents.

"Why, it's for the Chinese papers," he replied. Chinatown was going to see how Frederick, the devoted son, welcomed his mother to the New York shore. It was these moments that counted. The American Indians greeting the *Mayflower* were the subject of a historic painting.

"*Sei-lo! Sei-lo!*" sighed the mother. It was not enough that her son should kiss her but that the disgraceful moment should be published and immortalized! It was against all sense of womanly decency.

From that moment there was no peace among the party in the taxi until Daiko intimated that Yiko could keep the picture from being published and all agreed that he should. This was about the time they reached the Tom Fong Hand Laundry.

5

Things are never what they seem. The little rathole of a shop on a cross street near the corner of Third Avenue was a great disappointment to Tom and Eva and even to the mother. But it was not a rathole. It was a gold mine where the father and Daiko had made enough money for them to buy their farm in

Sunwei. Tom had had visions of a spic-and-span shop, all American style, crowded with hundreds of American customers, all talking the gibberish that was English. The basement shop was now closed. Tom tried to read the sign. He recognized the words Tom Fong. The next lines were still beyond his comprehension. They said, "Quick and clean. Try and convince."

Flora had at once taken a fancy to Tom. He pointed at the sign and asked Flora what it said. She merely smiled, for she knew only a few Cantonese words. Yiko answered for her.

"Convince means *seong sun,* like believe."

"What is believe?" asked Tom, gobbling up the new words.

"Believe means *seong sun.*"

"Why not say believe?"

"Oh, convince is a fine word. You say, I convince, much better than I believe."

It was the first English word Tom learned in New York.

The shop was in an antiquated three-story gray house, sandwiched between two red-brick four-story buildings. A staircase from the pavement led up to a dark hallway, through a door opened by buzz control. The family's home was on the top floor, consisting of three rooms and a very spacious kitchen overlooking a yard that was empty but for some clotheslines. The two children headed for the roof as soon as they discovered there was a staircase leading up to it. On the left were the backs of the houses on Third Avenue. Through a window Tom saw a woman in pink working in a kitchen and in another house, on the fourth floor, a girl was looking out of a window, her chin cupped in her hands resting on the window sill. Nevertheless, the yard gave a feeling of seclusion and peace. Their section of the yard, like the others, was enclosed by faded, discolored board partitions. A scraggy elm in the neighbor's yard on the right managed to breathe through its few branches of leaves. From the roof, Tom could come within a few feet of the leaves, and the roof was all their own. It was good and peaceful, and the sun was shining in the yard, and Tom was content.

6

Flora's heart had beaten fast when she went with her husband to receive her mother-in-law. In fact, her heart had started to palpitate some months ago when she learned that the China half of the family was coming. Loy had instructed her about the position of the mother in a Chinese family and had in a general way assured her that everything would be all right. His mother was a woman of great good sense, and why should not the young respect the old? It wasn't as if she hadn't met the family at all. But living with her husband and father-in-law was different; it was fairly simple, and Yiko led quite an independent existence. To live with her mother-in-law and the newly large family was another thing.

There had been considerable excitement about the arrangement of the rooms. Yiko had decided for himself that he wanted to take a room in Chinatown since there was not enough room for all. There was no question that the young children were to sleep in the room facing the street since that was the brightest and was to be the family sitting room. Besides, young children wouldn't mind the noise of the El. The two inside rooms opening on the narrow hallway were dark and stuffy, with single windows facing toward a brick wall one and a half feet away, but these rooms were quiet at night. There had been considerable discussion as to which was to be the mother-in-law's and which the daughter-in-law's room. One had a bath, the other only a washbasin. Flora had wished she could have the back room with the bath, but she had not said so.

Obviously, it could not be decided until the mother-in-law had arrived. When the question was put to the mother, she quickly replied, "You young people, you take the room with the tub. What do I need a tub for? All my life I have got along with a basin, and it is such a pretty white enamel basin, too. Besides, I want to be near the children." It was curious how such a little incident could sometimes be fraught with drama and deepest emotion. There were tears in Flora's eyes. The words "oh, Mother!" involuntarily escaped her lips. She did not realize that it was the first time she had called her "mother."

"Now, Tom and Abwa, wash," the mother commanded.

Mrs. Fong was an amazing woman. She had taken everything in at a glance. She had been disappointed at the puny shop, but she was not going to cry over it. Her mind was silently busy with a thousand things—family finance, this house, Flora, and the children—though she had not said a word. Foreign country or no foreign country, she knew this was her home, this her family, and she was responsible for all of them. One of her acts of unpacking as soon as she had gone through the house was to take out Tom's and Eva's toothbrushes and towels and put them near the kitchen sink. Tom had been his name even back in Canton; he used to be called *Shiu* Tom, or Little Tom, in honor of his father. Eva received her English name much later through a long evolution—Ahwa—Apwa—Abwa—Abva—Eva.

"Where shall we wash, Mother?" cried Eva.

"In the kitchen."

Tom and Eva obediently went, and the duty of washing themselves soon changed into the exciting game of turning the hot and cold faucets off and on and testing the little spray attachment and holding their hands under the spray to get a sweet tingle. They were lost in it for ten exciting minutes and came away with their clothes all wet across the chests.

"My, what have you done?" said their mother, her eyes resting fondly on the young boy. "And water costs money."

"No, it doesn't," said Tom. "Eva was told."

By a long series of circumstantial evidence, it became established that water was free, both cold and hot. Tom was told by Eva, who was told by Daiko, and the fact was finally referred to Flora, the authority on America, and further confirmed by the father.

"Washing is going to be easy," said the mother. "But it doesn't mean you have to be wasteful." Secretly she was reconciled to America.

Tom and Eva were now installed in the front room, which used to be Yiko's room, and as was to be expected, it was a little bizarre. On one side of the room, where the bed was, were a pair of red scrolls and a picture of George Washington gazing out of the corner of his eyes at a Chinese calendar exhibiting a colored print of a Chinese bathing girl, full length, clothed in a transparent veil of gauze, whose sweet eyes and enchanting smile were directed at George Washington in return. On the opposite side of the room was an enlarged portrait of the deceased grandfather, flanked by a multiplicity of pictures, mostly of the social and political activities of Yiko. One subject received particular attention in the form of a gilt frame, and that was Yiko shaking hands with a New York senator during an election campaign. Yiko had disappeared soon after they arrived because he had to attend to his office, and he was not there to explain. There were also clippings from Sunday magazines, of some half-naked women that Yiko liked, and that could not be removed without being torn. On the wall facing the street window was a print of a portrait of Sun Yat-sen under the national flags of the two sister republics, the Country of the Flowery Flag (the United States) and the Central Flowery Republic of China.

The room hurt the mother's sense of propriety on two scores. A Chinese bathing beauty on a colored calendar was an accepted thing in a Chinese village, but the pictures from Sunday magazines were obscene. Tom was assigned the task of removing those American beauties from the wall, a work that he did with a great deal of wonderment.

But the whole arrangement of the room was wrong. It had no sense of symmetry. Where were the seats of honor if a guest were to come in? So with Uncle Chan's help, the grandfather's portrait on the right and the red scrolls on the left were transferred to the central wall, looking appropriately and squarely toward the street. A table was placed exactly in the center under the grandfather's portrait, and two hard chairs were placed there, which were to be the seats of honor.

Uncle Chan had been wonderful. He had helped in lugging trunks and tables and chairs. He spun and rolled when he was moving the luggage, and it seemed to Tom that he could stretch or shrink his neck like rubber. When he was standing still, his two hands hung at his sides as if he were performing a balancing act.

When everything was over, Uncle Chan fell on Tom's and Eva's bed and began to snore peacefully, while Tom went to the window and took up his position from which he was to watch the fascinating world of his growing years go by. Across the street were a printing shop, a pet shop, and at the corner a bar. The rest were a series of neat, clean-looking five- and six-story gray- and red-brick houses. Only thirty feet away on the avenue loomed the dark steel trusses and bars of the Interborough Rapid Transit Elevated Railroad, with its lurching trains moving swiftly past his corner, carrying passengers seated at their windows. Tom was satisfied.

Chapter 2

I

TOM AND EVA TOOK SEVERAL WEEKS TO get used to the feeling of having a father. Tom had seen photographs of his father, of course, but to live with a man called his father was a different thing. The photograph was taken years ago when his father was younger. He was dressed in a coat and stiff collar and tie, holding in his hand a cane with a gold band. It somehow did not quite fit with this mental picture to see him working in his shirt sleeves, his head bent under the strong light of the blue-white globe, his broad shoulders casting big moving shadows as he stood ironing. After the first few days, Tom thought he could come down to help, but there was hardly room for him in that narrow basement shop. His father did not speak much to him, and somehow seemed distant to Tom. But his father's voice seemed rich and manly when he did speak to him. It seemed that the father took many days to know this youngest son of his. "Tom, you go out and play with Eva," was all he said.

But it did not take long to re-establish the dignity of the fatherhood of Tom Fong, Sr. The first week Tom and Eva found out what having a father meant.

"It is ten o'clock," said Tom's mother. "Tom, go down and ask your father to come up. I would not have an old man work that late."

23

"And shall I ask Daiko to stop, too?"

"He can work if he wants to."

When the father came up and was washing, it was Eva's job to place his slippers squarely before his bed. The mother always filled a basin with warm water for him and placed a towel and soap ready as if they were still in China, where providing a basin of hot water was a housewife's job when the husband came home. The mother always saw to it that the water was already turned on and the basin was clean, and that a pot of hot tea stood ready on the end table beside his armchair in the sitting room. In short, the coming upstairs of father at night was always a signal for certain petty household activities. It was the way the mother pronounced the word father that made it sound so solemn and important.

There were days when the father lay stretched on his bed, and Tom knelt beside him to tap his back and shoulders and waist as a form of massage. Clearly the mother was pampering him and changing him into a respectable old man. He had never needed a massage, but after he had had it, he admitted that five minutes of such tapping was very comforting and relaxing. The mother had shown Tom how to do it, with both hands curled closed and the arm held relaxed and flexible at the wrist so that the edge of the palm tapped the muscles like a rubber cushion. As the bed was low, Tom found the kneeling position the best. The first feeling of physical contact in tapping the shoulder blades and waist of a man who was his father was something Tom never forgot. Tom was good at it, and very soon he heard his father say to the mother when she was massaging him, "You are clumsy. Let Tom do it. A child's hand is nimbler."

Seated in the armchair in the evening after his work, with the bracket light above his head and a pot of tea at his right, Tom Fong, Sr., seemed a different person. Only Daiko and Yiko knew how great the change was.

The mother had provided the tea, Eva the slippers. The

mother was sitting as always, upright on one of the hard chairs. The children were ready to listen to what their father said. The father was lighting a five-cent cigar, his face relaxed and contented. Flora came in, unwrapped a package in her hand, and slipped a lamp shade over the light bulb. Turning around to the father and mother, she asked, "Do you like that?"

The mother went close to examine the shade. The children rushed to see.

"How do you put it on?" asked the mother, and the father translated.

"Just slip it on."

Flora showed how it was done, and the family was amazed.

"How much does it cost?"

"Ten cents," replied Flora.

The mother smiled. "It is pretty," she said. She looked around and continued. "But the room looks darker. It is a pity when we can have such a bright room that you can see a pin on the floor. With the shade on, now you can hardly see Grandfather's portrait. But it is pretty." The father translated again.

"It is prettier this way," remarked Flora. "The light is easier for the eye."

The mother surveyed the wall. "It does not look right. It lacks balance. There is no light on the other side of the portrait. How much will it cost to have another lamp on that side?"

"Fifty cents for the bracket, and ten cents for the bulb."

"Well, get another lamp for that side," said the mother. "Where will you get this so cheap?"

"At the five-and-ten-cent store on Eighty-sixth Street. We get everything there. Tell Mother to go and see it."

The father explained, but the mother said, "No, let Flora get it. I don't dare to go out yet."

"Go down to the shop, Flora," said the father. "Tell Loy to stop if he wants to. Tomorrow come, we iron again."

"Well, Tom and Eva," he said when Flora was gone. "You are now in America. How do you like it?" The father could trill the *r* after more than thirty years' stay in this country. It was his pride that he could say "America."

Tom and Eva were sitting on their bed.

"We like it very much, Father."

"You wanted to come, and now you are here. What do you want to do?"

"We want to go to school," said Eva.

"That I know. You go to school, a good school. In America you have school free. That is why I wanted you to come. What do you want to do when you grow up?"

Tom looked at Eva, and Eva looked at Tom.

"I don't know, Father," replied Tom.

"You don't want to do laundry?"

"No, Father."

"Is not laundry a good way to make a living?"

"No, Father. I don't want to be ironing all day, and I don't want to bother with women's clothes."

"What is wrong with women's clothes?" protested Eva.

"Women should wash women's clothes. I am a man," replied Tom. "Besides, I think women should wash men's clothes. Isn't that right, Father?"

Eva's eyes looked straight at Tom. She counted it one against him, but she said nothing.

"It is like this," said the father. "You wash clothes and are paid for it, whether you wash men's or women's clothing. It is a living."

"I shall charge more for washing women's clothes if I have to do it."

"And women should charge more for washing men's!" Eva suddenly cried because she could not restrain herself.

The parents smiled. "Well, Tom, that was what I was going to talk to you about. I don't want you to do laundry like Daiko. Daiko and Yiko had no chance for schooling. Now you, Tom and Abwa, can go to school. You, Tom, will not be a laundry-man like your father. You should think about it."

"What about Abwa?" Tom asked.

"Abwa is a girl. She will go to school, and then she will marry. If she marries a millionaire, she will be a millionaire. If she marries a grocer, she will be a grocer. If she marries a doctor, she will be in medicine. This is so in China or America."

"But, Father, why did you choose laundry?" asked Tom.

"I did not choose, son. And it is not bad as you can see. I have made a living, and now we are all here. There was no other way. All you have is a pair of hands, and you do what the Americans do not want to do and allow you to do. When they built the railroads in the West, there were no women there. Those American men! They could not cook, and they could not wash. We Chinese cooked and washed better, so they allowed us to cook and wash. Now we wash America and cook America because we wash better and cook better. I would have opened a restaurant if I had the money. Now you go to school, and you can be a doctor, lawyer, engineer. Henry Lee has a son who graduated from a Tech in Boston, and he is a bridge engineer. You can be anything you want to be and are good for. That is America, because they give you school free, and nobody bothers as long as you are honest, and you can be what you want. You want to be engineer, you are engineer. You want to be bad laundryman, you are bad laundryman. You want to be drunkard, you are drunkard. America is a free country."

"Can I be what I want to be?" asked Eva.

"No, you marry. You are free to marry. That is the freedom the American women get. But they do not get much help from their parents. They have to go and pick husbands for them-selves."

Eva, though she was only twelve, blushed and giggled.

That night Tom and Eva lay in bed and thought of all they wanted to be and were a little confused.

"I thought that in America men and women were equal," whispered Eva.

"You heard what Father said. We men pick our professions, and you women pick your husbands and leave it all to us. You ought to be satisfied with that."

Eva was a little mortified. "It is like China then," she said, greatly disappointed, and fell asleep.

2

Mother Fong had surveyed the situation and collected notes in her head. Many things were needed for the house and for the children. She had arrived with one hundred and fifty dollars in her pocket, for she had sold some of their property when she left. She could take out thirty or forty dollars to buy things. After all it was a new home, and Tom and Eva needed to have new outfits. They would not need overcoats yet; that could come in the autumn. But they had to have dresses, shirts, socks, shoes. She could afford to be a little extravagant. Flora knew a shop for children's clothes at the corner of Eighty-seventh and Third Avenue. There things could be had for cheaper prices, and there was the W. T. Grant store nearby. But they needed pillowcases and towels, and Eva said she needed a hairbrush like the one Flora had.

"We need more towels," Flora suggested.

"What towels? Isn't one face towel for each person enough?"

"I mean hand towels and a few more bath towels."

"You mean those things you wipe once and throw to the floor as they do on the ship!"

"I have never been on a ship. I guess that's what it is."

All this was carried on through the medium of Daiko's interpretation.

"*Hai-lo, hai-lo!*" Flora threw out the best Cantonese word she knew, meaning, "Yes, it is." Mother Fong laughed until her sides almost split.

"*Jan ho!*" she remarked. Flora understood that, too. It meant, "Very good." This was encouraging.

"We must go to Macy's, considering all the things we have to buy. We can do it all in one trip."

"What is Macy's?" Mother Fong asked, and Daiko explained.

It was then decided they were to go to Macy's on Saturday.

"We're going to Macy's!" said Eva.

"We're going to Macy's!" echoed Tom.

It sounded very much like saying they were going to town and bring the House of Macy down. Eva was promised a hairbrush and some pins for her hair, and Tom was going to have new socks, good American socks. It was like New Year's Eve.

Saturday arrived finally. Flora had to go as the guide and authority on American domestic purchases. Daiko wanted to go because he said he wanted to get some soap flakes and starch and bluing, but it was really because the family had just arrived, and he could give himself a half holiday. Father did not want to go, but since Yiko said he was going to take the family to dinner in Chinatown, why didn't he come along so that they could be together? Close up the shop for half a day? The father's heart was happy, and he would be extravagant. In the end, therefore, the whole family went.

There was no telling what would happen when the Fongs went to Macy's. Daiko had explained what a department store was. It was a place where you could buy anything from a garden shovel to a soda fountain lunch, from an egg beater to a complete suite of bedroom furniture. It was a heaven of goods. What were they going to do when they entered heaven? Mother Fong held tightly in her hand the handbag containing the money.

The Fong procession filed in at the Sixth Avenue entrance. There was a row of carriages with babies in them.

"You don't say they sell babies, too!" exclaimed the mother. Anything was possible in this country.

"Heavens, no," said Yiko. "Hold your hands, Tom and Eva, and don't get lost."

"No," said the mother. "Eva, you cling to Flora. And Tom, you cling to Yiko."

"Don't you think we'd better all stay together?" asked the father.

"Flora," said Yiko, "I think we'll save time if you take Mother and Eva to buy the household things, and I go with Tom and Father?"

"No," said the mother. "Tom is going to get socks, and I have to see them."

"The children's clothes are all on the fourth floor," said Flora.

So it was decided they were to stay together.

Flora wanted them to go to the basement first, and Yiko was for showing the children the escalator. There was a tug of leadership between Flora and Yiko, and Yiko won, as he always did.

Up the staircase to heaven they went in a crowd of women. The staircase to heaven was an interesting American thing. Up and up they went, while they stood still and felt as if they were being carried on a sedan chair to the clouds. Mother Fong thought the escalator was continuous, and when it hit the second floor, she fell forward.

"My handbag!" It had been flung to the floor. A woman picked it up for her.

" 'Kyou," said Yiko.

Mother Fong gave the woman a nice smile.

"Why did you say 'queue' to that lady?"

"It was to thank her."

"I see."

30

"There are many ways of saying it. You say 'thank you,' or 'many thanks.' But the smart way is to say 'kyou.' "

Up and up they went. When they reached the third floor, Eva got on the wrong escalator.

"Down and down I go. It is such a sweet sensation." She followed a lady in black whom she thought was Flora. The lady kept going down. All of a sudden Eva realized that she was not Flora. She turned her head and saw that she was alone. She touched the lady in front. She was frightened and began to cry.

"What is the matter, child?" said the lady.

Eva jabbered in Cantonese.

"Mother! Mother! Where are you?" she shrieked at the top of her voice.

A crowd gathered and a floorwalker came. He couldn't understand her, but he knew that she had lost her mother. He told her not to cry, but she continued to cry. Eva pointed upstairs. The floorwalker took her up.

Halfway up they heard a feminine voice crying "Eva! Apwa! Apwa! Eva!"

Flora had discovered at the fourth floor that Eva was gone. There was consternation. The family went down to the third. Yiko went round on the third floor. Daiko and Flora went down to the second. "Apwa! Apwa!" echoed through the crowd. Flora went back up to the third and down again.

Eva heard her voice from above, looked up and saw Flora coming down.

"There, there she is!" Eva pointed up. She stood calling to Flora, and Flora saw her. At the landing they met. Eva hugged her, and Flora almost collapsed. The floorwalker left Eva in Flora's hands and felt relieved.

Up they went again. At the fourth floor, they saw the mother anxiously waiting. She had been afraid, but she was angry when she saw Eva reappear. Eva explained. Somewhere the

31

words "Apwa! Apwa!" still went round. Gradually the family collected and the sounds ceased, but Yiko was not there.

A few minutes later, Yiko turned up with a detective and learned that his sister had been found. The detective started to leave.

"Have a cigar," Yiko offered. He pulled out his card. "I am Frederick A. T. Fong, Insurance Agent."

"Thank you," said the detective.

" 'Kyou," said Yiko. His firm handshake met the detective's firmer handshake, and the family was left alone.

The system of hanging together as one party did not quite work. After the children's clothes were bought, Flora wanted to take the mother to the basement, but Yiko wanted to show the children the toy department, and Tom wanted some pencils and erasers. Eva now would not leave the women and went with her mother and Flora to the basement, and the father and Loy also went with them. It was agreed that all would meet in the basement.

Once in the basement, the mother lost all will power. She could not resist buying a new teapot, with a set of cups and saucers. She could not resist buying a dozen glasses, all made in America. She liked the feeling of having new things. While Loy went off to buy bluing and soap flakes, and the mother and Flora dug deeper and deeper into their purses, where was the father to go? He contemplated the idea of buying a gold frame for the grandfather's portrait. Since they were feeling like having a new home, why not? Loy went with him.

After half an hour Tom came down and said Yiko would join them. The purchases were made, and Yiko had not come back, nor had the father and Loy.

"Tom, where did you leave Yiko?"

"I left him on the seventh floor."

Tom went up and Yiko came down.

"Where is Tom?"

"We sent him to look for you."

"Didn't I say we were all to meet here?"

Tom had gone to look for him. He had gone all over the seventh floor and could not find Yiko. Loy and the father came back and found that Yiko and Tom were missing. Loy went up to look for Yiko. Tom and Yiko met on the second floor and came down.

"Where is Loy?" Yiko asked.

"He has gone to look for you."

"I told you we would all meet here," said Yiko, exasperated.

Loy came back and the family was happily reunited. By this time everybody was hungry and everybody was exhausted except the mother. She found that she had spent the extravagant sum of forty-three dollars and seventy cents, and she was excited and happy.

"But where are the cups and saucers and glasses and the new kitchen clock?"

Flora assured her that Macy's would deliver them to their home.

"Oh!"

They went off to have their meal in Chinatown.

3

The time came when somebody from Macy's rang the bell and delivered the parcels.

"They are from Macy's," Flora declared.

The mother would not believe it, for the man had to make two trips up the staircase and he dumped four huge boxes on the kitchen floor. "It must be a mistake," thought the mother.

The excitement of the unpacking began. There was no mistake, but Macy's was extravagant. Really it was America that was extravagant. The toilet paper and the coffee took up a great deal of room. The dozen glasses were packed in a huge box, twenty-four inches wide, thirty inches deep, and they were wrapped in fine tissue paper and five pounds of sawdust.

"Do you mean that we pay for a dozen glasses, and they give us all this, too? Such beautiful paper, Eva. Smooth it and fold it up, and it will be useful some time. And such beautiful cord!"

They opened the smaller white box which contained the kitchen clock. The mother would not allow Flora to cut the cord, but untied the knot slowly. There was an ocean of fine snowy-white paper.

"What is it?"

The mother dug and dug. At the bottom of the ocean of white paper she found the clock. While she was slowly winding up the cord and smoothing out the paper, she saw Flora throw the box on the grating outside the kitchen. With a leap, she darted for it.

"My Buddha! *Tim ho hap!*"

Flora was surprised. She vaguely understood that her mother-in-law meant "such a good box."

"It will shorten your life to waste things like that," the mother said in Cantonese. Luckily Flora did not understand.

The box, blue with a cover of silver paper, was indeed an object of beauty and delight. Everything was new and fine. The printing was exquisite, the silver finish shining bright, and the clock itself chromium plated. "To get such a box free along with the clock!" The box became Mother Fong's sewing case and did good service for almost two years.

The cords were wound, the brown paper and tissue paper were smoothed out, folded and stored away. What were they to do with the cartons? They took so much room. After consideration, the mother struck a compromise with Flora and reluctantly allowed her to throw away one while the others were put with the excelsior and the clean fine-smelling sawdust in the roof hatchway.

In time, however, the mother succumbed. After she had accumulated five or six Maxwell coffee cans and a dozen pickle bottles, she lost heart a little. She knew she was doing the wrong thing. The trouble was that American things were too good. The cans were at least twice as thick as Chinese cans. How did America waste so many things and survive? There was enough food dumped into garbage cans in a small section of the city to feed a whole Chinese village.

These matters hurt Mother Fong personally and gravely. It was against all tradition, all conscience. America was a land of plenty, and Americans could eat very well if they knew how to cook. But they just didn't.

It may be said of Mother Fong, however, that she threw away no cords and no brown paper in all her life, not even when she was in America.

Chapter 3

꧁꧂꧁꧂꧁꧂꧁꧂꧁꧂

I

WHEN MOTHER FONG FIRST CAME TO
America, it was not as if she had not seen an American before.
In the celluloid, she had seen Jean Harlow, Clara Bow, and a
great many American beauties whom she greatly admired, as
well as a few tough men with hair on their chests, like Wallace
Beery, who frightened her. Tom and Eva knew them by name
in Chinese. Their mother remembered only one actor, Barry
Fitzgerald, who was known to her as "Fi-choy," though her
later passion was William Bendix. She had seen Barry Fi-choy
in a certain picture, then playing a minor role, and she liked
him so much that she remembered his name above all the
rest. "That is the good one," she said any time she saw her
Fi-choy appear on the film, and then she would smile. There
was something in Fi-choy's simplicity which struck her as
eminently like the Chinese she knew and therefore was easily
familiar. She could tell what Fi-choy was going to do; she
could never tell what Jean Harlow or Wallace Beery was
going to do.

She reflected therefore that there were foreigners she could
not understand and others that she could. She did not know,
when she came to America, whether she was going to meet
many Wallace Beery's or many Fi-choy's. Among the women

stars, she could not understand "those grown-up girls that do not wear trousers," but she could understand Ida Lupino. She had seen Ida Lupino in an English picture at Hong Kong. She was hoping that America was full of Fi-choy's and Lupino's.

The idea of having an American daughter-in-law had rather frightened her. She had prayed to God that she would not have one of those glamorous untrousered females for her daughter. As far as she knew, such females were everywhere strutting about in the streets, in homes, in hotel bars and lobbies, at swimming pools and on the beach. She had a fear of blondes; the fact that a woman's hair could be golden and her eyes blue was so fantastic that she gave up thinking. She had actually seen one American woman, the Irish wife of the missionary in her village, who had a carrottop and carried a kind of bronze flame on her head. Well, if it could be bronze, it could be gold, green, blue, purple, turquoise, or aquamarine. Moreover, there were several Catholic nuns in Canton who had blue eyes, though she could not see their hair. A load had fallen from her heart when she walked down the gangplank and was introduced to a girl with dark hair and dark eyes, who was her son's wife. She was not a glamorous untrousered female.

A sort of pantomime went on always in the kitchen. The mother-in-law could cook Chinese dishes and the American daughter-in-law could not. Therefore there was no question that the mother was the boss in the kitchen. Flora loved Chinese dishes, and she was curious to learn how the mother made Chinese gravy and prepared the mysterious chicken, called *sunfong gai,* which was roast chicken, yet more than roast chicken. So, by a natural law the mother became the chief and Flora the second cook.

The mother was a woman of steady temperament. Like her husband, she talked and moved slowly, steadily, and firmly. It seemed that everything was on a lower musical pitch, and the pauses were as long as the sentences themselves. Flora was a little gushing, and the mother thought that was because she

38

was an American. The Americans talked so fast, or it sounded so in her ears. The mother could not speak a word of English, and the daughter spoke only a few dozen words of Chinese. It was surprising how you could get along with pantomime within the confines of a kitchen. It was a continual guessing game. If Flora was willing to guess and guess again, and the mother was not irritated at her guessing wrong, it could be a lot of fun. The mother was not irritated because Flora had black hair and was a white woman, for whom there was a kind of natural respect, and Flora was willing to guess and guess again because the very first night Loy had told her that his mother liked her very much. So it was a pantomime with smiles. Flora thought it quite a change from the time when she had cooked alone and the kitchen was a place where one held communion with one's own soul—a change especially with Tom and Eva dashing out and in. It was a good thing, too, that one could not quarrel much in pantomime, not very well. You could sulk in pantomime, and you could breathe hard and communicate your impatience, but that was about all. No words said meant no words regretted. That is why no horse bears another horse a grudge for years.

But since the kitchen had been transformed into a school for learning Cantonese, with the most up-to-date direct method of teaching modern languages taught by an unquestioned native professor, it was not surprising that Flora picked up many words of the Cantonese language, which she promptly styled "hoi-polloi." If come was *loy,* open was *hoi,* drunk was *joy,* see was *toy,* vegetable was *choy,* and mustard plant was *koy choy,* then, obviously, the language was just hoi-polloi. All you needed to learn Cantonese was to keep to the *oy* pattern (remember the night-club artist Joy Toy?) and sprinkle some *aps, ucks, ums, ongs,* and *eongs,* and boom these syllables up and down through the air like a balloon, and you could deceive a Cantonese into thinking that you were talking his dialect although it might not make sense. Flora was so enthusiastic

39

over this discovery that she caught herself saying, "Look at the airplane in the skoy." Her husband was Loy, anyway.

Flora also learned her name in the family. When in the midst of a conversation in Cantonese she heard the word, *daisow*, she knew they were speaking about her. The *dai* being in the falling, and the *sow* in the rising tone, the word seemed to hit the ground solidly and then lift up with a snappy questioning tone so that the second syllable sounded very much like the English word *sour*.

"Why am I sour?" asked Flora of her husband.

"It means 'elder sister-in-law.' You are their *daisow*, as I am their *daiko*, the eldest brother."

That fixed her position in the family. Her husband and the parents called her Flora, but Tom and Eva were forbidden to call her that and addressed her as Daisow, and when the parents spoke of Flora to the children, they also called her Daisow because it identified her position in the family. Only Yiko, being fluent in American, preferred to call her Flora. Tom loved the name Flora so much that he asked one day, "Can I call you Flora?"

"Please do. Why not?"

"No, I guess I had better not."

But Tom continued to hear Yiko call Daisow, Flora. She was as much Yiko's elder sister-in-law as Tom's. Why couldn't he?

He asked his mother if he could call her Flora, and she said he could not. He asked his father, and he said he could not.

"Why can't I?"

"Because it is disrespectful. It shows no respect for your superior."

He asked Yiko.

"Yiko, you call Flora, Flora."

"I do."

"Can I call her Flora?"

40

"You can't."

"But why can you?"

"Because I am taller. I am taller and bigger than Daiko. I call her Flora. I call any American girl by her first name. But you are so small."

"Tell me, how do I say *put keng* in English?"

"You say 'no respect.' That is a common word. Do you want to learn some fine words?"

"Please tell me what I should say? I want to tell Flora why I don't call her by her name."

"If you want to use a fine word, you tell her it is because you don't want to be regardless. That means no regard. Or you say irrespective."

Tom learned the hard words and repeated them. Finding Flora alone, he came up and said, "Daisow, I have decided not to call you Flora."

"Why not? I don't mind."

"Because Father said it would be—"

"It would be what?"

"Because—because I don't want to be regardless and irrespective to you."

"What? Tom, you have learned long words!"

"Gee, I wish I could call you Flora. When I love a girl, I am going to call her Flora."

Flora kissed him on the head for that, and Tom dashed out of the kitchen.

2

For weeks Mrs. Fong would not budge again from her home. She was in her Chinese jacket and pants, and she would not be laughed at, and she was at an age when a complete change of her costume was unthinkable. Coming to this foreign country, her one guiding thought was that her family should be respected and honored among her neighbors. It was

41

not a conscious thought; it was her whole attitude toward life that no one, including herself, should do anything to disgrace the family. That was all she asked of life and of America. No son should dishonor her in the eyes of her neighbors; it was a divine and ever present law of society that no one should "lose face" before his neighbors, a law more valid and binding on members of a community than all the codes and statutes. The punishment for violation of this invisible law of face was laughter and ridicule. And yet here she found herself in a ridiculous situation. She felt her dress should conform, and yet she could not conform, and how ridiculous it would be for her to put on a hat! She had seen women's hats, and all of them looked ridiculous enough, in fact, entirely laughable. She had seen how some elderly women in Chinatown made themselves so by putting on a hat and a long black dress covering the ankles, like that worn by the Salvation Army women, and she concluded that she would keep her dignity by keeping to her Chinese costume. At least she knew how to dress in Chinese.

But it was not hard for her to stay at home. Women in China managed to stay in the house without going outdoors for months. She did not come to look at America; she came to be with her family. It was a surprise to her, however, that there were no such things as neighbors in New York City and that you hardly talked to the people next door or in the same building. That simplified matters for her since the family was left very much alone. Having no neighbors meant that one had no people before whom to lose face.

Often Mrs. Fong went to the window to survey the strange scene below and to watch Americans, men and women and children. In the mornings the street was quiet and clean. The sidewalks were cement, smooth like a house floor, and neat little garbage cans stood in groups before basement railings. Only a stone's throw away was Third Avenue, which was dark, noisy, and familiar. There was something about the darkness and familiarity and busyness of the avenue that she liked. She had never wanted to live in a deserted street, which meant that one was living in reduced circumstances. She had always wanted to live in a busy, prosperous thoroughfare, with lots of noise and people, and to be on the same footing with all the struggling millions. Third Avenue seemed to be just that. The shops—groceries, fruit stores, shoe-repair shops, upholstery shops, shops advertising men's two-pants suits, a supermarket—were all within half a minute's walk. Housewives with bags in their hands, fat women in black, young women in white and printed rayon, trucks, cars, horse carts selling fresh vegetables, barrel organs, all passed the corner in continuous procession. Up above, at five-minute intervals, trains carrying loads of people dashed past, swiftly, securely. All this rumble, this intense activity of people going somewhere, gave her a sense of excitement and of being in the midst of things. Where there were plenty of people in a city such as New York, she was sure there was money to be made. No wonder her husband had been able to send dollars home. Take laundry. There was so much to be washed in that one block alone. Her husband had spoken of washing America and cooking America. She needed only to wash the block, and perhaps, in the not impossible future, cook to feed the block. After eating American food on the ship, she was not surprised that the Chinese took to cooking for Americans. As she sat before the window, the conviction grew in her mind that there was plenty of money to be made in New York, and she was going to make it.

Yet there were "face" and disgrace even in this street of anonymous neighbors. As she watched out of the window and saw housewives emerge from this or that house, she could see which were neat and nice women and which were lazy, sloppy housewives. In this neighborhood known as Yorkville there were many Germans and Czechs, but all nationalities were mixed. There was a sweet young Belgian woman whose blond hair was always done up in a queue wound neatly round her head, an old Bulgarian woman whose white hair was gathered up simply in a tiny bun at the back, and there was a fat woman whose enormous outlines were casually covered by a dress that showed no recognizable difference from a nightgown or a sack with a V-shaped opening at the top.

Toward three in the afternoon the street suddenly sprang into life. Children appeared playing, chopping wooden boxes, skipping rope, roller-skating, playing cop and gangster, chasing, running, and screaming. Grown-up girls of sixteen or seventeen were not ashamed to be seen skating on the sidewalks like little children. Mother Fong surveyed it all. Clearly, there were face and disgrace. From the Idle Hour Tavern at the corner she saw drunken men, filthy and besotted, emerge staggering to stand or crouch on the sidewalk in various stages of intoxication. The young girls in the streets were prettily dressed, walking head up at a pace that sent their golden hair flopping up and down around the nape. It was the characteristically American gait. Before the third house, where the sloppy woman lived, a group of small children were playing. They looked filthy, and she was sure they were the children of the woman who looked like a drudge. Her guess was correct, because a few days later she saw the woman come out and spank the girl before she literally dragged her in.

Her idea of face was that she would never allow Tom and Eva to appear that way in the street. American clothes for boys and girls were pretty, and they looked well on Tom and Eva. Mother Fong admired the girls' ringlets, and Flora knew how to make them, so within a week Eva had said good-by to her pigtails. Even though other girls wore pigtails, she would never wear them again. As for Tom, as long as he could remember, the fortnightly Saturday haircut at the Lexington Avenue barber shop was a sacred and inviolable institution. His head was cropped clean and close at the back, and a small wisp of hair always fell across one side of his forehead.

44

"Look like a gentleman," the mother said. "We are Chinese, and you do not want to disgrace China."

Regularly at four o'clock the mother dressed them up, Tom with his hair parted and his neck scrubbed, and Eva with her pretty ringlets and a clean cotton dress. It is to be suspected that some advertisement tactics were involved. Clean children should emerge from a clean laundry. Were Tom and Eva to be walking signboards of Tom Fong's Hand Laundry? Mother Fong reasoned that people would not send their laundry to a place where the children looked as filthy as those in the third house opposite. Or was it a code of honor for a laundryman's son that his shirt should be superiorly clean, like a professor's son who is not permitted to say "he ain't" while other children do?

The children were not yet at school, and the mother had decided that they needed exercise. Regularly at four o'clock they had to go out of the house somewhere, no matter where. After staring at their eyes and noses for unclean spots until Tom felt the dirt would pop out of his nose if there was any, the mother commanded, "Now, Tom and Eva, march!"

"Where to, Mother?"

"To the Central Park. It is good for you."

"We were there yesterday," Eva protested.

"Never mind where you go. Now, march!"

Tom and Eva marched forward, past the toilet at the end of the hallway, down the staircase, and out into the street. Their mother's head was always at the window, and Tom and Eva always looked up and smiled, though sometimes, to their disappointment, their mother was already looking away.

Eva hated this marching business. At the corner, the question was always, "Where?" The East River and Central Park were approximately the same distance away and equally obnoxious. Eva liked the park well enough, but crossing the wide Park Avenue was always an exciting and trying adventure. Once arrived at the park, Eva and Tom enjoyed it, Eva

45

usually holding Tom's hand until they decided on a spot. She did not care for romping about, it was so childish and unwomanly. Boys should romp about; girls should not. So she often sat on one of the benches, guarding her ringlets and swaying her legs for exercise.

Third Avenue was a universe. From Seventieth Street to Ninetieth, bounded by Second Avenue on one side and Lexington on the other, the district was a universe for Tom's exploration. He reconnoitered it, played and worked and walked in it, tasted it, smelled it, swam in it like a whirling planet until he could recognize the very air he breathed. The smell of the Eighties was different from the smell of the Sixties, and he could shut his eyes and tell in which he was. Third Avenue was longer than the longest street in his home town, and the El seemed to cross its orbit and swim out of his ken into infinity. Only a few blocks away, he would come to the different and bright business district of Eighty-sixth Street, where neon lights and illuminated signs glared in competition from four movie theaters within a block of each other. Out on Lexington the vibrations were again different. Second Avenue seemed like a suburban district where there was more air and sunlight and the population moved on what was the periphery of this tense, exciting, brooding universe.

It was a little universe in itself in which babies were born, food was eaten, laxatives were taken, and the dead were embalmed, completing the life process. Several funeral parlors in the district attested to this last fact. A city hermit, choosing to live like a hermit crab, could live in one of these blocks and never go outside for what he wanted. Boys grew up and fought and burned wooden boxes in the street to melt the snow in winter and dashed almost naked through the water from the hydrant in summer, grown-up boys and girls had dates in dark doorways, and men toiled and sweated, and women scrubbed and cooked, and the old sat on the doorsteps in summer evenings. It teemed with life, and on summer nights it was wet with the perspiration of humanity.

Chapter 4

THE EL WAS NOT ONLY THE ARTERY OF this great cluster of life. It was, conveniently, also the connection between Tom Fong's family and the New York Chinatown. Tom Fong Senior had selected the location of his home because twenty minutes would bring him into the center of all Chinese life. Mother Fong's first sorties consisted of trips from her home a few blocks to the Eighty-fourth Street station, up the staircase, onto the El train, and off at Chatham Square to go into Mott Street.

Bounded by the Bowery and Canal Street, Mott Street, starting humbly beneath the shadow of the imposing Municipal Building, ran a distance of a block and a half, hit an old Spanish church, and swerved to the left until it abutted on the broad tangle of elevated rails and dark-canopied cobblestones called the Bowery. A little alleyway called Pell Street joined Mott Street (pronounced Mutt in Cantonese) on the left and branched into another shorter curving alleyway called Doyer Street. All these ended in the big dark sea of the wet Bowery population but seemed to hold back the sea whose waves broke only a short distance into Doyer Street and stopped at a Christian home for the unemployed.

The rest of Chinatown was all dry. Within the small area of

two blocks were crowded Chinese medicine shops, printers' shops, dry-goods stores, and some thirty restaurants whose brilliant neon signs blazed at night and which were jammed with customers on Saturdays and Sundays. On these days all the New York Chinese community poured into the narrow streets to see friends and talk business and eat a hearty meal. With the holiday spirit abroad, they refused to go home, but stood on the sidewalks to ease their eyes and rest their spirits and lose themselves in sights and smells that recalled old China after a week of toil. There was a kind of intense and luxurious idleness as if time stood still beneath the appearance of teeming activity. A man can stand for half an hour as immobile as a stork resting on one leg in the marshes, seeing the world go by and meditating the universe.

A short way on Mott Street on the north side of Canal Street was Flora's house, in the Italian section. The Italians penetrated Mott Street on the south side into the core of Chinatown, and the Chinese branched out into Canal Street on the north and across Chatham Square into Oliver Street, Catharine Street, and East Broadway up to the very shadow of the Manhattan Bridge.

So Flora's home was there, and Uncle Chan's shop was there, and Yiko had taken a room by himself overlooking Canal Street. If the Third Avenue El was like a single planet's orbit, Canal Street was more like the Milky Way, a corridor of constantly throttled yet moving traffic. On a white sign above a third floor window one could see the English words, Frederick A. T. Fong, Insurance Agent.

The family usually descended upon Uncle Chan's shop in Mott Street on Sundays. Relatives are relatives, and they just sat there for the day or helped in the shop. It was a prosperous shop; it sold everything from beef, poultry, chicken parts, pigs' knuckles, tripe, fish, shrimps, Chinese vegetables, to dry goods from China, salted eggs, preserved eggs, mushrooms, Nanking ducks, dried squids, sharks' fins, transparent noodles, and bowls, incense, laundry tags, medicine, and Chinese almanacs. In short, it sold almost everything the Chinese needed and found useful in America. The shop extended a long way back through a passage narrowed by a refrigerating room and became a general sitting and storage room with a table, a few chairs, a couch, and sacks, tins, and parcels stacked against the walls. At the dark end stood large vats growing bean sprouts. The family made the shop their headquarters while different members went out to do what they wanted. "Uncle's shop" was always the place for finding each other again or leaving messages. The parents always sent for Yiko through Tom or Eva and had him meet them there. Sometimes Uncle invited them to a dinner, and sometimes Yiko offered to pay.

Yiko was a wonderful elder brother. He took his parents and the younger children to see the show places of New York. Once, standing on top of the Empire State Building, he surveyed the city and pointed out to them his royal domain, from Chinatown up to Thirty-fourth Street, in which Frederick Fong and Frederick alone could sell insurance for Cornelius Underwriters.

"All this," he said with a sweep of his arm that took in the Woolworth Building, the City Hall, Wall Street, and the Statue of Liberty, "all this, from where I stand, is my territory." Tom and Eva and the mother, the new arrivals, were terribly impressed. "And I am a self-made man," he added.

Yiko smoked cigars and Philip Morris cigarettes indiscriminately. For what reason he smoked Philip Morris, Tom and the family could not make out. Tom liked the way he produced his gold-plated cigarette case and said, "Have a Philip Morris." Perhaps there was something in a name. He both loved Chinese food and condemned it. "Steamed turtle soup and bamboo shoots!" he said deprecatingly. "No nourishment. No vitamins. Good taste, that's all." He believed in beef and milk and tomatoes. He asked Tom to drink a great deal of milk.

"A glass of milk is equal to a pound of beef," he announced.

Conversely, "A pound of beef is equal to a glass of milk," when he urged Tom to eat beef.

But when he urged Tom to eat that foreign-looking tomato, acrid and sour, he said, "Four tomatoes are equal to a glass of milk and a pound of beef."

He had not yet acquired his enthusiasm for raisins, a package of which he later pronounced to be equal to a pound of beef, a glass of milk, four tomatoes. He did not make it quite clear whether he meant *and* or *or*.

Among the few books offered for sale at the uncle's store was a little pamphlet in Chinese, entitled *The Good Life,* no more than fifty pages, written by "Frederick A. T. Fong, Insurance Agent." It was said that the pamphlet was published at the expense and with the assistance of the Cornelius United States Underwriters. When you turned the first page, a photograph of the author seated at an office desk with a dial telephone looked at you with a firm, confident, friendly gaze. The booklet supplied a useful collection of proverbs on thrift, endurance, and success through struggle and had an interesting chapter on "The Forward-Looking Way," ("Chin Up," it said) with apostolic messages on courage, determination, and (this by Yiko himself) tips on personal appearance, and rules to give Americans the impression of the "Forward-Looking Way." Among the tips were "the heavy handshake" and "clutching the lapel" and "smile." It argued sensibly that the reason why more Chinese did not get on in this country was that the Chinese held themselves back too much. They did not know how to inspire confidence. Then it went on somewhat haphazardly and without too much logical connection to a chapter entitled "Love Thy Fellow Men," which opened with the undeniable and appealing maxim, "To help others is to help yourself." Christ, Buddha, Confucius, it said, all taught us to love our human brothers. "All Within the Four Seas are Brothers" was a quotation in large type. "Are we brothers or are we not? [The question was left unanswered.]

But if you follow Confucius and regard all men as your brothers, it helps to give you that forward-looking and confidence-inspiring smile." Thus the logical connection was finally established.

Really useful to Chinese readers were three appendices, one on Western table etiquette, one on general social intercourse, and one on "Essentials of Waitership." Someone at the Cornelius Underwriters had suggested the brilliant idea that putting in these appendices was sure to make the Chinese read the book.

The Western table etiquette was on the whole sensible and obviously correct, such as:

(1) Hold the plate with your left hand and take up the spoon with your right hand in the same way you hold a brush; scoop the soup and drink it. After drinking it, place the spoon face up on the right of the plate.

(2) Cut the bread with your knife before you eat it. You can also scrape butter or jam with your knife. Put it on the bread and eat it.

(3) Eat slowly and noiselessly even though the food is good. Eat quietly and do not discuss it.

(4) Cut meat into small morsels. Do not spit out things on the plate. Avoid bony parts. If you cannot disengage the meat, leave it alone.

(5) Do not talk while your mouth is full. Swallow it, say "excuse me" and then reply.

(6) At an American dinner, you are not allowed to stand up or leave the table.

(7) Do not bring children to a dinner to which only you are invited.

(8) Though fruit is on the table, do not touch it until the end of the dinner.

(9) Be respectful. In general, behave as during a ceremony.

Among the rules of social etiquette, the following are commendable:

Always allow a lady to go first on entering a car, a bus, or an elevator, or subway entrance.

Never ask a lady her age, and never ask if she is married or engaged. It may embarrass her because so many American women are unmarried.

Do not discuss age in general, especially before old people. They do not like it. Avoid the words "old" and "venerable" in general.

If Americans praise your wife and children, try not to look embarrassed. You may even praise them yourself. Be attentive to your wife in public.

Shave every day.

On a business call, tell them directly what you have come for. Americans appreciate it. Americans have no time for gossip.

Finally there was a full page advertisement of the Cornelius Underwriters, with the address of the office of Frederick A. T. Fong prominently displayed. On the whole, the pamphlet was a slick and effective advertisement, and it sold for a quarter.

2

The Sundays in Chinatown were wonderful and exciting. Flora always attended church on these Sunday trips and then went on to visit her family. Her aged parents lived alone in a flat four flights up. Flora never took her parents-in-law to her house, but Tom and Eva insisted on meeting Flora's parents and seeing her home, and so they went one Sunday with Daiko and Flora. They had grown very fond of her, and besides, they had never been inside an American home.

The sitting room was bare, the chairs old. On the top of a

piano stood some porcelain figures and a bust of Verdi. On the wall was a picture of the great Cathedral of Milan. Flora's father, Giuseppe Maggio, sold apples and roasted peanuts in shells on a small pushcart at the corner of Mott and Bayard Streets. When chestnuts were in season, he sold hot roasted chestnuts.

Bearded old Maggio had taken his stand there as long as people could remember, and sometimes Flora, sometimes her mother came to relieve him. Daiko used to buy peanuts from the old man, and he would stand at the corner on the chance that Flora would come.

"You go home and have your lunch. Mother is waiting for you," Flora had said to the old man.

When Daiko had heard that, it tugged at his heart. It was just just like hearing a Chinese girl say such a thing to her father. Beneath her foreign appearance, he almost saw a Chinese girl, and the picture of the little Italian family had fascinated him. But could he hope that such a healthy lively American girl would one day marry him?

And so it happened that between one and three o'clock on Sunday afternoons Flora always stood selling apples and peanuts on the corner, and Daiko always came to talk with her. After two months had passed, neither Daiko nor Flora could be found at the corner, and Old Maggio or his wife would appear, for Sunday was the good day for business in Chinatown.

That had been three years ago. Old Maggio had little to do with his daughter's marriage. Flora was twenty-two when she married. Old Maggio had seen so many Chinese for so many years that he did not think they were different, and he could judge Chinese faces as Chinese faces go. If his Flora could not pick a husband of her own, it was her own fault, and if she did, who was he to stop her? On the common level of life snobbery had no place. The Italians and the Chinese were

53

much alike in their pleasure-loving slow-paced living. Something of the old world met in Daiko and Flora.

Besides, the Chinese in Chinatown were making good money. Flora had a dream that one day Daiko might own a restaurant there. He was steady and loved her. After marriage, she found it easy because Daiko showed a special pride in marrying a white woman and Flora found herself mildly worshiped as any woman wanted to be worshiped. Her Western dress, showing her slim supple body, enchanted him, and every time her hair brushed his neck, it seemed to electrify him. He used to feel the strands of her hair and stroke her neck and Flora liked it immensely.

Tom Fong, Sr., was usually a silent man. When Loy married, he felt good. Flora was the first promise of a family of Fong grandchildren. The father felt toward her as an old tree trunk must feel toward a young new branch, expecting it to be fruitful. He wanted only a dependable and sober daughter-in-law; the rest he must leave to Heaven. He liked to see that Flora was helpful to her husband; he was distrustful of American girls, but Flora measured up well to old-world standards. The few times he reprimanded her were when she neglected her husband's comforts. Her help at the shop in keeping accounts and packing laundry parcels turned out to be an asset he had not expected from a daughter-in-law. He had asked for nothing for himself, regarding himself as an exile condemned to iron and iron until one day he should be able to retire to his own country.

But now there was a change. His family was established in this country. He began to feel at home, and he began to make plans for his children.

It was a great change for Flora, too. She had been greatly worried. Living with a mother-in-law was an accepted Italian tradition, and she had seen many Italian families where the parents continued to live with a married son, but she had not known how it was going to be with a Chinese mother-in-law.

54

With the best of good will and plenty of good sense she went to her job. Now it had turned out pretty well. There was no kneeling or kowtowing. She still went to her church and observed Mass, and she hung an image of the Holy Virgin on her bedroom wall. The family had completely ignored her religion and left her alone. The mother had taken over the cooking, and Eva helped with the dishwashing, and the children were very fond of her. In a way, it became easier for her when she had found her place in the family, and she was engrossed in watching this lively family life.

"Loy," she said one night to her husband, "when shall we be able to save up money and be independent?"

"What do you mean?"

"I mean have a shop and a home of our own—you know, independent?"

"Independent? Don't think of it."

"Loy, darling."

"What's wrong? Mother likes you very much, and I think you like her."

"It isn't that. I'm having a lot of fun. You really have a wonderful family, and I've nothing to complain of. But you know what I mean. Is this going to be forever?"

"Darling, don't you see? We are one family, and we all help one another. The money—it's your money, my money, Father's money. It's all the same. We work together, earn together, spend together. Tom and Eva now have got to go to school. But when they grow up they will have to help, too—perhaps even help support our children at school. We've got to work and help. Those who can, help more, those who can't, help less. You need a coat, you buy a coat; maybe I need a pair of shoes, I buy them, too."

"But is it going to be like this forever?"

"Nothing is forever. But while the parents are living we are one family. Then when they are too old to work, we've got to take care of them because they took care of us when we were young. That's the idea."

In a sense, what Loy said was true. She had charge of the money and took care of the checks. Only it wasn't her own money; it was the family money.

Chapter 5

I

ON A SATURDAY NIGHT IN JULY IT WAS extremely hot. All day the sun had beaten down upon the low houses and streets, heated the sidewalks and penetrated the walls until the whole street was like an oven. The heat was held imprisoned in the houses and yards and hallways without means of escape. A little cool air came from the East River and, thwarted and dispersed, became only a thin breath by the time it reached Third Avenue. Loy and Flora had gone to the roof, lugging a blanket with them. Tom and Eva were told to go to sleep, but half stifled, they could not.

The father and mother came to the front window and leaned their heads out to catch a breath of cool air. All was dark. Across the street some men and women had stretched out on the fire escapes and made themselves comfortable there for the night. A bald-headed old man in a broad nightgown had ingeniously arranged a table next to his window, so that his head and the upper part of his body rested on the iron grating outside while his legs were inside.

Some youngsters were yelling and singing in the street below, and now and then there was a silence, broken only by the intermittent rumble of the El.

They had come back from a hearty meal in Chinatown. Tom heard his father and mother talking before the window.

"Mother, can I go to the roof to sleep?"

"No, Daiko and Daisow are there."

"Why can't we?"

"No. Children, you lie still, and you'll soon forget the heat. This comes of your eating the ice cream. No wonder your stomach burns."

Tom had heard this frequently enough. He felt his stomach, it was true. All one needs to drive away the heat is to drink hot tea and perspire. One feels cool after a hot bath, hot after a cold bath. Better still, one should just keep perfectly still and do nothing about it.

"But I am perspiring," protested Tom.

"Nonsense. You have been playing with that shower in the yard ever since you came back. Lie still and you will be all right."

Tom said nothing more. He could hear his parents talking in the dark.

"Why, there is gold on Mott Street," said the mother.

The father was silent.

"You see the swarms in the restaurants. Uncle says they take in three or four hundred dollars a day."

"I know, I know," said the father placidly.

"How much will it take to open one?"

The father spoke as if he was speaking of events on another planet. "About ten thousand dollars."

There was a deep silence. After an interval the mother resumed. "I say there is gold on that Mott Street. It would be good to own a restaurant there one day."

"Where would you find the money?"

"I don't mean a big restaurant like the Pacific. We could start with a small one. How much will it cost?"

"That depends. You can't start a small one with less than four or five thousand dollars."

"We will find the way. I have been thinking. With me and Tom and Eva, there are three extra mouths to feed. Food is expensive and we are eating gold dollars. How are we going to meet the expenses and save? You and Loy are working your hands off to feed us all, and Tom and Eva are too young, and they will have to go to school. It isn't easy."

"No, it isn't easy," said the father.

Tom fell asleep.

2

When autumn came, Tom and Eva went to the public school on First Avenue, an old forbidding-looking dark red-brick building, and soon lost themselves in a world of American boys and girls. They had been to school in China. To their surprise, they found there was little work and much play at an American school. Classes were over by three in the afternoon, and all Saturday was free. Quickly, in a few months, Tom and Eva learned to understand what the teacher said and to follow their classwork.

Every morning Tom and Eva "marched" to school as they used to march at four in the afternoon. But it was a different kind of marching, and Eva no longer hated it. Something awakened in her. She had been a nonentity at home, a happy, dutiful child who was never troubled and caused no trouble to her parents.

Flora had never seen a Chinese girl at such close range, and she could not understand Eva. She liked Tom's bright eyes and his puzzled look; he knitted his forehead and bit his lips, puzzling over things, asking questions, and refusing to accept the answers. When Yiko said to Tom that four tomatoes were equal to one pound of beef, Tom gave him a straight look and said nothing until Yiko was embarrassed.

But Eva was different. She said nothing and seemed to accept everything. The father was indulgent and even soft toward her. A sort of pleasant, proud chuckle came from his throat when he held her hand. Yiko also played the big brother to her. But the mother was always a little hard on Eva because she was a girl, a *nutsai*. This word said so much. It was impossible to define it exactly. In Eva's mind it meant vaguely that a girl had to be put in her place. It meant that Confucius, the sage, was against her, had laid down the law that a girl should be quiet and good and hard working and silent. It meant that a girl should have good manners. Confucius did not say that a boy should have bad manners, but in practice a boy was excused for many things. A girl learned to be sober at an age when a boy was not. She had a different role to play, the role of the female—to be quiet and soft, to watch, to approve or disapprove, to sustain, to influence, to mother, and to guide. The role of the male was to be active, to create, to whisk about like electrons around the quiescent center. Whenever the mother uttered the word *nutsai,* she meant it as a sharp warning to Eva to prepare herself to be a good future wife and daughter-in-law. She had to answer when asked, not to answer when scolded, to talk softly, and sit properly with her legs close together. So when Yiko said something, Eva as a matter of long habit just said nothing. Yiko thought her a wonderfully quiet girl, but could not tell what was going on in her head. Her answers were "yes" and "no"—for the rest she had to watch, listen, think, and keep quiet.

This Doctrine of Female Quietude she carried to school and she never quite lost it.

"What poise that Chinese girl has!" remarked Mrs. Anderson. "I wonder if all Chinese girls are like that."

But indeed something had awakened in Eva. On the streets and at school, she saw hustling, bustling, boisterous, screaming, yelling, scuffing, ball-batting children, girls as well as boys. It was like seeing a blurring light. She could not detect that girls shouted any less loudly than the boys. American girls yelled at the top of their voices, and how proud and straight they stood! How fast they walked, with free swaying strides! It was a wonderful talking, chatting, romping, backbiting, and laughing world in which Eva quietly slipped by. On the park playground, she saw how the grown-up girls ran and climbed and tumbled, how other girls playing volleyball stood in bloomers, arms akimbo, legs wide apart, beautiful, strong, unafraid, and how other girls dived and swam, played hockey, roller-skated, rode bicycles and horses. It was bizarre, new, and strange. And she enjoyed it all as if she had discovered a new freedom, as if the magnetic field that had held her thoughts polarized had disappeared, and all was loose and free and, she could not explain how, hopeful. It was a new, fluid, untested world in which anything was possible.

So Eva was happy. She would not be late at school, and if Tom had to be late, she would go ahead, not waiting for him, and Tom would dash out later and perhaps catch up with her before she reached First Avenue.

3

Tom and Eva improved their English rapidly, as children do. In his third year, Tom had for his teacher in English one Miss Cartwright, a pale white woman, with a quivering voice from Litchfield, Connecticut. She was Tom's great discovery. He had never believed it possible that there were such Americans. Miss Cartwright spoke with a kind of angelic sweetness, and her lips tightened and dipped at the middle in a sweet smile when she spoke to Tom, and her eyes were a pale blue and widened when she was shocked, and her hair was a beautiful shining silver. When the boys annoyed her, she would open her mouth into a circle and a shimmering light would come into her eyes. When she asked her pupils to spell the word Mississippi, her lips moved ahead so that those who did not remember could always spell correctly just by lagging one letter behind her. Her accent was feminine, clear, softly vibrant, and seemed to Tom divine. She taught singing, too, and when she sang, what a thin, tremulous but beautiful voice came from her throat! That was the only time Miss Cartwright's body and head and hands swayed, for she seemed to enjoy herself thoroughly at singing—probably the only exercise she ever indulged in.

Tom worshiped her. In his mind, Tom established an equation—English was Miss Cartwright, and Miss Cartwright was English.

From his love for Miss Cartwright, he developed a love of English sounds, and from his love of these sounds, he developed a system for learning English words. It was the sounds that were most unlike Chinese which attracted his attention. One of the first words that fascinated him was *smudge*.

"Miss Cartwright, what is *smudge*?" he asked, when he found her free sitting at the desk after class.

Miss Cartwright looked up amused, her blue eyes wide open. A foreign boy who could ask such a question was worthy of some special effort. She took out a handkerchief, touched her lips, and made a red mark on her white hand and said, "That's a *smudge*. *Smudge* is a *smear*."

Tom looked at her white hand and saw the fine blue veins and the shining hair on her arm and wrist. "See," she said, applying the handkerchief, "I *rubidoff*."

Tom listened carefully, but did not quite catch the word the first time. He repeated it after her.

"You rubidoff."

He thought he had another new word and was fascinated. Miss Cartwright wrote it out for him, and pronounced the words separately and clearly for him, "Rub it off."

"No, you didn't say it that way," said Tom.

"What did I say?"

"You said *rubidoff*. I like it better."

He walked away, studiously repeating to himself *"smudge—smear—rubidoff."* The last word sounded fast and funny, and he shook his head, greatly amused.

The next day, he came to Miss Cartwright and showed her a page of his notebook and said to her, "I found these words in the dictionary. I like them."

Miss Cartwright looked. He had written down *"smudge, smear, smart, smack, smash, smuggle."* Opposite these words were Chinese words indicating their meaning, which he had found in an English-Chinese dictionary.

"Why did you pick these words?"

"I liked the *smudge* and *smear*. So I found the others. I chose the words which had sounds that I liked."

"Which one do you like best?"

Tom looked over the list. "I like *smack*."

Miss Cartwright was enjoying the words as much as Tom himself. She had never found a student like this, and she had never quite realized the drama of English sounds herself. Indulgently she closed her lips and suddenly parted them and said, "That's a *smack*." She whacked on the table, and added, "A *smack* is also a *slap*."

Tom caught the sentence like a string of pearls. "A *smack* is a *slap*. . . . And I like the word *smash*."

"Yes," said Miss Cartwright enthusiastically. "You *smash* everything in this room—that is *smash*. But I won't demonstrate it now."

Miss Cartwright tried to explain what the word *smuggle* meant.

"I know what it means from the Chinese dictionary."

"Why do you like the word?"

"I like the sound of it. We have no sounds like *gle* in Chinese. I like all the words like *giggle, juggle, jumble, scramble,*"

"Then you would like the word *snuggle*."

"What is that?"

"You look it up. I have an idea. Write down the words beginning with *sn*. Select the words that please you. Will you do that?"

Tom nodded. The next day, he came with *snuggle, sneak,*

sneer, sneeze, snicker, sniff, snivel, snore, snort, snuff. Miss Cartwright demonstrated to him what a *snicker* and a *snort* were.

It became a game between the two of them. Tom would pick a word he liked, and the teacher would write out words with similar sounds that pleased Tom. Tom favored simple, graphic sounds, like *chum, punch, munch, crunch, chump, hump, hunk, pump.* The word *bomb* was unforgettable.

And so Tom made rapid progress in his vocabulary. The English language was rich in graphic sounds. He could never forget the way Miss Cartwright taught him the meaning of *sway* and *swing.* She also made the other children relearn the value of their words better. She would give an ending like *—nch* and make the boys and girls write out the words they could think of. Tom got excited when such an exercise was on, and it became known as Tom's game. One day the teacher came to the class and found some one had written on the blackboard, "Tom Tunch, I have a hunch you munch your lunch, which is a bunch of spaghetunch with spinunch."

In time, the class came to know what was called "Tom's list of words" in testing a foreign student's command of the English language. It consisted of twenty-four words entirely of one syllable. A French girl who thought she was ready for advanced English failed miserably in this test of twenty-four monosyllabic words:

cot	mop	nap	slab
cop	throb	lap	stab
pod	lop	tab	scab
plod	pop	tag	scalp
prod	prop	nab	stack
sop	crop	snap	snack

Tom soon developed a system of his own for recording his vocabulary. He grouped words by their sounds, thus putting a new word like *gripe* on the same page with *tripe,* or with

64

grape, following his fancy. And he played with them as sounds. Thus he learned to connect the English sound—*ash* with a breaking, cutting, powdering movement after he collected *clash, crash, smash, slash, lash, hash, mash.* When he got a little confused by two similar words like *warble* and *wobble,* he would picture the *a* in *warble* as a little bird sitting by the branch with a bud, which was the *r,* while the *o* in *wobble* made him think of a goose's egg or the back of the goose itself.

4

Tom learned the American oath of allegiance. Whenever he came to the word *indivisible,* he said it very fast, tried to see how fast he could say it. He learned to salute the flag properly. It was a pretty flag, the flowery flag *(Wah kay),* by which words the American Republic itself was called in Cantonese. He associated the flag always with a playground, with a lot of boys and girls playing, tumbling, and hopping beneath it. The limbs of the children were as lithe and graceful and pretty as the flag itself.

"Gee, it's the prettiest flag in the world," Tom would say.

But his admiration for the flag was somewhat dampened by a little incident in school.

Tom was a pensive, meditative boy, somewhat aloof, and his fingernails were chewed short because of all the things that puzzled him. He was thought a little queer. He joined in the games and learned to catch and bat a ball, but fighting left him cold. He saw boys rolling on the ground on top of one another and didn't see the sense of it. "Why do men fight?" was one of the earliest questions he asked himself. Teasing and playing tricks were fun. But fighting and riding on the stomachs of smaller boys was unmannerly; sometimes it was brutal. What did it prove? That one boy was stronger than the other. What of it? When there was a wicked gangster in the movies, and the detective or a cop knocked him out with a thunderous smack on the chin and threw the thug reeling head over heels on the floor, you got a thrill. That was fine. But who would want to be a cop and a bandit chaser? Not an educated man! If a thug walked into a famous scientist's laboratory and threatened him with a revolver, what would the scientist do? He would of course submit to being bound and gagged if he was a good scientist. If he cracked the thug's skull instead, that did not make him a better scientist. Cops are hired to crack the thug's skull; that is what they are paid for. What Tom could not understand was why the American girls always applauded the bigger, stronger boy. What was even harder to understand was that in the movies a reporter or a soldier always settled questions by a sock on the chin. The fellow knocked out was sometimes a guard or a doorman refusing the reporter admittance in the strict line of his duty. Why did the audience applaud the reporter?

There was a gang of boys in the class, Jackie and Gus and Steve and an enormous figure called "Ziffy" Hruschka, who were the leaders whenever the teacher was out of sight. Steve was Tom's friend, but Ziffy was a bully.

The teacher had forbidden the students to use the words "Chinaman" and "nigger."

"Hey, Chinaman," said Ziffy in the noon-hour recess. "Go out and get an ice pop for me, will yer?"

"No, I'm going home," said Tom.

"Hey, what's the matter? Doncha know me?"

"Sure, I do."

"Well, I say, go out and get an ice pop for me, and beat it."

"I can't. I'm going home for lunch."

"I'm surrrprised!" growled Ziffy.

Ziffy came closer, hands in his pockets, affecting an easy, confident tone, "So you won't do what Ziffy tells you to do, is that it?"

"Leave him alone," said Steve.

66

"I'd like to know who's going to stand up to Ziffy." He advanced glowering and slapped Tom's cheek. "You Chink!"

Tom winced.

"Will you do it now or do you wanna fight?"

"I won't do it and I won't fight."

"Yellow!"

The other boys stood watching. From the yard Eva approached, wondering what Tom had got into.

"Say, is it true Chinese girls got two horizontal mouths?" Ziffy was bent on a fight.

"You stop that," said Steve.

"Say, you're not sweet on his sister, are you?"

"You don't have to pick on him. He's done you no harm."

"Tom, what's the matter?" Eva asked.

"Your brother is yellow, that's the matter. He's scared, that's what he is."

"Will you fight or not?" demanded Ziffy.

"What for? Suppose you win; that proves you got stronger muscles than me. That doesn't make you right."

The boys were confused. Some shouted one thing, some shouted another.

"Come on, fight me if you want to prove you're not a yellow dog."

"Let me see your arm," said Tom slowly.

Ziffy raised his arm, but Steve held him.

Tom raised his hand calmly and felt around Ziffy's biceps approvingly. "I won't fight you," he said. "You got stronger muscles. Makes no sense." Tom started to go away.

"So you *are* yellow."

"I know you got stronger muscles. I know it without fighting you. But that's all you got. I say I won't fight you, and I won't buy an ice pop for you. Get it yourself."

Tom pushed his way through the circle. Ziffy frowned miserably, his restive fists threatening action. Clutching Tom's arm, he said, "You're not going to get away like this. You Chinaman."

Tom turned round. "What's wrong with Chinamen?"

"You're a furriner."

"And you?"

"I'm an American."

"And your father, Hruschka?"

"I won't let you say anything about my father. He came to America."

"So did I, like your father."

Ziffy was furious. But Tom was out of reach already. Holding Eva's hand, he walked out of the school yard, to the amazement of all the boys.

"What was the matter?" asked Eva.

"It's nothing. He called me Chinaman. I don't see what's wrong with that. It's like Englishman, Frenchman, Dutchman, laundryman. I don't see what's wrong with the word."

5

One night he heard Yiko, who had come to see them, deliver a talk on standing up for yourself.

"De trouble wit' us Chinese," said Yiko, speaking now in English to them, "is dat we don't stand up for ourselves. You stand up and fight, dey like you. If you don't fight, dey don't. Hold your chin up and face de world. Dat's what I do. I see an Amelican. I go up to him and slap him on the shoulder and say hello. He act kinda scared and wonder who you are. See? If you stand up for your right, he t'inks you're right. If you don't stand up for your right and say nutting, he t'inks you're wrong. So long as you don't hit a lady, it's all right. You must act like a gentleman. Kinda proud and cheerful and unafraid. If dey are wrong, tell 'em dey are wrong. Impoliteness don't mean a t'ing. If you are good, say you are good. Your wife, your sister, your mother, all good and you're proud of dem. See? Amelicans are simple, honest people. Dey're easy to deal wit'. Impoliteness don't mean a t'ing. You got to know how to handle 'em."

"I've learned something at school," said Eva. "In the first year, when a classmate asked me what marks I got, I told her I didn't write a good paper. 'Oh, I'm so sorry for you,' the girl said to me. American girls, when they have good paper and get good marks, they tell you so. Now when I get good marks, I tell them so and they are no longer sorry for me."

"How you getting along in school?" asked Yiko.

"I'm getting along fine."

"How you like school now?"

"I like it fine. I was scared at first. But American girls are like Chinese girls, just about, except they are always excited about something. They've got to be thrilled or shouting at something. It's their way of expressing their emotions. They don't say they like a thing, they say they *love* it, and when they don't like a thing, they say they *hate* it. One day the teacher brought a white mouse into the class, and the mouse got away and ran all over the floor. They screamed. I don't think they were as scared as they seemed to be. They just had to let go. But we have lots of fun. If you like them, you talk with them; if you don't like them, you don't. They are very simple and direct and frank and easy to deal with."

"Tom, what's matter with you?" said Yiko, suddenly turning to Tom.

Tom could not understand Yiko. Yiko was some ten years older than he. The cigar in his coat pocket and his cigar cutter, his work and his manners, all puzzled Tom. He carried two lighters in his vest pocket in case one did not work. It was as if they lived in two different worlds. "Nothing is the matter," Tom answered briefly.

"Why don't you grow up faster?"

The question was one he could not answer. It was true that

Eva had grown faster than Tom. Yiko said it was the American milk. But Tom, at the age of sixteen, looked like an American boy of twelve or thirteen.

"You ought to drink plenty milk. It's good for you. I drink t'ree glasses a day and I never have a cold. I am full of vitamin, see? And you ought to get out and play more. Amelican children don't study. Dey play all day. Dat's why dey grow up so strong."

Yiko's face oozed a kind of animal energy. His cheeks were well filled, his nostrils extended, and his lips were thick, revealing his gums when he talked. His hair was thick and black, glistening with lanolin. His chest muscles bulged under his shirt.

"Take my advice and drink a lot of milk," Yiko said as he left them, walking, Tom thought, with a lot of vitamin.

Tom rather envied him, as the man who thought he completely understood America, had no questions and knew all the answers, and knew how to get along in this world.

Chapter 6

WHEN TOM WAS OUT OF SCHOOL, HE would go down to the basement shop and help in checking tags and keeping records. He was too small to do ironing. Fridays and Saturdays were the busy days. The wash came in big hampers, some to be hung up on lines close to the ceiling, some to be kept wet overnight under wet cloths. All was to be ready for delivery Monday morning.

When Tom was in the shop, he made answering the telephone his job. Customers would come for their own parcels. Some bundles would have to be picked up immediately and who was best for the job but Tom? Through the shop window he saw the legs of men, women, and children passing by on the sidewalk. Earnestly he wished some day that they could come up from the basement and own a shop on the street level.

Part of the ironing was done upstairs when the big wash came in. There was a system of communication between the basement and the top floor. Tom and Eva had fixed a two-way rope pulley holding a basket, which they could lower from the top floor to the back window of the shop and haul up again. The laundered semiwet wash would come up that way, and the pressed articles would go down the same way without any possible mishap on the dark staircase. A bell attached to the rope was useful as a lazy way to tell the members of the family down at the shop to come up for lunch or supper. Under Tom and Eva, the rope pulley became important and useful in other ways. A Coca-Cola bottle was used for notes, which were rolled and stuck in it. When Tom was in the shop and Eva upstairs, Tom would send up a message.

"Has Daisow returned?"

A jerk at the bell meant "yes," and two jerks meant "no."

"Ask Mother if we can go to the movie tonight."

"Mother says yes. Daisow asks if Daiko would come along, too. She is coming with us."

"Daiko is busy tonight. He says she can go with us. Tell Mother that William Bendix is playing tonight."

Sometimes the bell rang, and down came a question from Eva.

"Who shot Lincoln?"

"How do I know? Why don't you ask Daisow?" Tom flashed back.

She sent the answer. "A Chinese. Jimmy Wong Howe of Warner Bros. When are you coming up?"

Tom watched his father and Daiko at work in their shirt sleeves, ironing shirts, undershirts, towels, sheets, girls' dresses, workmen's blue denims, and ladies' silk pajamas. The winter evenings were comfortable, but the summer evenings were suffocating, and no breath of fresh air reached that little room. Tom saw his father and Daiko covered with perspiration, the heat from the pressing irons accumulating until they had to open the door. They had to keep the window shut to guard against the dust from the streets. Nor could they smoke while at work for fear of dropping ashes on the half-wet laundry. After an hour's work, Tom would see his father go out and smoke his ancient pipe, leaning against the railing or sitting on the steps.

Business was good, but with the rent, the food, and the children growing up, saving was difficult. Mother Fong had foreseen all this when she arrived. But so many mouths to feed meant also so many hands to work, she reasoned. And so she set to it. The hand was to feed the mouth, and there was to be no idle hand. So the upstairs became the women's department of Tom Fong's Hand Laundry, where she and Flora did the ironing. There were times when they had to forgo the Sunday trip to Chinatown in order to finish the work for delivery on Monday.

Mother Fong made the business expand, not only by taking care of more laundry and promising quick delivery, but by doing something extra to satisfy her customers. Her business principles were sound. If she kept a reputation for quick and clean laundry, the business was bound to grow, limited only by what the family, men and women, could do. She wanted to please her customers. She would not send laundry back with buttons lost or seams torn. This was a great extra inducement to housewives who sent their laundry to her, and she did the mending and sewing of buttons without extra charge. To regular customers she was willing to promise especially quick delivery when they wanted it. This anxiety to oblige was the secret of the increase in the business.

In June, when some of their customers on the Lexington Avenue side left the city, there was a decrease of business, and Mother Fong would say, "Well, we have enough work. And it would not be right to work too hard in summer anyway. A man must rest a little, as the plant breathes at night."

"Aren't you a little sorry, though?" said Eva.

Mother Fong smiled. "Well, a little," she admitted. "My Abwa can read a woman's thoughts."

When autumn approached and business started to pick up after hitting the low point in August, there would be great excitement over the returning customers.

"Nine-forty Park Avenue has come back to us!" Mother Fong would exclaim. She went by numbers, because personal names were too much for her. A few avenue names like Park and Lexington were possible to manage. She knew the arabic figures, and she kept all the address numbers in her head. Sometimes she would say, "Now we are washing as far up as Ninetieth Street." A variation of this was, "Now we are washing Ninetieth."

But somehow the business developed toward the south. One of Mother Fong's customers, a rich lady who was not the careful housekeeping type, once sent her housecoat to be washed, and in checking it, Mother Fong found a hundred-dollar note in its pocket. Tom was sent to return the money.

"My mother asked me to return this to you with her compliments," Tom told the lady.

The lady was struck by the incident. She spoke of "Mother Fong's Laundry" to her neighbors and friends, and they came to it.

"Now we wash 277 and 279 Seventy-ninth," Mother Fong said with great satisfaction.

And yet, when the work was over and all the finished and unfinished laundry had been put away for the day, Mrs. Fong was the wife of her husband and mother of her children. Loy and Daisow had to relax in the evening and went to the movies by themselves, but Tom never saw his mother tired. There was always the supper hour when all the family gathered together, and the evenings when the father and Daiko had come up, which gave the children a home, intact and inviolable, just as if they were in China. Tom and Eva had a safe corner in this foreign country in which they were happy and secure. The neighborhood came to be familiar and Tom loved it. His position at the street window, the kitchen, the dark staircase, the yard and the roof were as familiar as life itself.

2

On Mondays, and usually on Thursdays also, it was Tom's job to deliver the laundry when he came back from school.

Tom did not want Eva to go along because she walked too slowly for him, though she could help carrying the parcels. Only occasionally, when Tom was not able to go, did Eva deliver the parcels in his stead.

It was a new experience for Tom. Eva was sent to the nearby blocks, but some of the addresses were farther away, out toward the East River, and up as far as Ninetieth, and these were Tom's job. Most of the business, however, came from Lexington and Park Avenues. For the first time Tom penetrated these imposing apartment buildings and came into contact with a new class of beings—doormen, service-elevator men, janitors, maids, rich men's wives, and bachelor girls. There were all sorts of women. Tom usually pressed the back door bell, announced, "Laundry," and stepped out again. But some maids and some wives, caught by Tom's bright eyes, would talk to him and ask him his age, and whether he went to school, and would give him a nickel or a dime. There was a woman artist living on a top floor on Lexington who always asked Tom in, offered him a "coke," and asked him all sorts of questions about China. And there was a bachelor girl who had a beautiful apartment on Seventy-ninth Street, and who would come to the door in her house gown. She called him Tom.

"Tom, come in."

Her laundry was never ready. Tom would go into her bedroom closet and jam her laundry in a bag. She would be in all stages of undress and Tom dared not lift his head. It was a beautifully furnished but disorderly room. Papers, jewels, and many things were lying about, and the bed was unmade. Tom saw the glass table with cigarette butts lying on it, the white lamps and heavy rugs. The woman had golden hair. Once while Tom was collecting the laundry, he looked up and saw the woman's nude back. She went into the bathroom, turned on the faucet and threw the soiled towels out.

"Tom," she said from the bathroom door, "take these things

and get the pajamas from the bed, and close the door when you go out."

Tom turned all red and dashed out of the bedroom and left, his heart beating wildly. He went home, excited, and told nobody about it. He could not understand American girls. They didn't mind being seen nude, this was evident. It was the first time he had seen a woman with so little on, and it was not like seeing them in pictures. Something deep and vague and compelling stirred in him. He longed to catch a sight of that woman again. This was his biggest secret.

Tom, and for that matter Eva, who had slept in her mother's room since she was thirteen, never had any illusions about the mystery of how babies came into the world. One of the most fantastic things he learned was that children of ten or twelve in this country still did not know how babies came. The stories Tom's playmates had heard about the connection between the stork, the cabbage, and the coming of a baby sounded like savages' explanations of rain and measles and seemed just as superstitious and less plausible, more childish, more naïve. How was it possible to deny the father's part? What did the American parents try to conceal? How was it possible to let the American children see the earth and not the sky? How could a child feel filial piety and kinship toward his father unless he knew he came from him as well as from the mother? The *Classic on Filial Piety* clearly says, "Your body, your hair, and your skin come from your father and mother." Every child in China knew this. It was sex, of course, and sex was always slightly funny, but the children were never disturbed by it. It was just one of the funny things grown-ups do. But there was no unspeakable shame. "Why, that was how Father and I have you," Tom's mother had told him. It was one of the elemental facts of life.

"Mother, American children are superstitious like the savages. They believe babies come from cabbages or from Macy's,"

76

Tom said one day to his mother in the hearing of Father, Mother, Flora, and Eva.

This was the most fantastic thing he had learned about America. One day, after spending two years in this country, he suddenly realized that he had never seen an American mother suckle her baby in public, while of course in China this could be seen anywhere in public, in the family sitting room, and on the streets. The Americans were the funniest people. You could show on the screen a man and woman sleeping in bed and kissing each other in the most intimate scenes, but you couldn't show a mother suckling her young. Where did the mothers go when they suckled their young? Did they lock themselves up as if it was something obscene—this most natural and innocent and even beautiful deed of motherhood? The Americans would proclaim, display, exploit, and blazon sex from the skies, painting a girl's breast on a dirigible, but they pretended to be ashamed of suckling their babies and knew nothing of how babies came. Displaying a woman's "undies" in public was not obscene, but suckling a baby was. Tom concluded that the Americans are ashamed not of sex but of childbirth.

3

Tom was carrying his parcel one afternoon across one of the streets where a gang of boys was playing Indians. He walked past them when all of a sudden a young boy shot water in his face from a squirt gun. Tom was taken unaware, and when he discovered that the packing paper was wet, he hastily took out his handkerchief to wipe it off.

"Hi, you're a laundryman, ain't yer?"

Tom did not say a word. The boys laughed, and he ran. Stopping at the corner, he carefully examined the wet spot on the package, hoping it would not be serious. He ran on to the apartment where it was to be delivered.

"Mrs. Renke," he said to the woman who opened the door. "I'm awfully sorry. The package, I'm afraid, is a little wet. I was coming along when some kid spurted water on it. Will you open it? If it's too bad, I'll take it back and have it washed again."

"Well, I never! Those kids are just a bunch of savages. Let me see."

She opened the package. Only the top dress was slightly wet in one spot.

"It's all right," said Mrs. Renke. "Was that your voice I heard on the telephone at the shop? What's your name?"

"Tom. I'm Tom Fong, Junior."

"Well, Tom, you're a nice boy. You must stop those scalawags, and don't let them do it again."

The following week he met the same gang playing again, led by a loutish boy of thirteen or fourteen in a red-and-black check jacket. Tom saw them whispering and grinning. It looked ominous. Perhaps he should not have run the first time. He could not decide what to do.

"Hi, Chinaman, what are you stealing in that parcel?" said the leader. "You're arrested."

The other boys closed in.

"Please, this is laundry."

"Laundry, eh? So you're a laundryman."

"What's wrong with that?"

"You're a Chink, that's what you are." The leader grabbed his arm firmly. Now Tom was really angry. He wanted to defend himself, but he had to protect his parcel.

"Leave me alone." He tried to push past them.

"Not so fast. You're arrested."

"You are not a cop. This is a free country, ain't it?" Tom quoted the sentence most frequently heard in America.

"This street is ours. We don't want furriners slinking around here."

Tom cuffed his way out. It was a signal for attack. Someone

78

tugged at his parcel and tried to tear it away. Tom hugged the parcel closely to his chest and couldn't fight back. Someone grabbed his leg, and he fell head on to the ground and dropped the parcel. In a sheer vandalistic outburst the gang tore up the parcel and scattered the contents in the dust of the pavement. Tom was in tears. He picked up the soiled articles as the older boy kicked the things toward him, saying, "So it is laundry. You're released. But that will teach you not to come here again."

"Come on. Let's beat it before the cop sees us."

The boys disappeared. The laundry articles were hopelessly soiled. Tom put them together in the torn brown paper and returned to the shop with his face bruised and smeared.

"Why, what's happened?" his father asked.

When Tom told him, the father was in a rage.

That evening at supper there was a hot discussion.

"I was afraid something like this would happen," said the mother. "Those boys play mountain robbers with guns all day, and no one stops them."

Yiko happened to be present. "How big are dose kids?" he asked in English.

"They are not big. Just my size."

"De only way is to fight 'em. I told you de Amelicans like fighters. Dey don't respect you if you don't fight back."

"I don't want to fight. What for? It's so silly."

"You can avoid them. Don't go through that street again," said Loy. Flora listened keenly.

"It is true that he does not have to go through that street," said the mother in Chinese. "I would not suffer the disgrace of having my children seen fighting in the streets."

"But it is the way here. You have to hold your own," said Yiko, in Chinese.

The mother was firm. "What would you have Tom grow up into? A mountain robber or a soldier?"

"Mother, you don't know this country. Don't you see the

movies? American parents teach their children to take off their coats and fight back when they are bullied by somebody."

"Well, that is not our way. My Tom is going to be a scholar not a hoodlum." The mother's tone was final.

The father spoke. "Why all this fuss? If it's a bad street, you don't go through it. Isn't it simple? The Americans do it one way. We Chinese do it another way. That's how we get along. That's how the Chinese get along anywhere. In my days, it was much tougher for us out on the West Coast."

"Father, I was told they robbed, killed, stole, and beat up the Chinese workers," said Tom.

"Yes, it was tough. But I survived, didn't I? If you had bad luck, you got killed. But not all of us." His voice was calm; he enjoyed telling the story. "I got away through the back fence of my garden in the dark, and hid in the bushes during the daytime and walked at night. But I got away. Old Tuck didn't get away in time. They caught him hiding in one of the corners of the shack, covered with a blanket. They dragged him out and after burning his shack, ran him between thirty or forty men standing on both sides of the road, and they kicked him in turn. Then they fell on him and mauled him so badly that they left him to die, lying with half his body submerged in a river. But he didn't die. He is still alive, too."

"Where is he, this old—what's his name?"

"Old Tuck. He is here, in Chinatown. Some day I'll take you to see him. He is about seventy years old now."

The story so enchanted them that Tom's troubles were forgotten. The practical conclusion was what Tom Fong, Sr., had said, "If it's a bad street, you don't go through it." It was as simple as that.

Thereafter in delivering packages to Mrs. Renke Tom always made a detour.

80

Old Tuck was a legend in Chinatown. He was probably the oldest man living in that community. Few people saw him, and he appeared in the streets only once or twice a year. Since he was of the Clan of Ng, the Ng Guild, which had a large membership, took care of him. He had no direct descendants, yet all the Ngs were his relatives and called him old granduncle.

It was said that he had been to Alaska, Vancouver, and Portland, and had led a band of Chinese workers across the Wyoming wilds. They had stolen and fought their way to Illinois after losing half their men and finally established themselves on the South Side in Chicago. In his late fifties, Old Tuck came to New York. He was known for his physical prowess, but by the time he reached New York he was a cunning, wise old man, as if he had read the three thousand years of Chinese history. It was reputed that he made himself study ancient Chinese at the age of thirty-five, that he met Sun Yat-sen in Chicago, and that after the revolution of 1911 Sun Yat-sen had offered him a post in the government, but he had declined. He was a natural leader in settling disputes among the tongs. Actors sought his patronage, his name was wanted on the sponsoring committees of all philanthropic activities, prominent Chinese lawyers listened to him, and the New York police counted upon his co-operation. It was said that during prohibition he kept Chinatown dry, though speakeasies were to be found over on the Bowery side, and easy money was to be had. Old Tuck would not permit it. Some said that in doing this he greatly disappointed the police. He was the inevitable figure at weddings, delighting the guests with his raw Cantonese sallies. He was easily the most popular leader of Chinatown despite the fact that he had one glass eye. But Old Tuck was gettin too old. He had given up work and given away most of his money, and for some years now he had been retired and was seldom seen.

Tom insisted that his father take him to see Old Tuck.

He was led up a dark staircase to a temple on a second floor. Latticed panels serving as part of the front wall admitted a dismal light from a green veranda. Red sharp-pointed strips of silk hung in front of the Western Queen Mother of Heaven, with the popular God of War and Justice on her right and the God of Medicine on her left. A wide horizontal silk panel, neatly embroidered with gold threads, with circles containing Chinese characters cut out in black velvet, stretched the length of the room and half concealed the foreheads and faces of the fierce-looking idols. Joss sticks were burning on a porcelain tray standing on the old, faded, red altar.

Tom heard a cat mew somewhere, and it startled him.

"Father, where is Old Tuck?"

"Don't call him Old Tuck. You should call him Granduncle Tuck. I thought I should show you the temple first. He is inside there. He has been in his bed all winter." The father pointed toward the red hangings.

Tom pictured a one-eyed old man putting his face out somewhere among the idols. The cat mewed again. It sounded very close.

"Father, I don't want to see him!"

"Hush, he can hear you. Remember that he is one of my oldest friends. We made the journey together from Alaska to Vancouver."

"Is that you, Tom Fong?" came the voice of an old man from behind the idols.

"It is I," replied Tom Fong.

"Why don't you come in?"

"I am showing my son the temple. He wishes to come to pay his respects to you."

"Where is he?" whispered Tom ever so lightly, holding his

father tightly by the arm. Tom heard a knock on the boards behind the idols and saw the red hangings shake.

"Come with me," said his father.

He led Tom out to the staircase landing and stopped before a door that led into the room back of the temple.

They might have stepped into a hermit's cave. A dim light came through the half-drawn shade at the only window of the room. On the bed, half covered, sat an old man in his Chinese jacket, with a hoary, frosted head, his eyes closed. Tom waited for his eyes to open to see the glass eye, but when they did open, he did not know which was glass and which was genuine.

"Go up and shake hands with Granduncle. This is my son Tom."

Tom sidled up and stared. The old man's hands moved. "Come closer. Let me look at you."

Old Tuck's face was all wrinkled, and he appeared to have an enormous torso. Tom could not tell whether the old man saw him or not. The eyelids seemed to open wider and give him a cold stare.

Old Tuck held Tom's hand and smiled behind his white walrus whiskers.

"Well, I'm glad you've come to see Granduncle. Tom, your father and I are great friends."

Tom sat gently on the edge of the bed.

"How are you these days?" the father asked.

"Just as usual," Old Tuck answered in a thin, whiskered voice. The cat peeped out of the bedding from his seat on Old Tuck's chest, and the old man stroked him. "He is a good animal. He keeps an old man warm."

When Old Tuck said "just as usual," it sounded as if he had lived an infinity.

"Granduncle, what do you do all the time?"

"What do I do? My son, I think."

"Granduncle, are you not lonely, living here all alone, and are you not afraid?"

"What do I have to be afraid of? This is a wonderful place." He knocked on the board partition. "I am as near Heaven as can be. The Western Queen Mother of Heaven is right there and Kwan Yu is beside her." Kwan Yu was the God of War, the model soldier of China's history, protector of the just and a scourge to the mean and dishonest. When Old Tuck gave away his money and retired, it was his wish to have this room because he was a great admirer of Kwan Yu, and the guild had asked the tenant family to vacate in his favor.

"Is it true that you led a band of Chinese from the West?" Tom had lost his fear now.

"Yes, I did, in my young days."

"You did it! But it is thousands of miles."

"Son, the Union Pacific was built then. We had a free ride." The old man seemed suddenly to come to life as he laughed a genuine laugh.

"You had a free ride?"

"Yes. Those who have money pay for tickets, and those who don't, get a ride all the same. Those days were fun—we slept on hay, and you looked out from under the horses' bellies to the starry skies above."

"You slept with horses, Granduncle? Didn't they step on you?"

"Oh, no. Horses are good animals. They are your friends, and they don't go to sleep. When you want more room, you push their legs, and they make way for you. I slept with one arm holding a horse's ankle, and he didn't dare move for fear of hurting me. Horses are your friends, son. Yes, those were great days."

Tom's heart was filled with admiration.

Old Tuck began to ask Tom Fong, Sr., about his family. "It is my only regret that I have no son as you have. That comes of not marrying when you are young. When you light a fire, you want it to go on and you have to light another stick before the one burning goes out. Ah, Tom, you are lucky to have a bright young son like this one."

Turning to Tom, he said, "Son, you should be a filial son to your father and carry on the Fong name. This is a great country. You and I and your father are all guests in this country. You like this country, don't you?"

"Sure. I see so many new things."

"Yes, it is a great country, and you are lucky to come here and learn things."

At this Tom was surprised. "Granduncle, do you really believe this? Didn't they beat you up and almost kill you?"

"Yes. But they could not kill me, could they?" Old Tuck laughed. "You see, son, you are young. You would not understand. I sit here all day and think. There are no bad people in this world."

"Weren't they bad people who tried to kill you?"

"There are cutthroats in every country. But cutthroats are not bad people. There are no bad people. Nobody is bad. All people are very much the same. Some are a little better and some a little worse. That is all. Some are richer, some are poorer, but they are much alike. They are born, get married, breathe for fifty or sixty years, and go away. Do you know, I am as rich as Rockefeller. I have all I want. You would not understand."

"Why do you say this is a great country, Granduncle?"

"I have lived here most of my life, and I know. I came at the age of eighteen to the Old Gold Mountain. I have seen this country grow. There were no motor cars, no movies, no radio, no railroads. They were just building the Union Pacific in my time. There was no electricity such as you see today. Just nothing but land and men in red scarves and woolen jackets. All the West was full of men in red scarves and woolen jackets, with guns and horses, and very few women. Men fought like dogs and were killed like dogs. The stronger dog won. But I have seen how this country has changed. They have the law now, and so long as you obey the law, nobody can do anything to you. You get your school free, and you can be anything you want. You need not be afraid of anybody but yourself. Son, you want to make your father proud of you. You want to make the Fong name shine."

Tom came away greatly excited, and he saw his father's face shining as if he were indeed already proud of him. He asked how the granduncle was taken care of, and his father said that the family upstairs was entrusted by the guild with the sacred duty of attending to his wants. The old man did not have to worry about anything.

Chapter 7

TOM NEVER TOOK HIS CLASSWORK VERY seriously, but he did his mathematics and English and science well. He grew peas in a bottle, and he once bought an ant nest in a glass case, and for a while he lived with the ants. He studied how the ants greeted each other and bred, and imagined himself an ant. In spring, he would always buy a pot of pansies. The velvety feeling of pansies and their fine coloring excited him; in fact, all flowers and insects excited him.

On Fridays, when Flora ate fish, he always told the fishmonger to leave the head on. His father loved a big carp's head, and his mother made a delicious dish of it with an incomparably rich and pungent sauce. When it was a small fish, the head was always Father's. Father declared that there was a fragrance and delicacy of flavor in a fish's jowl that nothing in the world could compare with. But the fish's head was usually quite messed up when it was served. The eyes were usually missing, and the jaw was often broken.

"What has happened to this blind fish?" asked the father at dinnertime.

"Tom took the eyes out," Flora explained.

"Whatever for?"

"I am studying them," answered Tom.

Tom always cut the eyeballs out. From the balls oozed a kind of sticky, transparent liquid. Sometimes he could see his own image in the fish's eye. Sometimes he wondered how he would see if his eyes were arranged on the two sides of his head like the fish's. He put away the liquid in a small wineglass.

"What you do that for?" asked Flora.

"It's like the albumen of an egg. I want to collect it."

"Tom, you are still so childish. You want to make a scrambled egg with it? What for?"

"I dunno."

A liquid so transparent and clear was wonderful. He dreamed that he might discover a magic elixir of eternal youth, or at least he could make good glue out of it.

He failed in history. The only thing interesting about Charlemagne was the peculiar pronunciation of his name. And he called Napoleon "Napkins Good-by." He took Bonaparte apart. "Bon" was "good" and "aparte" was "separate." "Napkins" expressed his contempt for the great conqueror. Why should he want to conquer the world? He read about the Battle of Waterloo and got some satisfaction from learning of the defeat of "Napkins," and he thought St. Helena a good place for him. He got an E, which was unusual for him.

"What's the matter with you, Tom Fong? You are a bright student, but you don't take your schoolwork seriously," said the history teacher, who was a man about fifty.

"Because there are too many interesting things to learn." He was thinking of his pansies and his ant nest and fish eyes at home.

"But wasn't Napoleon interesting?"

"What's interesting about him? He was so short."

"He did many great things."

"He killed so many people. He wanted to be bigger and stronger than the others. That was all."

"Don't you want to be a great man who changes the history of mankind?"

"No," answered Tom slowly and thoughtfully. The thought of wanting to change the world's history had never crossed his mind.

"But you look up to some great men, don't you?"

"Yes, I do."

"Who, for instance?"

"Newton. And Watt and Edison and Singer."

"What Singer? I never heard of him."

"I thought he invented the sewing machine. I bet Napkins couldn't do that."

"Who?"

"Napkins. That's my name for Napoleon."

"What's wrong with Napoleon?" asked the teacher, bewildered and amused. After thirty years of teaching about Charlemagne and Napoleon, he felt this an insult to his profession.

"He was on the side of Louis XVI. The revolutionists killed the king and Napkins killed the revolutionists. They all killed each other. They killed the people and the people killed them. See what I mean? He was crazy."

"Who was?"

"Napoleon. He thought he was bigger than all of us. Perhaps God wanted him to be king or something. And he landed in Alcazar."

"In what?"

"In Alcazar, that is, St. Helena. It's all the same thing, where all the lunatics ought to be shut up."

"Well, in a way, I suppose, all great men are a little crazy."

"Not Thomas Edison. He is right; he has proved that he is right. The Singer man was right, too. I mean all these fellows who wouldn't leave us alone. Like Ziffy Hrushka."

"Tell me about Ziffy Hrushka."

"He wants to bully all the boys. He and Gus want to be the leaders and won't leave us small fellows alone."

The teacher never thought much about Hrushka except that

he always failed. The truth was that he didn't know a thing about what the pupils did outside his class.

"You say Ziffy is the leader of the boys?"

"Yes. He wants to be governor or senator or something when he grows up."

"And you never want to be a leader of men?"

"No. I can't."

"Well, between you and me," said the teacher, screwing his eyes into sharp slits, "I don't want to be, either. I merely study these heroes objectively."

2

But Tom was absorbing new ideas. When he was in the ninth grade, he had to study more American history. It did not seem close to him. He had to wrestle with the Declaration of Independence. He had never read anything quite so difficult and obscure, and moreover, it was not the kind of English he liked. He went to his teacher for assistance. The teacher this year was a young radical, who wore spectacles. Tom had difficulty with the very long first sentence, which was a stately and cadenced period.

"What is 'to dissolve the political bands'?"

"That means to break the ties, ties connecting England and the Colonies."

"And this: 'a decent respect to the opinions of mankind requires that they should declare the causes which impel them to the separation'?"

"It means that we owe it to the other fellows to tell them why we did it."

Following Chinese tradition, Tom tried to read the sentence aloud to test how it sounded " '. . . requires that they should declare.' It sounds nice. But what requires?"

"Respect requires."

"Requires them to declare what?"

"Declare the causes which impel—"

"Respect requires you declare causes which impel." Tom drawled. "Mr. Watson, this is just like ancient Chinese. They make it so that you don't understand and will think the writer is very learned."

The words "unalienable rights" took the teacher a long time to explain.

"Why are they unalienable rights?"

"Because nobody can take them away from you. Life, liberty, and the pursuit of happiness. They are yours when you are born. Nobody can take away your freedom from you. Nobody can take away our right to be happy."

"Nobody?"

"Nobody," said the teacher firmly. He had an idea that this sounded terribly strange and revolutionary to young Tom.

"Who said so?" asked Tom.

"The founders of the Republic said so."

"Is that what you believe?"

"That is what all Americans believe. Remember, *nobody*," he added. "And that is why we have the United States of America today." The young teacher's face was inspired.

"And if somebody should try to take them away from you?"

"You throw them out. Read further. A government exists to protect these rights. A government has no right to govern unless the people want it to govern. And whenever any government destroys these things, the people have the right to change it, to throw it out, and get a new one."

Mr. Watson saw that some new ideas were penetrating Tom's mind. He went over the entire text with him and talked to him more than he ever talked to the class, because Tom was listening. It took an hour.

"Taxation without representation is tyranny," the teacher repeated. That was almost the strangest thing that Tom had ever heard of in all his life, so new that he literally gasped. "The taxpayer is the most important person in the United

States. He pays the taxes and chooses the government he wants." He could hardly believe it. "That is the basis of American democracy."

So when the next day the teacher said, "Tom Fong, stand up and tell the class what the Declaration of Independence says," Tom gave everybody a surprise.

"Who was the English king, Tom?" Mr. Watson began.

"George III."

"What was he like?"

"He was a moron. He couldn't even speak English well."

The class roared.

"And his queen was a flibbertigibbet," Tom added, using a new word that he had recently found in the dictionary. The class roared again.

"Well, why did the American people declare their independence from England? What does the Declaration say?"

Tom paused a while, and began. "When one people wants to break the ties with another people, they owe it to the other fellows to tell them why they did it. A government exists to protect our rights of life, liberty, and the pursuit of happiness. Nobody can take these rights away from the people. When any government takes these rights away, the people must throw the government out and get another."

The class listened closely. No student had thought the Declaration could be put so plainly.

"Go on," the teacher said.

"Well, the people of the Colonies put up with it until they couldn't stand it any longer. You know people are usually too lazy to change things. Now the Colonies would no longer put up with it. George III wasn't playing fair. He tricked them and gave them dirty deals one after another. He robbed them of their rights. Here are the facts. The king said laws were no good until he gave his okay and he didn't give his okay to laws that were good and needed and important. He said they would have to wait till he thought them over and okayed them, and then he forgot all about them. He called meetings of the representatives at the strangest, most unheard-of and faraway hick towns where they couldn't get at the necessary papers, just for the fun of wearing them out and making them give in." Tom gave as many facts as he could remember and concluded, "Every time he did one of these things we told him not to do it. We begged humbly in fact, and every time we begged him not to do it, he went ahead and did it again. A prince who was every bit a tyrant had no right to rule us. And we appealed to the English people, too, who had the same blood we had, and they didn't care. The people of the Colonies were sick of it all. They decided to throw out the king and declared themselves free."

The teacher's eyes were bright and his face was happy as he heard Tom express so clearly the ideas he had taught him the day before.

3

"Daisow," said Tom to Flora, at home. "Is it true the taxpayer is the most important person in the United States?"

"Yes, it is true," said Flora.

"Are you a taxpayer?"

"Yes, I am."

An idea so new took days for Tom to absorb and understand. The words of his teacher. "Nobody can take them away from you, nobody," rang in his ears. He thought he understood now why everybody in America was so proud of himself and would not yield to anybody and preferred to fight, and why American girls walked so straight and held their heads so high. He had long ago read in Chinese schoolbooks of George Washington and Abraham Lincoln and "government of the people, by the people, for the people." One often understands the words without understanding what they are meant to say. But this was clear. The taxpayer pays the money to support a government for his protection; he elects the government and tries to keep it in line, and if the government fails in its job, the taxpayers throw it out and elect another. Now he understood.

He thought of Ziffy and his gang, so arrogant and ready for a fight, like the white men he had seen in the streets of Canton where his own people always yielded. While boarding the steamer at Hong Kong, he had seen a white man in a sun helmet and shorts. A husky Cantonese sampan man brought his luggage to the ship and asked for more money. Whether the white man wanted to give more or not was up to him. The white man settled the question by a brutal blow on the boat-man's shoulder. It was lucky that the boatman did not strike back with his strong brown arms.

Tom's mother always told him to avoid a fight. And not only his mother. In any quarrel, whether of grown-ups or children, the party that "first raised the fist" was adjudged barbarous, no matter what the provocation. Was Ziffy then a good American? Tom was confused. Perhaps, he thought, the American people would throw Governor Ziffy out. And he felt a little better.

One day Daiko brought home a bilingual edition of the Confucian *Four Books,* with the Chinese text on the upper half of each page and the English translation on the lower half. No one in the family had really read the teachings of Confucius. The father had told Daiko to read it when he was of teen age, but the father himself did not know how to read it and could not teach him, and Daiko glanced at it and did not understand much of it. It was all "Confucius says." Some was obviously good sense, some seemed meaningless. Yiko had no interest in it whatsover and never touched it.

Now the father's eyes brightened when he saw the book.

"Make Tom read it. There is very good teaching in it. It teaches you how to be a gentleman. And Eva, you must read it, too."

The book was a great curiosity in the family. It said a lot of things about government and ritual and benevolence and righteousness that were merely words to the children, even with the help of English. It was also a bad translation, designed to be scholarly and unintelligible.

Eva had a few looks at it and lost interest. She pronounced her judgment: "Confucius says a lot of things—all about gentlemen. A gentleman does this, a gentleman does that. Nothing about ladies at all. Confucius is not interested in ladies, and I am not interested in him. I won't read him."

Tom struggled with the book and was quite bored. The aphorisms were terribly dull. The superior man blames himself; the inferior man blames others. This was awful. It sounded like Mrs. Dennis at the morning assembly. The *Book of Mencius* was a little better. It had longer passages, and there was one at the beginning where Tom made out that the King of Chi had a private park seventy *li* square and Mencius thought the King ought to make it into a public park and share his pleasures with the people. Mencius said that poachers in the King's forest were killed, and that was "like setting a trap seventy *li* square in the middle of the kingdom to trap his people." This Tom understood and liked. He never learned whether the King did or did not make it into a public park. Probably he didn't. Then he also left the book alone.

One night, the father said, "Tom, I don't see you reading the *Four Books.*"

"I don't see what's in it. A brother should be brotherly, a wife should be wifely, a father fatherly, a friend friendly. Of course!"

"Well, I can't teach you. Confucius was the wisest man. All the scholars admire him. Some day perhaps you ought to get a Chinese teacher. Are not the things he says in it very wise?"

"I dunno."

Tom turned to his ant nest.

Chapter 8

I

AS THE YEAR WENT ON TOM'S VOICE GREW hoarse. It was about this time that he became interested in girls. The world changed in depth and dimensions. It was bigger, better, and more complicated and more interesting than before. Vaguely he felt that he wanted something, missed something. He was leaving his fish eyes and his ant nest alone. He grew a little sad and sentimental. The world seemed full of mystery and unknown beauty, and he was seeing it for the first time. He learned that there was someone called God who was the source of the power and the mystery of the universe.

Flora frequently mentioned God to the family, both as a real being and as an English figure of speech that had nothing to do with religion, such as "for God's sake." (It was usually anybody's sake except God's.) Flora went regularly on Sundays to the Italian church in Chinatown, and Daiko sometimes went with her. When she went to special services and to holy communion, she always went alone. The Fongs knew well enough that Americans are Christians and Christians believe in God. There was nothing to argue about. It would be strange if the Americans did not believe in a god. Flora did not have to convince them that God exists. That Flora believed in God, that she prayed, that she had an image of the Virgin in her bed-

97

room, did not surprise them a bit. They let her religion alone. The women in China believe in Buddha more than the men. Men don't bother, but women do. This was just like China.

There were times when Flora got especially religious. That was always in the spring. It was as if something big was coming. She would pray more and go to church more often. When the Holy Week came, she went to church every day. That was when she lighted white candles before the image of the Virgin. Flora was a different person during that week. She always got a new hat with pink flowers on it. School was closed, and Tom and Eva saw Flora the whole day. She was a little nicer than usual, more forgiving, and kinder to everybody. When Easter came, Flora got up at five o'clock in the morning to attend the service at dawn. She put on her new bonnet and went with Daiko and the children to walk on upper Fifth Avenue.

Eva had put on a red Chinese dress that her mother had made for her. She was still slim, but her figure was developing. The children were walking with Flora while Loy walked behind with his parents.

"You must believe in God," said Flora. "Don't you believe God exists?"

"Of course I do."

Flora could get no more from them. The family accepted the existence of God. It was like accepting the existence of the father and the mother and the Third Avenue El.

"If you become a Christian, you don't cheat, don't gamble, don't drink."

"But good men don't cheat, don't gamble, don't drink."

"If you are a Catholic, you believe in marriage. The Protestants have divorce. Catholics don't."

This was the first time Tom learned there was any real difference between Catholics and Protestants.

"You see, it is good to believe in something."

In her Easter bonnet Flora looked happy and even beautiful.

"Daisow, you are a good woman," Tom said after a while. Flora smiled. "Am I?"

"You are not like American women. You are a good sister-in-law, and you love your husband."

"What makes you think American women don't love their husbands?"

"Isn't it true? You see it always in the movies. I saw one last week. She threw things at her husband, and they argued and yelled at the top of their voices, and he went out and slammed the door and went to some other woman. Are many husbands and wives like that?"

"I suppose so," Flora answered hesitantly.

"Do Americans beat their wives?"

Flora was horrified. "No. Gentlemen don't beat their wives. The law would not permit it, and American women would not put up with it. Do Chinese beat their wives?"

"Of course not. Chinese shout a great deal when they quarrel. That's all. You are happy with Daiko, aren't you?"

"Yes," replied Flora.

"You are a good daughter, too, to Father and Mother. Mother was scared when we were coming on the ship and she thought she was going to have an American girl for a daughter-in-law."

Flora was touched. She thought of many things, of the times when she had to control herself and keep quiet.

"Gee, Daisow, you are like a Chinese woman."

"What do you mean?"

"You work hard all day and have no quarrels with your husband and the parents."

"That's because my family is Italian. In Italy, my father tells me, children always obey the parents. A *padre* is a *padre*. It sounds different than in English."

"Do you speak Italian?"

"I speak a little. Papa and Mamma talk Italian at home, but it's all mixed up with English. If it's shoeshine or applesauce

99

or hot dogs, we say 'shoeshine' and 'applesauce' and 'hot dogs'."

"Italy must be a beautiful country. I have read about Rome and Florence and Venice."

"Italy is a beautiful country, and life is good there, Papa always says. He came from Milan. He and Mamma often talk of Italy when they have had a little wine. Life is good and easy there, with olive groves and good food and songs, and cathedrals and convents, and the whole population believes in God. The people are contented. It makes me want to go and see my mother country."

"You have never seen your country!"

"No. I was born here. I am an American, and I feel like an American. But some things that Papa says make me feel I am Italian, too. It's all sort of mixed up."

"Is your father happy here?"

"Well, he is now," said Flora. "He has Mamma, and that sort of makes it all right for him."

2

The midautumn night that year was particularly memorable. Uncle Chan had presented them with a set of moon cakes, and Tom Fong had invited the uncle to join the celebration at home. The uncle brought some crabs which he had seen that day in a Chinatown shop. These made it just right. The crabs were a little small, but the meat was good and they added to the atmosphere of the festival. The moon cakes were a complete set, specially ordered, and were to be played for in a game with six dice.

With the crabs and the dinner of special dishes cooked by the mother, including a fish cooked in chicken fat and a whole casserole of steamed turtle soup with ducks' feet, which Yiko despised but ate heartily, everybody was in a cheerful mood.

Uncle Chan had not been to visit them for some time. Tom

Fong had closed shop for the day and upstairs all the ironing boards and baskets of laundry had been cleared away. A silvery full moon had come up and seemed to hang on the top of the tree in the yard as they looked through the window of the kitchen where they ate.

"You've got a good brood, sister," said Uncle Chan.

"My Tom and Eva already speak English like American children," said the mother proudly.

"When will you be grandma?" asked the uncle. For some reason he used the English word "grandma." Flora understood and blushed.

"I don't know," commented the mother dryly.

"Hurry up, Loy," said the uncle. "It is about time you got a *sailokok* [a boy]."

"We can't afford it," said Daiko. The mother looked at him.

"You are all wrong. You all behave like Americans. You get a *sailokok* and become a father. What is life for anyway?"

The uncle stood up to help himself to another turtle paw and sat down. His rubbery neck stretched and shrank again.

After dinner they played for the moon cakes. The first prize was a large cake about eight inches in diameter, and the others decreased in rank and size, all named after the different degrees of the imperial examinations. There were a great many cakes of the lower ranks, and each time one threw a four in red, he was given something, depending on what went with it on the other cubes. The ranks went up according to the number of cubes that turned up with the same number. But there was only one first prize, which was the *chuang yuan,* and no one could claim it for his own until the end of the game when, in the case of a tie, the contestants had to throw again for decision. The first prize required the throwing of four dice turning up the same number. The cakes were filled with sweetened pea flour, and the third rank was a beautiful thing filled with lotus seeds, higher than the others and shaped like a drum. Everybody played for the first prize and there was great excitement. Eva threw a *chuang yuan,* and there was a great shout. The largest cake went to Eva when the game was over.

While the children ate their cakes, the uncle sat down to talk family business.

"How about the restaurant sister was talking about?" asked the uncle. "If you move to Chinatown, we'll have a lot of fun together."

"Not so easy," said the father.

"But you are doing well."

"Yes," said the mother confidently. "We have always new customers. It will take a few years yet."

The father's eyes looked up surprised at the mother's confident tone. "You talk as if you are sure of it."

"Why not?" said the mother. "I will bide my time."

"It is not easy with such a large family. The children are growing up. We have been able to save a little sum, but it is a long way yet. Happily no one is ill, but Eva had a tooth pulled out. It cost us five dollars. She has been wanting to wear a brace to keep the teeth straight. I told her we cannot afford it."

"That reminds me," said the mother. "A tooth has been troubling me. Chan, will you pull it out for me? It has been shaky for some time."

Uncle Chan was glad to have the rare opportunity of pulling out a tooth. He rose and crossed the room. "Let me see it." He felt it. "It moves," he declared. "It is easy."

Bending over the mother, he said, "Close your eyes." He put his finger into the mother's mouth. The mother yelled. The uncle was firm. The mother yelled again. The uncle was still firmer. After a third prolonged yell, the uncle drew out his fingers.

"It is out!"

He held a saucer before the mother's mouth and said, "Cough hard," and gave a powerful slap on her shoulder. She coughed and out fell a tooth into the saucer.

"It is a racket," said the uncle proudly. "American doctors charge five dollars to pull out a tooth. It is a racket."

His round, shiny frame swung around and slumped into the big chair.

Mother Fong, still suffering from the shock and pain held a hand to her cheek.

"It is a racket, I say. Go and wash out your mouth, and in a few minutes you won't feel anything."

"You didn't have to strike so hard on my shoulder." She got up and went to her room.

"You feel the pain in the back and don't feel it in the tooth; feel the pain in the tooth, and don't feel it in the back, see?"

When Mother came back, Yiko said, "You ought to have an artificial tooth filled in there. Otherwise the upper molar has nothing to grind on."

"Don't make me laugh," said Uncle Chan. "If you lose a molar, you lose a molar. So what?"

"I don't need a false tooth," declared the mother.

"But if you lose another molar?" said Yiko.

"I don't want any false teeth. You leave my teeth alone. I can bite my way for another twenty years yet."

"Your mother is right. Don't you go near a dentist. When he sees your teeth, he will pull a half a dozen of them out and make you pay for pulling them out. If you get a small hole, he first drills to make it bigger. Then he makes a bridge, and the bridge grips your good teeth and presses them until the good teeth get sick and the dentist can pull them out too. You leave your teeth alone, sister."

"I am ashamed of you, Uncle," said Yiko. "You have been in this country so long and still talk like that. Americans are scientific. Dentistry is a science."

"A science!" The uncle's lips spluttered in a series of explosions.

"It is a science," Yiko insisted. The uncle spluttered louder than ever. "Like insurance," Yiko went on. "It is a science, too. Father, if you are thinking of saving money to open a restaurant, you ought to take an endowment policy. You ought not to put your money in rolls in your drawer. You ought to let it draw interest for you."

"Are you trying to sell insurance to your own father?"

"Yes, but you never will listen."

"Trying to sell *insu* to your own father. You are no son of mine!" *Insu* was a Cantonese word taken over from the English.

"But it is for your good, and for the family's good."

"A son trying to guarantee his father's life! What is the world coming to?"

"It is not for me. It is the Cornelius Underwriters, the biggest and best company in New York."

"As a respectful and dutiful son, you leave your father's life alone, will you? If I die—"

There was a stir of "hush-hush" from the uncle and the mother and Daiko. It did sound very gloomy and even sacrilegious. The father was not permitted to finish his sentence. Yiko was discomfited.

"I mean an endowment, savings for yourself. I don't mean—" He could not finish. The subject, bordering on sacrilege, was dropped.

"Nobody wants to talk about that tonight," said the mother. "It is midautumn."

3

The children had been plotting to go up to the roof tonight. Seeing the father upset a little, Tom asked Eva to bring up the question because she was the only girl in the family and the father was always indulgent toward her.

Eva went up and whispered to the mother if she might ask Father, and her mother told her to speak to Father directly.

"Father, this is midautumn. Don't you think it a good idea if we all go up to the roof to enjoy the moon?"

"We ought to be thankful that all the family is together tonight. We should enjoy ourselves," said the mother, supporting her daughter's suggestion. She was feeling happy herself.

The father did not say no. A cheer went up from the children. They helped carry the blankets and pillows to the roof and brought along a pot of tea and cups and the cakes. The family emerged from the attic staircase. The roof was enclosed on both sides by the walls of higher buildings. The outstretched branch of the neighbors' tree had grown perceptibly bigger and nearer, and was now a mass of white, shadowy forms reflecting the silver moonlight. Above, the moon rose sharp and clear and round against the dark side of the corner of the neighbor's house and flooded half the roof with its light. The air was perfectly still, and the night was cool, calm, and beautiful. Below, the boarded-up yards were cut into squares of white with sharp shadows.

The family arranged itself on the roof. Only Mother Fong sat and refused to lie down. Lying there, the family talked of home and of relatives in Sunwei.

Tom could not quite realize where he was. He told himself he was with the family in New York, that he was in school here in America, but his mind drifted back to his home, the farmhouse at Sunwei, the village street, the lichee forest behind their house, the games played there, the playmates whom he had left behind in China. He remembered them so well, so clearly, including the number of windows in the schoolhouse and the clock in the tower. It was a red-brick building with a playground at the back. He had had to memorize these details when he was coming to America, to meet the test of the immigration authorities. In fact, he had had to write them down and memorize them on the ship. It was almost a matter of life and death. If his father should have told the authorities that there were ten windows in their house and he should tell the immigration authorities there were twelve, or if he said the main street led north and south instead of east and west, or missed a few other such details, he might be shipped back across the Pacific.

Now he could even see the footpath that led to the five lichee trees and the birds' nest on one of them. He told Flora, who was lying next to him.

"Daisow, we had a big house at home, because father sent us money, and there is a duck pond near the lichee forest and Mother used to raise ducks and we had to chase the ducks home at night. Eva, how many windows are there in our house?"

"Ten."

"And the main street?" Tom asked again.

"The main street leads east and west and ends in the school-house on the west side, and the schoolhouse has fifteen windows and a clock in the middle, and the playground is at the back." Eva rattled it off.

"You miss something."

"Yes, I know. And there is a church, and the church has no belltower but is enclosed all round by a wall."

"Pass!" said Tom.

Flora did not understand. "What are you doing? Is it a game?"

Eva explained.

"How many windows are there in our house?" Tom asked Flora.

"How do I know? Let me see."

They tried to count but could not agree whether the skylight should count or not.

"You'd better find out when you go to China. We wouldn't let you land in China if you guessed wrong."

"If I go, I go with Daiko. I'm not afraid."

Tom laughed. "No, I was just fooling you."

The children felt like listening to tales. Mother Fong always told them tales in the summer evenings.

"Mother, tell us about Chang-O, the beauty in the moon."

"You have heard that story."

"Tell it again."

So the mother again told them of the Archer and the beauty Chang-O, how the Archer fell in love with the girl and chased her, how she was afraid and fled and the Archer still pursued her, until Chang-O flew far up into the clouds and reached the moon, where she is now sitting under the laurel tree. Once there, Chang-O could not fly back, and so she can only sit under the laurel tree and think of her lover. That is why the moon always confers the magic of love on young men and maidens.

Lying there, Tom admired the heavens, the unspeakable beauty of the pale stars, and the serene moon moving silently across the sky.

"Tom, what are you thinking about?"

"About up there," he pointed to the sky. "Isn't it wonderful?"

"You see, there is a God," said Flora. Her voice was calm and the sentence was spoken simply, naturally, without intention of saying more.

"Do you believe?" she asked Tom.

"I believe," said Tom hesitatingly.

"Do you believe?" she turned to Eva.

"I believe."

"What are you children talking about?" asked Mother Fong.

"Daisow is asking us if we believe in God."

"Don't be silly. Of course there is a god. If you are a good man, you go to Western heaven, if you are a bad man, you go to hell."

"But God takes care of us if we pray to him," said Flora.

"Of course. What use would he be if he didn't?" said the mother.

Flora did not say more.

"Flora, I like your religion," said the mother. "It makes you a good woman."

Flora could not say what she wanted in Cantonese. "Tell Mother," she said to her husband, "that the Catholic religion is the true religion."

"Any religion is true if it makes you a good man," replied the mother. "The Catholic Church is a good one if it makes you good."

Tom was not thinking of the goodness and badness of man. He was thinking of this life and this vast world, of which he was such an insignificant part, and of the beauty and power and mystery of the magnificent universe.

Tom's family, like many other villagers, had hated the Christian religion, more as a social than as a religious fact. The American missionary and his wife in his native village were no better and no worse than the Chinese in their personal relationships. They lived mostly apart from the Chinese and had contacts only with their Chinese assistants. The wife was a kind person, and she played the organ and taught at school. The missionary was seen walking in the country with big fast strides, wearing a helmet and shorts, hell-bent to save the heathen. Yet in spite of his shorts and his fast strides he was dignified. He could preach a sermon in Cantonese if he had to, but usually he simply attended the service and let the Chinese preachers preach for him. His job was to administer funds, and he bickered about the wages of the local teachers, like a businessman, and when he bickered, he blasphemed under his breath. According to the house servants, he was known to have flown into a rage at home and shouted in his wife's face. The non-Christians did not like the Christians because the latter cut themselves off socially from the rest, did not join the village festivals, and were a closed community by themselves, and there was always a feeling that they were relying on foreign protection from a power represented by gunboats. Christianity was a hundred years old in Canton, and yet this flavor still remained.

Only when Flora pointed to the heavens and said softly, "You see, there is a God," it sounded different. Tom was confused.

Chapter 9

WITH TOM'S ADOLESCENCE, THE AWAKENing of his life, his head grew very busy. It was as if he had left the child's world, had shed it as the cicada sheds its skin and comes forth in a new dress. The world grew bigger, more complicated, more fraught with urges, powers, and meanings. The child's world of physical sense, of touch and smell and color—the smell of fish and meat and onions, the smooth touch and the hues of pansy petals, the shape of everything he examined with his fingers—the world of physical senses was still there but it had lost its novelty. It seemed as if he had a new vision and could see further, and a new heart and could feel more deeply, and a new brain that began to puzzle over invisible causes, origins, meanings, and purposes, beneath the surface of shapes and forms.

Since that night on the roof when Flora had said to him, "There is a God," he had felt a certain restlessness. It was as if he were presented with a vast and complex algebraic problem, and Flora had said the answer was x = 349. But to know the answer was one thing; to work it out through four pages of mystifying equations was another. The fact that the answer was provided in a textbook prepared by the first mathematicians of the times would not make any difference. It would not satisfy Tom's inquiring mind. Why are we born? Why do men live and die? If they die, why do they live? If they don't die, how do they continue to live? Do we know the meaning of why we live? Is our life snuffed out at the end of our days, like insects'? Tom was seized with a vague feeling of great sadness.

He went to Central Park, chiefly to look at the zoo. He would stand for ten minutes fascinated by a pink-bottomed gibbon or a chimpanzee and imagine how the animal thought and what was going on in its head. At the circus he always wondered what the lions thought of the human orchestra and the blazing lights. He could not take his eyes off the rhino and the hippo. Once he went to the Bronx Zoo where he saw a group of flamingos and was so overcome by the serenity and grace and color of these pink birds and the reality of life to the flamingos themselves that he came home dazed with the mystery. Was his life the same as that of the flamingo, or was it more true, more real? He was not quite sure. Do the giraffes look down upon us as queer pygmies? Probably yes, but more probably they do not care who we are. Why did the bison look at him as if he hated him? How does the spider invent a chemical glue that never dries in the air?

There was one special problem that bothered him, to which no one provided the answer. When he was in the Bronx Zoo, he went into the house of tropical birds. He saw some South American fishers that had enormous, powerful bills ten inches long, and he saw humming birds whose bodies were hardly two inches long, and a pink parrot who wore for his crest an extravagant Parisian hat that would make Fifth Avenue ladies swoon with envy. The triumph of it, and the pride! But he was struck particularly by a detail. A meadow lark had an eyebrow, a sharp, clear black streak above its eyes as if it were painted with a painter's brush. All of a sudden he was brought up short. How did the bird get the painted eyebrow? He examined it. The black line consisted of a great number of fine feathers crossing it at certain points. The feathers turned black on entering that line and turned white again after leaving it at an angle. And all these feathers coming at an angle were so arranged that the beautiful black line was formed. He was sure the lark did not know how he did it any more than he himself knew how his own fingernails grew. The birds and animals were too real, too complete in themselves, for him ever to believe that the lark sang and painted his eyebrows for man's enjoyment. The male bird painted that unexcelled eyebrow to bewitch the feminine heart of the female, so as to reproduce more young birds. But why more young birds? Who cares? They call it instinct, but that doesn't solve anything. Tom called it the problem of the feathers.

Once he saw the problem, he saw it everywhere. The same problem was presented by the golden rings on the peacock's tail and by the stripes of a lake perch. How did the birds do it? He went to the Public Library and read and read, but there was no answer. Blind but numberless chance variations, the books said, and survival of the fittest variation. He refused to accept this. Did the spider discover the permanent adhesive and did the poisonous snake discover his fatal venom, which is a highly complicated chemical formula, by chance, through numberless "blind" variations, until he hit upon it? And after accidentally producing that venom, did he accidentally possess the mystic gift of passing on his secret formula to his young so that his young should manufacture a venom quite as good as their father's, so that generations of vipers might survive in a most fitting fashion? The poison as poison was superb, deadly, infallible. It was not the problem of the survival of the fittest, but of the *arrival* of the fittest, not how the fittest survived, but how the fittest ever *arrived* at all. Not how the giraffe survived by his long useful neck, but how did he *get* it? How did the jellyfish get his sting, and the electric eel happen to shoot a current of several hundred volts, and the deep-sea fish happen to carry an electric lantern before his

113

eyes? Surely, life contained a secret. The answer was woefully inadequate. Do the men of science know that they don't know? This problem worried him for years until he met a girl named Elsie.

So whenever Tom went to Central Park, he had a new feeling of wonder and sadness, that he did not know the bottom of it all. He usually went to the rocks near the Seventies and he liked to get himself lost in the winding footpaths and rocky streams. Sometimes he would lie there, feeling a kinship with the soil of this good and beautiful earth, lying on the cool cushion of green blades and watching the clean furs and bright eyes of the squirrels. There he could see above him the serried windows of the skyscrapers. How men worked and squirrels played! Something about this was wrong, he thought. On cloudy days the skyscrapers were half hidden in clouds. Then they were prettier. The sharp spires of the edifices would emerge above the sailing clouds, and they would have a certain awe-inspiring heavenward lift and glory about them. Or when the setting sun shot shafts across them, with sharp perceptible shadows and dark areas in the air, and there was a clear sky, then the proud structures seemed to move in the sky like the masts of a ship at sea.

2

When Christmas came, the family went to a Christian service. The father had been in this country for more than thirty years without ever being inside a church. Once he had peered in at the door for curiosity. He knew it was a church, but it had nothing to do with him.

Tom and Eva and their mother had once been persuaded to go with Flora to the Italian church in Chinatown. Very few Chinese were there. There were many poor people in it, and the majority of them were women. Mother Fong thought it was like being for the first time inside Western society, meeting Americans indoors, and not just seeing them on the streets. The poor old women, their black long skirts almost covering their ankles, were just like Chinese women. Some were infirm, or had swollen ankles, or walked with shaky frames. Others were young housewives. These were people just like Chinese people. There was something about poverty that made everybody familiar and easy to understand as if you knew their hearts, their struggles, and their secret self-pride, and life was a long and never-ending process of struggling and maintaining that pride. Things happen to poor people, accidents, deaths, mishaps, loss of a job, and the poor struggle on so that they can keep afloat on the stream of life and not be entirely submerged, and things continue to happen to them one after another. And these struggles give them a common stamp of humanity, but each conceals his individual sorrows and fights for his chance. So Mother Fong lost all her fear, even though it was like meeting American society for the first time.

Not only that. The church was dark and old, and the light from the stained-glass windows left many patches of dark in different corners. All was quiet, though a few whispered. The men and women sat with their heads bowed in silence. Mother Fong had the feeling that she was inside a Chinese temple. The altar, the candles, the dim light of a red glass hanging near the altar, like the "everlasting lamp" before a Buddha, the images, the priest's cassock were all reminiscent of the Buddhist symbols of worship. Dozens of small candles flickered in the semidarkness before altars on the side. The church was very poor. In the niches and on the pedestals stood painted images of saints. An old staircase on the right, probably dangerous for use, was blocked up with boards and planks. Flora knelt down before one of the statues and prayed. Mother Fong was glad to see her daughter-in-law kneel down and pray like a poor woman.

But this Christmas they went to a big cathedral on One

hundred and Twelfth Street because the service there was beautiful.

Tom and Eva had been three years in New York. Sounds and faces had ceased to be strange. Everybody talked Christmas and felt Christmas three weeks before it came. At school and in the shops they heard about Christmas. They had bought and sent Christmas cards to their friends. The cards were pretty, with cottages in snow and golden bells and reindeer. The day before Christmas vacation they had a Santa Claus at school; then they saw the same Santa Claus outside of Bloomingdale's. Flora bought Eva a bright red beret and Tom three pairs of socks. So Christmas had come even to the Fongs.

They went up the high stone steps. The mother was properly warned to cover her head with a black shawl, which Flora had thoughtfully brought along. Tom stopped to gaze at the sculptures in the doorway. The cathedral was jammed. It was so big and the roof was so high that one felt more like being in a court with tall columns than in a house. People stood and walked about, though an effort at silence was made. Far off, about two hundred feet up the aisle, there was a shining altar of gold, and the figures of boys in white were moving about, and a voice came from somewhere in that direction and boomed down the aisle. Tom and Eva were awed.

When they had taken their seats, Tom could not take his eyes off the magnificent tall columns. A feeling of grandeur seized and inspired him. He strained his eyes to look. In the far-off chancel before the altar there appeared a little shack with human figures in it, and a donkey. Tom recognized the scene as a miniature stable, with the Virgin Mary holding a baby and three resplendently dressed old men. Then the organ pealed. The sound came from aloft and filled all the corners of the church with its vibrations. Tom's pores opened. Soon a heavenly strain of voices, boys' and men's, arose. It was unspeakably beautiful, this singing of men and boys in peace and harmony in common tribute to something great and inspiring. He had never heard such a chorus of voices before. The singing of the oratorio lasted for some time. While the boys' voices trailed up and down, the men's voices responded, majestically marking the rhythm, and while the men's voices rumbled, the soprano voices soared again to ever new heights. All the time the bass drummed in certain short quiet phrases, but the soprano strain went on its way, seemingly ignoring it but really supported by it. Then the boys' voices stopped and picked up a low, familiar melody, as if complaining and yet telling a heart-warming story. The pace quickened, and Tom's eyes filled. Something, the voices said, something great was happening. All the voices broke out in a thrilling and triumphant full-throated chorus, united in glad tribute to something greater than all of us.

When the singing was over, a priest appeared at the pulpit in the middle of the aisle. The Fongs were sitting far back, but Tom listened and caught sentences he could understand.

"Christ was a poor man. He was born not in a palace, but in a stable, in a little shack in Bethlehem, surrounded with horses and hay and the smell of manure. He had nothing to do with kings and the great of the earth." Tom became interested. "All his life he lived and mingled with the poor, and he went about ministering to the poor, the sick, and the lowly. He drank with sinners and sat in taverns with the publicans, and he allowed a prostitute to anoint his feet. He loved the poor because he understood them, and he understood them because he lived with them."

The worship in its beauty and majesty was the most inspiring thing Tom had ever seen, almost the biggest show next to a sunset over the skyscrapers of New York.

The family left the church, and Tom was silent all the way home. The fact that people could unite and sing was so moving. What the priest had said about Christ being a poor man brought it very close to him. If religion stood for poor struggling men and women, it was all right. The Christian religion, he thought, was not difficult to understand. He wished life could be all as beautiful and simple and true as that.

3

As Tom and Eva grew older, they began to take longer walks. Eva was seventeen and grown-up, and it seemed that the older she grew, the less she was inclined to walk, but the older Tom grew, the longer walks he took. He needed someone to walk with him. Once he exasperated Eva by suggesting, when they had got through the Bronx Zoo, that they go on to the Botanical Gardens.

"Tom, you are dreadful," said Eva, and he had to take her home.

They often went on Sundays along the upper East River. There was no highway then, and the river edge was partly filled with garages, warehouses, and shabby tenements. Still it was in the open and one had a clear view across the river of Welfare Island and Randall's Island. In the distance the Hellgate Bridge of the Pennsylvania Railroad stood, where a train could be seen crawling, and sometimes they could hear its whistle. There was an asphalt motor way and along its side the footwalk was a good place for rambling in Chinese style.

Nearer home, at Seventy-eighth, a ferry on the East River carried visitors to Welfare Island. On Sundays there were usually bigger crowds going and coming over. Tom and Eva would come to this part on summer days when there was a steady cool breeze and watch the river traffic of coal barges and refuse barges and tugboats pushing sections of trains along the river. The east bank was always in the shade in the afternoon, and they pretended sometimes to fish in the deep waters here, but there were no fish. To the south, the Queensboro

Bridge spanned the river, and beyond, where they could not see, were the Williamsburg and the Manhattan Bridges.

Sometimes Tom walked alone to the head of the Queensboro Bridge, drawn by a mysterious power like his early fascination with the El. The bridge leaped some sixty feet above him, a mass of black crossed steel trusses, supported by heavy black stone towers that might vie with kings' tombs and medieval châteaux in their size and height. Tom loitered under the shadows, a tiny figure by comparison, wearing a loose sweater. He looked up. He saw that the bridge had the sweep of the sea, the grace and strength of a great work of art, the independence and pride of a beautiful woman, the leaping power of a leopard. The steel tower rising solid into the clouds must have been a hundred and twenty feet high from the ground. Traffic went on, trucks, street cars, automobiles, thousands of tons passing over it, and the bridge received them and did not even tremble. The bridge was a product of the human mind, impossible in any other civilization. If it had been created a thousand years ago, it would have become renowned as the greatest single wonder of the world, greater in size than the Pyramids, more wonderful than the Leaning Tower of Pisa, more majestic than the palaces of Assyrian kings.

Tom looked at it with puckered brow, admiring it and not understanding it. The bridge contained a mystery, a secret of human knowledge in a vast realm that he did not understand. There were so many things he wanted to study and understand, and he hated it that there were things he did not understand. The bridge itself became a symbol of the power of the age of machines and what makes the wheels of modern civilization turn.

The first thing that had impressed him on his second day in America was an electric orange squeezer at a lunch counter. Americans squeeze oranges by machines, mix chocolate drinks by machines, sell stamps and peanuts and Coca-Cola by machines, shovel earth by machines, haul cargo by machines, sweep snow by machines. He went all the way to the Pennsylvania Station to see the electronic door. It was ghostly. All these things he did not understand. Would he be an engineer one day when he was a man?

Chapter 10

FLORA WALKED INTO THE LAUNDRY ONE afternoon, whispered a message to her husband, and went upstairs. A mysterious smile hung on her face as she passed out of the door.

"What is it?" asked the father.

Loy went on ironing. He took a few seconds before he could open his mouth.

"What is it?" the father repeated.

"Father," said Loy, setting down his iron. "Flora is going to have a child."

"Good! Good! Good!" the father said three times. He felt happiness welling up from his toes to his heart; his face was flushed, and his nerves were taut.

"She just came back from the doctor," added Loy calmly, not to show too much excitement.

"Good! Good!" The tone suggested triumph, success, achievement, good luck.

"Does your mother know?" he asked.

"I don't know."

"Go and tell Mother. No. I'll tell her."

The father dashed out of the room. Then he turned and said, "Never mind the laundry. Never mind anything. You come up too."

"What? Close shop?"

"Yes, close shop, for all I care." The father's face was eager and excited.

"You go up, Father. I'll come up later."

"Aren't you happy?" There were shimmering tears in the old man's eyes.

"Yes, Father. But I had better stay here." Loy was actually feeling shy.

Flora was in her room, and Mother Fong was in the kitchen. The father broke in panting hard.

"What is the matter?" said the mother, turning round and keeping her hand on the iron. "Has anything happened to my Eva? Or Tom?"

"Has Flora told you?" cried the father.

"No, what? You must speak."

He came close to her ear, trembling.

The mother gasped and then a broad, blissful smile started from her lips and spread all over her face. "Heavens!" she exclaimed.

"But where is Flora?"

The mother went with hurried steps to Flora's door. It was closed.

"Flora! Flora!"

"I'm here, Mother."

Mother Fong opened the door and went in. Flora was lying on her bed, in tears.

The mother went and sat on the bed and sought Flora's hand and held it.

"My daughter!" the mother said. "God bless you! How old is it?"

"Only two months."

"Are you sure?"

"The doctor said so."

The mother went to the image of the Virgin and knelt down.

"What are you doing?" asked Flora.

"Offering thanks to God."

Flora saw the mother draw a cross on her chest.

"Is this right?"

Flora was so taken by surprise she could not say anything and merely nodded. "M-hm!" she said, and her voice was that of a woman in surprised satisfaction.

"I shall come to your church and offer thanks to God with you. Whenever you are ready, I shall come with you."

Flora got up with a new pride on her face. She had wiped away her shame, the shame of sterility. She wanted to cook lunch, but the mother would not allow it.

"I'm perfectly well," Flora laughed.

"No, not today."

At lunch Loy came up, and the four of them sat together.

"Flora, you pray for us," said the mother.

Flora had been used to say grace silently by herself merely as a gesture of habit. "God is merciful," she began and stopped. The rest was in her heart.

"It is a good god she worships," said the mother.

Loy for some reason was bashful and silent. The father said, "Loy, you must take good care of Flora. It is a father's order. You must not excite her. Make her happy while she is bearing your child. And Flora," he said with a serious face, "you must take good care of yourself. Do not go dashing down the stairs the way you do. We will do all we can."

To Flora it seemed silly for the family to make so much fuss over her as if she was very sick or very important. But the seriousness with which the Chinese took the situation was shown in the fact that the father did not go down to the shop after lunch. Loy thought this silly, too. He wanted to go down and finish the laundry.

"Go down if you want to," the father said.

The father sat in his chair in the sitting room. Suddenly he thought of something. He got up and went up to the roof.

After a while he came down with a piece of board and looked for the hammer and saw.

"What are you doing?" asked his wife.

"I'm going to fix that broken stair."

He chopped. He sawed. He measured. He went down the stairs and came up again. It took him more than an hour.

Tom and Eva came home to find their father bending over the dark staircase.

"Why, Father, what are you doing?"

"I am fixing that dangerous board."

"Let me do it," said Tom.

"You go up. Mother will tell you."

"Tell us what?"

"Ask Mother. She will tell you."

Tom and Eva went on while their father hammered in a nail.

"Come back!" he said and straightened himself. "Tom and Eva, I want you to be very nice to Flora."

"Has she done something wrong?"

"No, no! I just want you both to be nice to her. And don't rush and bump into her. Go on, Mother will tell you."

Tom and Eva were completely perplexed until they learned the news from Mother.

"Tom and Eva, you are going to be young uncle and aunt. Go and congratulate Daisow."

"How?"

"Go in together, and congratulate her. Say what you want to say in English."

Tom and Eva stood solemnly before Flora's door.

"May we come in?"

Flora saw them and broke into a laugh. "Come in."

Solemnly Tom and Eva approached. Eva's eyes were fixed on Flora's body with a quiet wonder.

"Congratulations, Daisow," they said together.

124

Flora hugged them. "Thank you." Suddenly Tom broke away as if he were frightened.

"Are you going to be sick in bed?" Tom asked.

"No, Tom. I'm perfectly well."

When they came out, Mother said, "Now go down and congratulate Daiko."

Tom and Eva dashed down to the shop.

The father went out after he had fixed the staircase. At about six o'clock, he returned bringing a big roast chicken and merely saying that he had been to Chinatown. He also brought a new pipe with a jade mouthpiece, which was evidently a celebration gift to himself. The features of his face were subtly changed, and he smelled of drink. He wore a devil-may-care expression, like that of a scholar who had passed the imperial examinations at the age of sixty after forty years of failures. When Flora had been thought to be sterile, he had not said anything, but it had hung like a load on his chest. Now the surprise almost overwhelmed him.

That night smoking his new pipe in the lamplight, the father announced to the family firmly, "I am going to raise a beard."

The idea of her father having a beard was repugnant to Eva, but they were all completely awed by his voice, and no one said anything.

A week later Flora went to see Father Bosco. She found him in the rectory adjoining the church. He was an old man, with a clean-shaven, gentle face.

"I came to see you about my mother-in-law," she said.

"I remember seeing her with you in church. Why don't you bring her more often? And your husband does not come regularly."

"Father—I am expecting a child."

"Well, that is good news. I'm glad to hear of it. May God bless you."

"And when I told Mother, she prayed to the Most Blessed Virgin."

"That is good," said the priest. "A heathen can worship according to his own light. God is opening the way. Perhaps —we don't know."

"Father, my mother says she wants to come to the church and offer thanks to God."

"We should give thanks to God on all occasions. The expectant mother is sanctified by the Most Blessed Virgin's own experience as a human mother. After it is born, I know, you will want the child to be baptized."

"Yes," Flora answered with a little hesitation in her voice.

"That is good!" said the priest. "But I am a little surprised."

"I can't quite explain. My family leave my religion entirely alone. They believe in God—in a general way."

So the next day Flora took the mother to the church. Mother Fong said she would donate to the church ten dollars, and she also had a great many candles lit for the occasion. She knelt and looked up at the image of the Virgin, and she said in Chinese, "Dear God, take good care of my daughter-in-law. I pledge that if Flora gives birth to a boy, I shall donate fifty dollars, and if she gives birth to a girl, I shall donate thirty dollars."

Father Bosco watched the woman as she prayed on her knees. She was honest and devout and sincere. Certainly she believed. After the pledge, Mother Fong got up and fumbled in her pocket and handed the priest a ten-dollar bill, in full view of the Virgin.

2

Flora became unwell. She seemed to suffer much from nervousness, indigestion, quick breath, lassitude, fatigue, and vomiting. She was also restless, and once she went and stayed with her parents for a change for nearly a week. She had not known what pregnancy was like, and she drew some comfort from the light way in which Mother Fong dismissed her pains and troubles.

"The best way to expect a baby's coming is to forget it," said Mother Fong. "We country women work right up to the day of labor."

Nevertheless, Flora knew that the mother was very pleased and she was treated as a special person. Mother Fong told her to stop work when she was tired, and she went with her to buy a new coat. She was fed systematically, Flora thought, almost like a prize dog before a dog show, or a champion boxer training for a fight. Father Fong himself went to a medicine shop on Mott Street to select the best quality of "Indian bread" (food for the fairies) and *tangkwei* roots (*angelica sinensis,* supposed to be good for the breast), matrimony vine, and a black shining root called *tihuang* (*rehmannia glutinosa*)—all tonics for the woman's system, especially during pregnancy. He tested the black root at home by putting it in water.

"See, it sinks. This is the best quality, grown in Huaiking."

All these herbs tasted mildly sweet and had an exotic medicinal aroma. Flora didn't believe in them and yet she didn't quite disbelieve. They seemed to do her good, to tone up her whole system. The best part of it was that the sliced roots were cooked with chicken, freshly killed at the live poultry yard in Chinatown. The fact that the chicken was freshly killed made all the difference. It was steamed, and the soup was carefully kept simmering, so that for hours the smell of *angelica sinensis* filled the whole flat, and Flora's mouth watered. The soup was served in the earthen pot in which it was steamed, and it was all for her and for her alone. Father Fong would get the wings of the chicken because of their delicacy, and also the gizzard. When it wasn't a special "tonic" chicken, the mother saw to it that Tom got the breast and Eva a drumstick. But when there was a smell in the house of *tangkwei* and *tihuang,* it meant that the whole chicken was for

Flora, though Mother Fong still managed to give the wings and the gizzard to the father, who protested and then ate them with great gusto. A mysterious importance, of great gravity, attached to the fact that Flora was fruitful and promised to bring forth a new branch of the Fong family. Through her the Fongs would multiply.

Fresh color came into Flora's face. It was summer and the days were hot, and Flora was inclined to take long rests. But seeing that the daughter-in-law was in good health, the mother said, "You should not lie too much, Flora. You should get up and move about. The child is in you. Through your motion, your child moves. Through your life, your child lives."

It was in this period of Flora's pregnancy that many things happened. It seemed to Tom, looking back, that the promised birth of the grandchild was a signal for many things to happen to the family. Yiko got engaged. La Guardia was re-elected Mayor. In China, war broke out with Japan. And later there was an accident which brought a great change to the family.

Chapter 11

✳❀✳❀✳❀✳❀✳❀✳❀✳❀

I

TOM SAW SING TOY AT A DINNER IN
Chinatown given by Yiko for some American friends. Yiko
was a little proud of Tom and Eva and invited them to come
along, since it was Sunday. Flora had heard that Sing Toy, a
night-club artist and a girl friend of Yiko's, was coming, and
she and Loy also came. Only English was spoken.

"Dis my kid brother, Tom. And dis is my kid sister, Eva."
Yiko introduced them proudly. "Dey are in Amelican school."

"Dis is Miss Sing Toy."

Sing Toy sang and danced in a midtown night club and
was therefore thoroughly familiar with the paraphernalia of
female charm. She was in an American evening dress cut so
low that it hung precariously over her shoulders, and by the
exquisite calculations of feminine costuming was fated to be
held up on one side and to slip down on the other. She had
what may be called a semistage make-up; her lips were a deep
red and the shadows on her eyelids and her stained eyelashes
had a kind of sophisticated elegance. Her teeth were even and
her hair was upswept, with bangs in front which gave her a
China-doll effect. The trouble with such a make-up was that
it was rather obvious. It seemed to say, all this is, of course,
illusion, but by all known and tested records men fall for it,

and women admire it. Tom and Eva had never sat close to a woman with such a low-cut dress, and it made them both uncomfortable. As if all that was not enough distraction, Sing Toy had green fingernails. Flora saw at once that she was not in a class with Sing Toy, and she quaked.

If Sing Toy knew her trade well, as was to be expected, she was also very charming. She had a well-rounded small oval face, with a weak chin, and her well-manicured fingers were constantly waving and gesticulating before her face while she was talking. If you looked closely enough, her eyes were small and dark, with a brightness that did not necessarily say anything. They were bright only with youth. She was not reserved or proud; she was anxious to entertain and to please. When she was with men, she was like a seal in water. Her movements and her talk had a certain swimming motion that went on at an even pace and with an undulating form until the men left or she left the men. She was quite aware that Yiko, whom she called Freddie, admired her. They liked the same things.

One of the three Americans present was Sandy Bull, a colleague of Yiko at the Cornelius Underwriters. They had first seen Sing Toy together at the midtown night club. Having known a few dancing girls in Shanghai, Sandy liked her, and the two men had come to know her.

"You know what, Toy?" said Sandy. "You'd be the queen of Shanghai, if you were there."

Sing Toy was flattered. She did not take it seriously, but she thought men were wonderful all the same. "Do you think so?"

"I know it is so. You remind me of a girl I knew in Shanghai. We called her Queenie. Say, how about calling you Queenie, Baby?"

"I don't mind. Queenie to you, hey!" She raised her glass high.

"Queenie to me!" Sandy raised his glass and they drank. Sandy, sitting on the other side of Sing Toy, put his arm around her, and she shook it off. "Please behave yourself, Sandy," she said with a piqued smile that showed that she did not altogether dislike it.

"Say, Sandy, she's my girl, don't forget," said Yiko.

"Say, wait a minute," protested Sing Toy. "You guys seem to know before us girls whose girls we want to be."

"Okay, Freddie. Okay, Queenie, you're his girl," said Sandy, rolling his words together. He raised his glass. "*Ganbay!* [bottoms up] I drink to you both. I'm a married man. I told you, Queenie, I'm married. I like the Chinese. I don't know why I like the Chinese."

The little incident was over and they went on with the food in an atmosphere of gay frivolity. To Flora, who was always a little excited when men were present, but was not used to such society, all this was unexpected. Tom's and Eva's eyes were wide with curiosity. Jokes went round the table. The funniest jokes were always about wives who deceived their husbands. The men always roared aloud and enjoyed them immensely. What was so funny about a wife being faithless? Tom wondered. There was no point except the bare fact that the wife was faithless. One of the guests told a joke about a test-tube baby. On being told what a test-tube baby was, a man said, "It is a pity. The old way was so nice." The whole table roared, that is, the whole table except Flora and Tom and Eva.

After some more drinks and perfect hilarity had been established, Sandy rolled his words together again. "All right, it's clear. You are Freddie's girl. He is sweet on you, honest, Baby, he is sweet on you, but you are goddam pretty, no misunderstanding, you are goddam pretty and you are Queenie to me."

There was something bullish about Sandy that reminded Tom of his name, something in the way he rolled his words together as if he was going to ram somebody. Sandy was a confused and frustrated man in his forties. In China he had been connected with an English newspaper. Being fairly intelligent and considering himself an intellectual, liberal, pro-Chinese and pro-Russian, he had risen to the position of editorial writer. He had a fluent if undistinguished command of vocabulary and a colloquial, glib style, and he had pleased some readers and offended others by the use of "hell" and "goddam" in his editorial column. He was always angry at something, ready to fight for something, to debunk something. An American in Shanghai would sometimes come up to him and say, "Hullo, Sandy, I don't see the word goddam in your editorial today. You're not goddaming somebody. What's the matter?" But somehow his mind remained at the level of his speech. At forty he suddenly discovered that he did not know what he stood for and was left without convictions. He fell to the level of his business associates and took to drink, divorced his first wife and remarried. His pro-Russian pro-Communist attitude was about all that he had left; it seemed to him his only title to being called a liberal, and for his self-respect he clung to it with tenacity. But his pro-Communist attitude got him into difficulty with the owner of his paper, and he gave up newspaper work and came to New York, where he found a job writing insurance publicity for Cornelius Underwriters. He was put on the work having to do with the Chinatown community, as one who had lived in the Orient and was therefore an expert on China. He was at this moment both pro-capital and pro-Stalin. He was broad-minded and a Christian and a man of evident good will. He knew how to get along with the Chinese, loved to pat them on the back, and thought the Chinese loved it. He could say *ganbay* and was very sure that he knew all about China. The technique of patting the back happened to work with Yiko, and they had become great, good friends.

2

Flora came home with her husband and the children, feeling like a country girl who had seen city society at close range for the first time. She was uncomfortable. She did not at all like Sing Toy, her hairdo, her dress, and particularly her green fingernails. She thought the jokes at the table had been vulgar, leaving a foul flavor about the whole dinner.

"Her fingernails!" Eva gasped the moment they entered the El. Their disapproval was unanimous.

"Do you think Yiko will marry her?" Tom asked his eldest brother.

"I dunno. If he likes her, Father can't stop him. It's he who will marry her, not us."

"He will have to get Father's consent, won't he?" asked Flora.

"Who's going to force him?"

"As his elder brother can't you talk to him?"

"You know he never listens to me—or Father."

Flora looked straight ahead and said nothing.

That night in bed she said, "Loy, I'm thinking."

"Of what?"

"Of that girl with the green fingernails. Do you think her pretty, prettier than me?"

"Oh, Flora."

"Do you think her pretty?"

"She is a night-club artist. Why do you ask?"

"I don't think her ears are pretty. And she talks with her lips glued together at the sides. I'll show you."

Loy watched and laughed. He took a cigarette, lit it, and puffed.

"It's all her make-up," he said.

"I'm glad you see that."

"Flora, you are different. You are not that type." Loy patted her hand, and she felt comforted.

"You men don't see such things, but I'm glad you see that. The way she kept tugging at her dress at the shoulder made me feel immoral. If a girl wants to wear a low-cut dress, let her wear it, and not call people's attention to it all the time."

Flora straightened her pillow, and putting both hands behind her head, began to slide down into resting position with a sigh, half of admiration, half of annoyance. "Gee, I did admire her dress. It must be expensive for Freddie to go round with such a girl. Loy, I'm not complaining. But I don't understand. Freddie—"

"Why talk about him?"

"Do you think it is quite fair? Freddie's independent, and he looks after himself, while you have to work for the family."

"Yeah, it looks kinda strange to you." His voice, as usual, was calm and slow, even placid.

"It certainly does."

"Well, as I told you before, we grew up differently. I came over with Father when I was thirteen and have always been with him. When Yiko came over, he was on his own from the very beginning. He didn't want to do laundry. He served as a waiter and got himself a job. Father depended upon me always. I've never thought of leaving Father. It would not be right."

"But now Freddie is independent, and he is not helping the family, while we share everything we have."

"He says he has to save up now for his marriage. Flora, we're doing all right. We are able to save, with Father and Mother and you all working. It's all right with me."

"I'm not complaining. Only it looks odd to me. If it's all right with you, it's all right with me. But with that girl, I don't see how he is going to save."

"I don't think he will. That's his business."

"Is he really serious with her?"

"I hear he's been going round with her a lot. They go gambling together. Father knows, too."

"They say there's a black sheep in every family. Does Father approve?"

"Of course not. But what can he do? Freddie has always

been apart from the family, and Father is different toward him."

Flora snapped out the light and said, "Well, all I want is that they are fair to you," and slid down in the bed and fell asleep.

3

Yiko was having a wonderful time. He often said, "Life is kind to me." Another variation was, "Life is treating me fine," or "New York is treating me fine." Tom once saw him in his room, his hair ruffled, his long legs stretched out on top of his desk, while his tight shirt moved up and down. His voice was naturally big. It was all American milk, Yiko declared. "I'm a package of vitamins. Never a cold, or ill for a day." He indeed looked like a package of health. The more Tom examined Yiko, the more he was mystified.

"Are you happy?" Tom asked.

"Happy? What do you mean? Happy about what?"

"About what you are doing and all the people around you and what makes life go?"

"Tom, you are funny. Why should you care what makes life go? As you can see, I'm doing well. I make a lot of money. De Amelicans like me. I have a good position."

"I don't mean that. What do you do when you are alone here?"

"What do I do? I turn on the radio."

"Don't you think of things?"

"T'ink! I am too busy to t'ink. I'm getting along fine. I never went to school and here I am. Do you ever see me open a book? Tom, I bet you never seen me open a book since you came to de U.S. I'm doing too many t'ings, too successful, to t'ink, dat's what."

"Don't you have problems?"

"What ploblems? I never let ploblems stop me."

Tom could not express quite what he meant. "A man must have all sorts of problems, personal problems—how you want to live, get married, and such things."

"Sure, I want to get married."

"I don't mean . . ." Tom stopped. They were talking different languages to each other. Life must be good or bad; it must have a meaning of some sort. He could never make Yiko see what he meant.

"By de way, what do you t'ink of Sing Toy? Do you like her?"

"Not too much," said Tom, putting it mildly, and as honestly as he dared. "You see, isn't that a problem?"

"Dat's not a ploblem. She is a nice girl, young, like an Amelican girl and full of fun. Well, if I like her, I go and marry her."

"Does she like you?"

"Dat's a funny question. Of course she likes me. I'll offer her a home. A two-room apartment, dat's what I'm t'inking about. And I'll be proud to go out in the street wit' her. She speak very good English. She's born here. She walk straight like an Amelican. You must tell Eva. She still stoops a little."

"Do you love Sing Toy very much?"

"Sure, I love her. She's a nice-looking girl, good figure. And she loves the movies and dancing. She can jitterbug, too. I guess I'll take her to the movies or some dancing halls in de evening and, boy, dat is life! We'll be as happy as a pair of lovebirds."

"Are you going to marry her?"

"I t'ink so. I like to keep her waiting. Let her wait a little. And whenever I feel I want to marry, I'll propose to her, and we go to a justice of the peace and be married."

"You are sure she will marry you?"

Yiko dismissed the question by clicking on the radio and he listened to the jazz music being played.

"Tom, you ought to learn to dance. It's a lot of fun."

136

Sing Toy was very happy, too. She had discovered herself. Why, before, she was nothing but a common waitress on Grant Avenue in San Francisco, and now American men were at her feet. She could joke with them, and they could joke with her.

While she lived in San Francisco, her parents had died, and she had only a brother. She had been a good girl, working eight hours a day at the restaurant; she was still a good girl, as modern standards go. She wanted to get along and find a husband. One day when she was twenty-one she read in a Chinese newspaper that a night club was hiring hostesses. Night clubs had suddenly sprung up in San Francisco Chinatown and were doing good business. Night-club patrons paid handsome tips. There was a demand for Chinese girl entertainers. Singing torch songs was easy; the audience wasn't exacting if the girl was young and had pretty legs and if she had a slightly cracked, hazy, wet, clammy, lachrymose voice. More essential to singing were good limbs and "pep." The "pep" was easy, too, if she followed the jazz-band conductor's shaking knees. Could she dance? She could not tap dance. But this dancing was only a matter of tossing the legs and shaking the hips in rhythm. There wasn't anything in singing and dancing of the sort that other grown-up girls of good figure did that she could not do.

One day it seemed as if scales fell from her eyes. She found she lacked nothing she needed; nature had equipped her. It was simple and it was delightful. In entertaining men she was entertaining herself. It wasn't as if she had to go to college for four years to learn to make a living. Sing Toy was not much given to thinking. She had heard it said that the earth was round, but she knew that it was flat, and on top of this flat earth there were men and girls walking erect on two legs, and the men liked the girls when they were young. She called it nature. If the men like it and pay money for it, let 'em have it.

She moved to Los Angeles, and then she moved to New York as the demand for Chinese hostesses spread from the West to the East. There were too few Chinese girls to meet the requirements and she had no difficulty in finding a position. She already had a dozen clippings about herself from the evening newspaper columns.

Then, for no reason that she could make clear to herself, she thought she would like to marry. Now that she was twenty-five, she dimly perceived the truth that entertaining men in general was all right but to marry a man was still better.

Freddie had come to the café several times. Freddie thought her wonderful and his eyes told her so.

Back in the dressing room, she told Vicky. "He is here again."

"You mean Freddie?"

"Yes, isn't he exciting? He is taller than most Chinese and quite handsome. Don't you think he is handsome?"

"Well, don't miss your chance if he is serious. Now if you don't throw all you've got at him, honey, you're dumber than I thought."

So when she went out to do her number, she darted a glance at Freddie, and Freddie's big heart opened, and he said to himself, "There is the girl for me. I am lucky. Frederick A. T. Fong is always lucky."

She came to sit at his table after her last number.

"Well, I'm all through for the night," Sing Toy gave him a full smile. Her eyes glistened in the dim light like a huntress approaching her cornered prey. It was literally true: Frederick A. T. Fong, the luscious prize, was seated in a tight corner.

"Have a drink. What will you have?" Freddie spoke as if a spirit had ordered him.

The band played. The dimmed lights made the girl shy and bold alternately. The wine flushed and the muted music soothed. Her mascaraed eyelashes drooped. Her hand lay limp on the table. Freddie gently touched and squeezed and then smoothed it. They were sitting so close that he felt the fragrant warmth that came from her body.

"Do you love me?" Freddie asked suddenly.

Sing Toy suddenly came out of her happy stupor.

"What did you say?"

"Do you love me?"

Sing Toy thought it a strange beginning. It would have been better if he had said, "I love you." How was she to reply? She merely looked at him, the huntress sizing up the game lying at her feet.

Freddie put his arm around her waist, and she did not resist. He felt that it would be good to have a wife like this, to sit in the evening at home and put his arm around her thus.

"Darling," he said. "We are bot' Chinese. Life is kind to me, and I have a good position. You don't have to work here."

"Is this a proposal or what?"

"Well, it is. If I can't sell myself to you, how can I sell insurance? Darling, do you love me? If you love me, we'll be married. I can support you, and we'll have a two-room apartment, and we can spend all our evenings togeder. Toy, I t'ink you are wonderful."

"Oh," said Sing Toy. At last, it came, not quite a declaration of love but something quite near it.

"You have not told me whether you love me," she demanded.

"Why, of course. Or I wouldn't have come here so many times. You are wonderful, darling. We'll have a wonderful time together. Will you marry me?"

Sing Toy was silent. "I'll have to think about it."

"Why t'ink about it," Frederick pressed, following the psychology of salesmanship as he had been taught. "What is dere to t'ink about? You love me, don't you?"

It was the third time he had put that question. He was good game; she did not want to lose it after hunting it down, yet she did not feel satisfied. She remained silent.

"Come on, have a drink. It will pep you up. I want you very much, darling. I want you very much. Marry me."

"I'll think about it. All right?" Sing Toy glanced at him, this time fully.

"Let me t'ink for you. When I'm married, I get a raise of fifty dollars. I shall be having a salary of two hundred and seventy-five, plus commissions. What do you say? Are dere more questions you want to ask?"

"No, it isn't that. I want time to think."

Freddie left, feeling not too well pleased, as he felt when he came home from trying to sell a policy but had failed to clinch the sale. He had not intended to propose that night, but he had done it. They had left on good terms and she had promised to think it over. It was somewhat of a surprise to him that when Frederick A. T. Fong had proposed the girl had not had the sense to accept at once. He was sure that Sing Toy had been a little surprised too, and she needed time, as so many prospects did who in the end were sold a policy. But, after all, luck was always with him. He had found a Broadway celebrity, and how many of his compatriots could marry a Broadway celebrity? It was as good as though she had accepted him.

The thought of marriage suddenly overwhelmed him. As he lay on his couch, a smile broke over his face. The thought of having a girl like Sing Toy living with him, in the house with him, serving him, was delicious. He put his two hands together like a boxer acknowledging applause after a fight and congratulated himself. He even thought of how he was going to have a model modern home and be a model father of adoring children, and he would come home like a model husband and be met by a model wife. He would kiss her when he left for the office in the morning, and his wife would kiss him when he came home, "just like Amelicans."

"Boy, I'm going somewhere!" he exclaimed.

Suddenly he remembered that he had only about two hundred dollars in the bank.

"Vicky, Vicky, he proposed to me!" Sing Toy cried when she went back to the dressing room.

Vicky Lamore was much older than Toy, but her age was a secret between herself and God.

"Did you accept him, honey?"

"No, I said I would think it over."

"Don't be a sap! Tell me, how old are you, honey?"

"I'm twenty-two."

"Honest?"

"Honest."

"That's it."

"What do you mean, 'That's it'?"

"I mean you are too young to know how good a proposal from a man is. Isn't he about your age and making a good living? How much is he making?"

"I suppose he must be making four hundred a month."

"What are you thinking it over for then?"

"I thought it was funny he asked me three times if I loved him and never once told me that he loved me."

Here the conversation became a little confused, for both girls were speaking, and neither was listening to the other.

(Vicky) "When a man proposes to a woman, isn't it
(Sing) "He did say, though, that he wanted me

(Vicky) enough? Of course, he loves you. And
(Sing) very much. He did say that. It was like

(Vicky) don't you stand on a high horse and try
(Sing) saying he loved me, wasn't it?"

(Vicky) to high-hat him. When I was younger, I had a number of suitors. But I was a sucker, just like you. A guy proposed and I said I would like to think it over. Well, I thought too darn long. If I were you, I woulda fallen on his shoulder then and there and stepped on it good and fast till he was done brown. That woulda fixed him for good."

Since Vicky outlasted Sing Toy, the latter got the full sense of what she was saying.

Freddie stayed away for about a week. His bank account slightly worried him, but it wasn't only that. The next morning he realized what he had done. He did not know why he had proposed. The whole thing just came up bang in his face. He went over last night's scene. He remembered how delicious the new thought was, the new vision of having Sing Toy with him always. Then he remembered that she was taking time to consider. He had not prepared to sell her something last night, he had meant to keep her waiting. Did she sell herself to him last night instead? He was sold on her, he figured. But when he tried to sell her on the proposition of becoming Mrs. Frederick A. T. Fong, she said she would take time to consider! Well, then, he would not be too anxious about it. It's good psychology, he told himself. So he stayed away.

6

In the course of human events it can never be established whether women are the pursued sex or the pursuer. Authoritative opinion varies; men and women themselves disagree. All that can be said is that, one, if the female sex is the pursued, it exerts all its energy to be pursued; two, if the pursued isn't interested in the pursuer, she stops and meets him, and there is no game; and three, if she is interested in the pursuer, then she runs, but the more she runs the more she must keep herself in sight of the pursuer, nor should she let the pursuer out of her sight. Since the human race began, all games of love have been played according to these rules.

On the seventh day Sing Toy was a little worried. "Well, if he wants my answer, he knows where to find me," she thought. She would not call Freddie first on the telephone, but she was within sight, strictly according to orthodox tactics.

Freddie walked into the café with a generous forgiving heart, thinking that seven days' waiting was enough punishment for her wish to think it over. A mysterious power drew him to her. He had resisted it long enough, and now he came. Without understanding why, he was nervous. He had never been like this. A week ago he had had the courage to propose, and he had not been nervous at all. But now, as he sat in an obscure corner, he felt sanely, with the cold eye of reason, the importance of what he was going to do. He fidgeted with his key chain and his cigar cutter. If only he saw Sing Toy once more, he would know whether he was doing right, whether he wanted her forever. Perspiration broke out over him as if he were a boxer going to meet a challenger in combat. "Silly of me to feel like this," he thought. He was giving something, his name, the promise of a home, and yet he was nervous like this!

Sing Toy came out on the floor with six other girls, in a midriff outfit. She was the smallest of them. Her small oval face, her eyebrows, her almond eyes, gave her a cute Oriental look, but her movements and gestures were all American. She had a full bosom, and when she turned her head right and left in unison with the other girls, her neck was supple and graceful. There was a fast number in which the girls bent forward from the waist and clapped their hands while alternately resting on their right and left legs. The saxophone blared, the kettledrums rattled, the girls grinned. There was a glad show of limbs in rhythmic movement. Everybody was pleased, and Freddie was enchanted. Then the girls walked in a circle close to the tables. Their right hands were resting on their hips, and they passed by exactly as horses parade for the judges before a race. The best horse's haunches always compel admiration from the judges.

Freddie forgot his nervousness. He felt immensely proud that he knew one of these girls, that one of them was considering marrying him, with almost the pride of a horse owner or a prospective horse buyer at a race. He was proud of her stature, her looks, her grace of movement.

Sing Toy did not see him. But later in the evening she came to his table.

"Why, Freddie, I was wondering where you've been?"

"I've been out of town on business. I'm very sorry." He was sincerely sorry, now that she was so close and smiled up at him. Sing Toy was very sweet. At his little questions she just dipped her head and answered, with closed lips, an attractive and wonderfully effective "hm, hm." She put her arm round his shoulder.

"Well, have you considered?"

"Hm, hm."

"Will you marry me?"

"Hm, hm."

They embraced, and Sing Toy, remembering Vicky's advice, covered him with a spray of kisses like buckshot, deliberate and well aimed, just to make sure there was no mistake, and the chase of the pursued and the pursuer was at an end. "That fixes him for good, as Vicky says," thought Sing Toy. So Freddie succumbed. It was several minutes before he recovered from the fumes of the buckshot.

He sat up straight and took a comb from his pocket to restore his dignity. He ordered a bottle of champagne. "Let's celebrate."

Suddenly he felt like a conqueror or a hunter who has taken his game, thus reversing the process. He was immensely satisfied with himself.

"I felt kinda jealous a while ago, you know."

"Jealous of what."

"Everybody saw your legs and your whole body."

"Was that a surprise to you?"

"No. I just felt it. Now we belong to each other and you'll be Mrs. Frederick A. T. Fong. Gee, it's wonderful to have a celebrity like you for my wife."

"When shall we get married?"

"Not for a while yet." Freddie's voice was a little low. "But I'll get you an engagement ring right away."

"Oh, Freddie!"

Sing Toy had a well simulated technique, especially under the influence of liquor. She had a cultivated drawl, the low, lazy, and soft drawl that men like. It was like an invisible coil of feminine sound that tingled Freddie's senses and wound round his heart. Her head reclined on Freddie's shoulder.

"You are so handsome, Freddie," she cooed.

"What did Sandy say to you? You should be the queen of Shanghai. But now I shall take care of you, and you are all mine."

"Hm, hm."

"And don't forget we are Chinese, and you will obey me like a good wife."

"Hm, hm."

All of a sudden Sing Toy raised her head from Freddie's shoulder and sat up.

"What's matter?"

"Nothing. I just want to sit up. Come on, let's dance."

They went to the dance floor and danced. Sing Toy nestled very close to him. Freddie seemed just the right height to dance with. They did not say many words but danced in a close intimate enchanted world of their own. And Sing Toy held him, and it seemed that from the fascination of the perfume of her flesh he could never get away.

"We're engaged," Sing Toy announced to Vicky after Freddie left. "He's mine now."

Vicky congratulated her heartily. "What did I tell you?"

"Thanks for the advice. He's tall and handsome and socially

very active in Chinatown. Don't you think him very handsome?"

"Yes, he is. You're lucky, Sing."

"Freddie is funny. I really don't know him too well. You know what he said to me? That was after I said yes to him. He asked me to promise to obey him like a good wife."

"Ho, ho!" Vicky laughed. "And did you promise?"

"I nodded."

Vicky laughed again, as if she was greatly amused. "I'm glad you did. But it is really so funny."

"What is funny?"

"Funny for him to think of that. Look here, honey, when you marry a guy, you should worry about that. The difficulty is in hooking a guy to go down to the altar with you. Well, lucky for you! I'll be kicking my legs here for some time yet and see what kind of sucker comes along. Good night!"

Chapter 12

I

IN JULY, 1937, CHINA SUDDENLY BECAME
front-page news. War was begun with Japan. The Fong family
and the whole Chinese community caught the fever of it.
Chinatown was a seething cauldron of demonstrations and
patriotic activities. The Chinese papers printed extras or wrote
out the latest news flashes and pasted them on walls, and a never
ceasing stream of people came and stood about to read them.

The overseas Chinese, as usual, organized themselves, collected funds, and poured American dollars into China. They
did so with a fantastic generosity, difficult to believe. Money
collected from laundrymen and restaurant keepers and waiters
was paid regularly by the month. By the end of 1940, it was
estimated, the overseas Chinese (all over the world) had sent
three hundred million dollars to help fight the war. By the
time the United States came into the war they were sending
home, in American dollars, about seven million dollars a
month. Of this a substantial part came from the Chinese in
America, and of this the principal sources were the Chinese
laundrymen and restaurant keepers. The Manchu Empire had
been overthrown, as everybody knows, largely with the laun-

drymen's money, and now they gave again to save their country.

Tom Fong, Sr., raised his head high. He had never bothered about politics. Ten years ago he had been glad when the Nationalist Revolution started from Canton. Revolutions seem always to come from Canton. The revolutionists marched north and unified China. He was glad and that was the end of it. But now suddenly something happened that was very close to him. He had been pushed about in this country and he had made his way like water, that symbol of Taoist wisdom, seeking the low places and penetrating everywhere. Laotse's philosophy, as he heard it in Chinese proverbs, was the first philosophy of camouflage, of seeking the lowly and appearing foolish, of the strength of the gentle and the blessedness of the meek, the apparent dumbness of the truly wise, the stupidity of the garrulous, the tactical advantage of lying low, and the futility of strife and contentions. That philosophy was, in truth, Tom Fong's philosophy of living. Laotse was right; those who occupy the lowly places can never be overthrown.

> How do the rivers and seas become the Lords of the
>   Ravines?
> By being good at keeping low.
> That was how they became the Lords of the Ravines.

And so Tom Fong and his people sought the lowly places and penetrated everywhere and survived like the sea.

> The best of men is like water;
> Water benefits all things
> And does not compete with them.
> It dwells in the lowly places that all disdain
> —Wherein it comes near to the Tao.

How does the common sparrow multiply and spread and flourish everywhere? How has it lived so near to men unharmed and yet has become the most numerous species in this world? Because its feathers are gray, because it does not contend and is unnoticed of men.

Tom Fong had been so used to being called a Chink that it did not really hurt. He had not himself read Laotse's statement, "Who receives unto himself the calumny of the world is the preserver of the state." But it was in his blood. "The honest I believe; the liars I also believe." What could the world do to Tom Fong, armed with an unpierceable armor of knowing and pretending not to know?

But Tom Fong was also human. Minding his own business and not caring about politics, he did wish his own country to be strong. The overseas Chinese had been hounded out of the West Coast, murdered and robbed and driven out of Mexico, out of Australia, out of New Zealand, out of Africa, and their own government could never afford them protection. When China wanted to isolate herself from the white man, the white man knocked at her gate with gunboats. When America wanted to isolate herself from yellow labor, she simply shut the gate. It was this long suppressed feeling of unequal treatment, of being kicked about and called Chink, that caused the overseas Chinese to pour millions of dollars into China when there was hope of doing something to make China strong. Tom Fong felt it, and every laundryman abroad felt it.

All of a sudden the American attitude was changed. The Chinese Army was fighting and clinging stoutly to Shanghai when Chapei and Kiangwan were turned into an inferno of bombs and shellfire. Stories of Chinese heroism poured in daily to the newspapers. Americans began to pat the Chinese on the back, and they were sincere. "Tom Fong, thumbs up. Your country is fighting the Japs!" Tom Fong felt a glow of national pride as something surprising, something he had not expected. He was not enough of a Taoist philosopher to know that those who pat you on the back today can slap you in the face tomorrow.

149

Tom Fong no longer stooped and looked at the pavement as he walked the streets. He held his chin level and met the eyes of the people who passed, and he knew that they were admiring his people for fighting. Americans applaud anybody who puts up a fight. That he knew. The American missionaries who went to China to preach a gospel of peace called their mission a "challenge," as if heathendom were challenging them. The North Pole or Mount Everest was a "challenge" to them. Did heathendom and the North Pole ever care? But they had to put it that way to stir the missionary's blood up to preach peace to a people who never believed in fighting, or even in raising a fist in an argument. Now there was no escaping the fact that China was fighting heroically and was being admired. In the El passengers looked at Tom Fong and smiled at him. He felt as he had never felt before. It was as if somebody had put a flower in his buttonhole, had taken notice of him, Tom Fong, whom no one had noticed before. Every additional week the Chinese Army held on at Woosung and Kiangwan added to Tom Fong's wonder. When people said to him, "Your country is fighting the Japs. Good work!" Tom Fong answered, "Yeah, China fighting now." Quietly, he put up the Chinese flag of the blue sky, white sky, and red earth in his basement shop window, and below the words Tom Fong Hand Laundry he painted "Yeah China Fighting Now."

And so the war fever reached the Fong home. If the father and mother took the war with great pride and dignity, it shook Tom and Eva, particularly the quiet Eva. Where did Mayor La Guardia stand? He was campaigning for re-election and he was for help to China against Japan, and he was of Italian origin, as Flora was. And so the family felt warm toward Flora, and she was proud and happy.

If the United States was not yet at war with Japan, China-town was. Being the center and source of all Chinese activities, Chinatown became a place of tense emotions, as if there were in the air an invisible power that drew all Chinese to its vortex, all except the wealthy Chinese families who lived uptown. Loud-speakers in the street blared forth war news in Cantonese. Flags waved, posters covered the walls, a white cloth banner hung across the street urging subscriptions. Somebody made large profits out of making and selling Chinese flags and buttons.

2

Freddie got himself appointed to a committee. He knew everybody in Chinatown. He knew the "unofficial mayor of Chinatown," and he knew the addresses of all Chinese south of Thirty-fourth Street. A campaign was going on to raise funds for sending gifts to the Chinese soldiers who were still clinging to the Kiangwan line around Shanghai. One day he appeared at his father's home.

"Father," he said, "I'm on the committee to raise funds. Everybody knows you are my father. How much can you give?"

The whole family was in the sitting room.

"How much do you think?" asked the father.

Freddie had in mind one hundred dollars, but he said, "I know we are not rich, but as a member of the committee I ought to set an example. I say two to three hundred. It is for our soldiers."

The father's mouth tightened, and he smoked his pipe silently and looked at everybody and puffed again.

"Don't know if we should touch the savings," said the mother, fixing her eyes on her husband.

"We have pledged to contribute five dollars a month. Five dollars a month as long as the war lasts," the father said and resumed his pipe.

"The savings are for the restaurant Mother is planning to open," said Loy. Flora and Tom and Eva watched with excitement.

Slowly the father got up, went to his room, and came out with a cloth parcel. He unwrapped the cloth and revealed a brown envelope with many Chinese figures scribbled on it. Breathing very hard, he looked at Freddie and said, "What did you say the money is for?"

"For taking gifts to the soldiers at the front who are bleeding for the country, dying for the country."

The family knew about the cloth parcel but had rarely seen it. The money was always kept in a drawer to which Father had the key.

There were more than twenty-four hundred dollars in the cloth. Tom Fong had a checking account at the Manhattan Trust Company, on which Flora drew their checks, but he never left more than two or three hundred dollars there. The rest he put away in fifty-dollar bills.

Business had been good. Father and Mother Fong had a simple system of finance, which was to spend less than you earn. The principal thing was regularity and avoiding extras. If a person could save regularly fifty dollars a month, he would save six hundred a year and six thousand in ten years. What was ten years? It would be entirely against all their principles of finance to make an exception. So tenseness was seen on everybody's face when Father Fong appeared with the cloth parcel.

The father sat down. He took out two fifty-dollar bills and put them on the table. Freddie's eyes brightened.

"Father, it is for our soldiers."

Tom Fong, Sr., was fighting mad. The children had never seen such an expression on his face. He took out another fifty-dollar bill and then another, and slapped each down with a smack as if he were laying a great wager or providing money to marry a daughter. "There! And there! Two hundred!" he exclaimed and said nothing more. He panted with satisfaction, and the family was silent.

Freddie took out his contribution book and wrote a receipt.

He preferred to sign his name in English because he was good at it. He crossed the T in a bold straight line and brought the final g in a beautiful, forceful loop way back to and beyond the beginning of his name. But the sum was not yet filled in.

"Father, I am getting engaged," said Freddie.

"Engaged? To whom?"

"To Sing Toy," said Loy.

"A Broadway star, Father. She's very famous. I can show you clippings."

"You have not told me," said the mother. "Are you already engaged?"

Freddie nodded. He had always been remote from his mother. Now she flew up at him. "Ah-Tong, you are almost like an American. Who is this girl who is going to be my daughter-in-law without my seeing her?"

The family was in an uproar. Freddie took Sing Toy's photograph from his wallet. It was a portrait of her face looking over a bare shoulder. Mother Fong could not have felt more queer if Freddie had gone out and married an American blonde.

"Isn't she cute?" asked Freddie proudly. "Mother, you ought to be proud that your son is engaged to a star. I love her and she loves me."

This declaration of love, so shameless and so unnecessary, was really too much for the mother.

"Ah-Tong, if you are going to marry a daughter-in-law without your parents selecting one for you, you will be ruined."

"We'll talk about it later," said the father. "You finish the receipt."

"Father, that was what I was going to speak to you about. I have never taken money from you these years. Now I'm getting engaged. I need some money."

"Fill out the receipt. What has this got to do with it?"

"Well, I thought perhaps you could give a hundred more."

"This money is for the soldiers. Give me the receipt!"

Freddie hesitated. "Of course it is for the soldiers," he explained. "Only when I was making the receipt, I thought I ought to contribute some, too. And I have no money left on account of the engagement ring, which isn't fully paid for. If I didn't tell you about the engagement, you would not understand."

"I am giving this money for the war. Fill out the full amount. If you take a penny out of that sweat-and-blood money of mine—"

"Father, will you advance me a hundred dollars as my contribution to the war? I will repay you when I get the money. I am on the committee and should set an example."

"It is not for the ring, then."

"No, it is for my contribution to the war," Freddie said in his most professional reassuring tone.

Everybody was confused, and Loy and Flora had a suspicion that something was wrong.

The father took out two more fifty-dollar bills and gave them to Freddie, and he filled out the receipt.

A week later, when the list of contributions was published in the local Chinese newspapers, Tom Fong, Sr., was enraged. Listed among those giving a hundred dollars was Frederick A. T. Fong while listed among those giving fifty dollars was his father.

The father summoned Freddie to appear before him.

"What is the meaning of this?" the father asked.

"Father, I will explain."

"This is criminal. What are you doing?"

"Let me explain. Father, I shall return you the hundred dollars. You don't lose anything."

"I don't lose anything? You wheedled two hundred dollars out of me for the war. You handed in fifty and took a hundred and fifty for yourself. Don't the soldiers lose something? I have your receipt. If I went with that receipt to the Benevolence Association, do you think you could explain it?"

"Father, you know I would not do anything dishonest. I am honest with everybody. I have a perfect record."

"You are not honest with your own family."

"Father, don't be angry. You would not spoil my reputation. I needed the money very badly. When I compared your contribution with those made by other laundrymen, you were among the top ones with fifty dollars."

"And you made it appear that you contributed a hundred."

"Well, it is different," Freddie's voice came out a little hard. "You see, everybody knows who I am. I had to give a hundred. But you are among the top ones, and the Fong family gave a total of one hundred and fifty. My honor is your honor. No other laundryman's family gave more. And I needed the extra money for the ring."

"If you have no money to buy a ring, you don't have to get engaged," the father said angrily, but feeling a little helpless. He knew that he was not going to expose his own son, and knew that his son knew.

"What about this girl you are going to marry?"

"Father, you don't know what she is like. She is a very nice girl and you will be proud of her."

"Did I ever see her?"

"No. But you will. She is a very patriotic citizen of China."

The episode passed. The only person who was left really angry was Flora. She had never yet had a diamond ring for herself, large or small.

3

Someone uptown had organized a Chinese Women's Committee for War Relief, a branch of which met in Chinatown.

On the Women's Committee there was a girl who taught in the Chinatown school. Elsie Tsai had been brought by the school all the way from Shanghai because the elders of Chinatown wanted someone who could speak and teach mandarin, the national language of China. Few in Chinatown spoke anything but Cantonese. The classes were held in the late afternoon. The Chinese children, after leaving the regular school each day, had to go to these classes between four o'clock and suppertime. Elsie had been recommended by her college for proficiency in speaking and teaching mandarin. The elders believed in the classics, and Elsie came from a scholar's family in Fukien. Her background had given her a knowledge of ancient Chinese that even most modern Chinese college students lacked. She was still only a sophomore at college, but when she heard of the chance to go to America, with passage paid, she worked hard to get it. And she came all alone.

It was Tom who discovered the Women's Committee in Chinatown. One day, passing through Mott Street, he stopped on the sidewalk to read the war news posted on the wall of the little schoolhouse. He saw a beautiful young Chinese girl come out of the narrow door, gingerly holding in her two hands a paste pot and a poster, the characters on which were freshly written and not quite dry yet. Her hair hung straight and long over her shoulders, only slightly curled under below, and she wore a beige Chinese gown, simply but effectively trimmed in black. She was so intent on the poster that she did not see Tom. Her bones were smaller, her face was more delicately moulded, her eyes were quicker and at the same time there was an instinctive modesty more marked in her than in the Chinese girls he had met. It seemed to Tom as if a girl had stepped out of a picture in the old woodcut-illustrated novels that he had seen, someone remote and subtly charming. As he watched, she took the brush from the paste pot and slapped it gently and most unprofessionally on the wall, holding the poster in her other hand by dexterous use of two fingers. Very slowly her brush went over the wall. There was something odd about the way she held the brush. She held the handle as she would hold a writing brush, with the peculiar motion of the wrist and position of the thumb and fingers that good calligraphers betray even when they are not writing. Her small, tapering fingers were white as onion. The jade bracelet on her arm slid about as she drew the paste right and left.

Tom was fascinated. It was like hearing exotic music that he had known and forgotten, had hidden somewhere deep in his being, and now he heard it and recognized it as something belonging to other lands, other times. He was seized emotionally, by he did not know what. The girl still did not look at him. She was holding both the paste pot and the poster in her other hand. He wanted to help her, but something held him back. When she had applied the paste, she bent down to put the pot on the ground. Tom wanted to hold it for her, but again he dared not. She smoothed and pressed the poster gently with the tips of her fingers and the ball of her thumb, once, twice, three times.

The poster had a feminine touch. Drawn at the top was a modern girl's head, done in sharp black outlines, and the text below was a call for women volunteers. The girl stood staring at her own handwriting. She saw to her annoyance that in smoothing the poster over the wall, she had accidentally touched the still wet red circles beside the headline, and the red ink began to dribble. After some hesitation, she regretfully decided to tear it down.

"Oh, no!" Tom involuntarily exclaimed.

She turned round and saw his flushed face.

"It's spoiled. I'll do it over again." She spoke in mandarin, and Tom hardly understood what she said.

She bent down to pick up the paste pot, and Tom rushed forward to help.

"Let me get it." She looked at him directly and smiled shyly. His shirt collar was open, without a tie, and he wore no hat, looking very much like a college boy.

"May I take it in for you?" Tom essayed in Cantonese in a more than respectful voice.

"If you like," the girl replied softly.

Tom followed her into the building and into the teacher's room. He did not know what to say.

"You want women volunteers?"

"*Hai-lo! Hai-lo!* You've read it."

She spoke Cantonese with a foreign accent, as a foreigner does, and Tom could not help smiling. She knew her Cantonese was funny, but she enjoyed talking it because it was new to her.

"You are laughing at my Cantonese, I know," she said with a smile.

"Oh, no," said Tom. Then he added, "You speak the language of Tongshan [China] like a foreigner."

"Do I? And you are a son of Tong, and you cannot even speak the language of Tongshan." She got through the long Cantonese sentence safely.

Which was the language of Tongshan? Tongshan was China. In the Tang Dynasty, which the Cantonese called Tong, the Chinese Empire expanded, and the southern Chinese who went overseas always spoke of themselves as Tongyen, or sons of Tang, and of China as Tongshan (Tang Land).

"If you need women volunteers, I can bring Eva here."

"Who is Eva?"

"My sister."

"Where do you live?"

Tom told her. "And what are you going to do now with that poster?"

"Do it over again."

"May I watch?"

"If you like."

As she took another sheet of pink paper and began to write on it, Tom stood near and looked on, fascinated by the way she wrote, the way she drew, and by her whole figure. He watched beneath her dark tresses the soft contours of her small face and her pointed nose, and how her lips moved with the strokes of her brush. To see a modern Chinese girl holding a Chinese brush, her hand bent at the wrist at a steep angle, writing such fine Chinese characters, was like entering a world unknown to him. Not only her writing, but all her movements and gestures had something of the old China about them, with a delicacy born of a different century. When she talked to him, she did not turn her face toward him, so that most of the time, Tom saw her face at an angle, and her eyes more often looked downward than up. Without unnecessary movements, she expressed everything through her eyes.

"You are the Chinese teacher here, aren't you?"

"Yes. And what are you?"

"A laundryman." Elsie gave him a look of half belief. "Laundryman," Tom repeated, as if he wanted to throw the word carelessly at her and see how she took it.

"You are so young. You ought to be studying," she said.

"I am studying. My family is here, and I am at school. Where do you come from? You are not a Cantonese."

"I am from Fukien, your neighbor province. But I grew up in Shanghai."

"May I know your name?"

"Elsie Tsai."

"Which Tsai?"

Elsie wrote the character for her name on a piece of paper. "Oh, Choy! Miss Choy."

"Don't call me Miss Choy."

"Why not?"

"It sounds awful. And besides, we are sons of Tong and ought to speak the Tongshan language properly. My name is Tsai. You ought to learn to speak mandarin."

"I will if I can find a teacher."

Elsie Tsai looked up quickly. There was a bright twinkle in Tom's eyes.

"I teach mandarin here," she said quietly.

She finished her poster, and Tom held the paste pot, and

together they went out to the street again. When the job was done, Elsie said to Tom, "Bring your sister. We need a lot of help."

In this rather abrupt businesslike way, she said good-by to him and went inside.

Chapter 13

I

TOM WAS SO OCCUPIED BY A NEW SENSA-
tion that the jerk of the El waked him before he realized that
he had reached the Eighty-fourth Street Station, and he
quickly dashed out just before the train started to move again.
Indeed, he did not know how he had got on the El. Tremu-
lously he went down the stairs. He felt that he had lost something, had found something, and was ashamed of something.

Miss Tsai had chided him for not being able to speak Chinese. This was not quite fair. Cantonese was as much Chinese
as mandarin. Why should he care? But it was something more
than that. He knew that mandarin was spoken by nine tenths
of the Chinese people. He had grown up in Canton, and it
seemed to him that there was a vast China which he did not
know and of which Elsie Tsai had reminded him. He could
not shake the image of Elsie from his mind, her writing, her
accent, her different costume, the jade bracelet on her arm. He
remembered how he had felt when he first met his father. It
was the same feeling he had now, a feeling that there was a
world of which he had heard often, but which had only now
become real through this girl teacher in the Chinatown school.
But she had given him a cold and formal good-by. Why should
she so upset him?

For no reason, he felt guilty when he reached home, as if he were bringing with him a new secret. During the dinner he said very little, until suddenly he remembered that he had something important to say.

"Mother, there is a Women's Committee at the school in Chinatown. There is a poster there asking for women volunteers. I told the teacher—she is Miss Choy—that Eva could help." He stopped and blushed slightly at the name Miss Choy.

"Mother, can I?" Eva was all excited. "I want to do something. Mother, I must!"

"What about your schoolwork?"

"Mother, you must let me go. You must." To everybody's surprise Eva was almost in tears.

"Why, what is the matter?" said her mother. "I never saw you so excited. You are getting to be like an American girl." Then she added, "Be calm, Apwa. Nobody has said you cannot go."

Eva smiled through her tears and hugged her mother and kissed her face, which she had never done in public before. "Mother, I promise that I'll do my lessons as usual. I can arrange the hours."

At the age of seventeen, Eva had changed, as if all of a sudden she had reached maturity. She had the same poise as in her childhood, but the American schooling had taught her a sense of independence and self-confidence. She talked with an almost perfect American accent, and she could say the New York "yeah," and "kyant" with a nasal twang instead of "can't," and she could imitate her Irish music teacher who said, "It's a saad day," and reproduce a Brooklyn "oily boid that catches the woim." She had learned to make her own dresses and to cook an entire dinner by herself. In the family she had become known as the expert packer, and she could call up the Public Library or the Post Office for any information she wanted. At home, she had begun to make fun of everybody, and at times she shouted as loudly as an American girl could. She walked straight and unafraid like American girls and with the American gait.

She became very valuable on the Women's Committee. Her knowledge of written Chinese was no better than Tom's, but her English was useful to the committee. She could type letters, and there was no better person for checking index cards, counting stamps, and wrapping packages. The best of it was that she was always punctual on the days she promised to come, and she would clean up the unpleasant part of a job that someone else had left. Mother Fong who had been hard on her in her childhood now began to speak of "my Eva" with special pride and confidence.

The work of the Women's Committee, co-operating with the Chinese Women's Committee for War Relief uptown, began to multiply. Many other Chinese women from Manhattan and Brooklyn began to join. It was inevitable that Flora too was called in, as someone good in English was needed on days when Eva was not there, and after that Mother Fong herself joined. Almost every afternoon a member of the family went to Chinatown.

Flora's symptoms of malaise had disappeared and she was feeling well. The office at the school building became a kind of club, where the women could have something to occupy their minds while they were gossiping. These meetings were never dry and dull, and Mother Fong and Eva never came home without having heard that someone was engaged, or had a baby, or broke her arm, or without learning news about the mistresses of prominent political leaders.

Mother Fong's circle of acquaintance began to expand. There were days when she had to go to the committee and Flora would be busy with unfinished laundry. Then Eva would say, "Mother, you can go. I can help pack the laundry. And I'll have the dinner ready when you come back."

On these days when Mother Fong went to Chinatown, it was Tom's privilege to accompany her. He seemed very willing to go. Sometimes he offered to go again to bring her home. "I don't like Mother to go up and down those crowded stairs alone," he said.

In the late afternoons the class in Chinese went on, and Elsie Tsai was always either in the classroom or in the office next to it. She usually managed to come into the office for ten or fifteen minutes when the class was at its work. She was the Chinese secretary of the committee, responsible for writing Chinese letters and copy for the Chinese papers. She always gave Tom a smile of recognition when she saw him, but his sense of her mystery and remoteness, strengthened by the barrier of language, never quite vanished. Once, when he met her going back to her class, she asked him, "Can you copy Chinese addresses on these envelopes for me?" The other Chinese women could not write beautiful characters. Nor could Tom, but he did his best because Elsie had asked him. When she had to correct a character because he had written one stroke too many, he was embarrassed and felt badly for a long time.

2

Double Ten, the October tenth festival celebrating the founding of the Chinese Republic, was coming. The celebration this year was to be the biggest Chinatown had ever known. The Chinese Army had not yet retreated from the Kiangwan battle line at Shanghai. A giant parade was being organized to raise funds for war relief. Long before the day came, the Chinese women both uptown and downtown were very busy. A thousand details had to be attended to. There was to be a street collection. A gigantic national flag, thirty feet wide by sixty feet long, was to be made. All available young girls and women of the Chinese community were to be called out, some to solicit contributions with cans at street corners, and forty or fifty of them to carry the flag flat through the streets for people to throw coins on. To make the flag, sewing machines had to be borrowed and transported to the school building. Because the school was the center of the preparations, classes were suspended for a week. Posters, pins, collection cans were piled up in corners, and the sounds of scissors, sewing machines, telephone bells, and women's laughter filled the hall.

During that week Tom came to help every day after half past three. Elsie was particularly busy with posters and mail, and somehow Tom was always standing by when the poster was to be pasted up or when there was mail to be taken to the letter box.

One day he came in lugging a bundle of bamboo poles for the flags and bumped into Elsie. He heard a voice cry out and recognized it as Elsie's. The bamboos had struck her on the head, and as they dropped from his hands, Elsie almost fell forward, dragged by a stick entangled in her hair. Tom rushed forward to disengage it.

As he exclaimed, "I'm so sorry," Elsie caught a look of tenderness on his face.

"It's all right." She began to rub the back of her head.

"Are you hurt?"

"No, it doesn't matter."

"But you are hurt," cried Tom as he saw a tiny trickle of blood run down her temple. "There," he pointed to the spot.

Elsie put up her hand, then she went into the teacher's room and took out a hand mirror to look at her wound, and wiped off the blood with her handkerchief. A look of great concern hung on Tom's face.

"The bleeding must be stopped," he said.

Taking her eyes from her mirror to look at him, she said with a laugh, "Why do you look so anxious? It's only a scratch."

Tom stuttered. "I'm so sorry for what I have done. Have you got a Band-aid?"

"Yes, upstairs in my room. Will you be so good as to get it

for me? It's in the medicine cabinet above the washstand."

Tom rushed up the stairs. He saw for the first time Elsie's bare room. There was an old desk and a wooden bed, and a screen behind which stood a hatrack serving as clothes hanger. The desk was neatly arranged. Some copies of old Chinese poetry and a number of novels stood on an unpainted shelf above the bed. Except for some feminine garments, one would not know it was a girl's room.

He dared not loiter and rushed down with the Band-aid. Elsie was rearranging her hair when Tom came dashing down, tearing the little package open.

"May I put it on for you?"

He borrowed a pair of scissors, studied the wound, cut the plaster into a small piece, and began to apply it very gently.

Eva, sitting nearby among the women working at the big flag, saw her brother occupied in this pleasant task and giggled. Tom demolished her with a look across Elsie's shoulder.

"Tom, Tom," Eva snickered, as she stabbed a stitch into the red cloth and then dropped her head on the table in an uncontrollable laughter. The women understood what Eva was laughing at and smiled silently.

The job done, Elsie studied her face in the hand mirror. Eva lifted her head, wiping tears from her eyes, and went off again in badly concealed laughter. Elsie looked around and saw the looks on the women's faces.

"What is everybody so happy about?" she remarked. Turning to Tom, she said, "Thank you, Tom."

Elsie went to the telephone and dialed the uptown office number of the Women's Committee for War Relief.

"Hullo, Mrs. Yang," she said in mandarin. "Have you been able to get more girls for the street collection? Yes. Yes. And the parade, more women must march in it. There are not enough. We have forty girls and women to carry the flag, and only thirty for can collection, and there won't be more than eight or ten for the parade unless . . . Of course, of course I

166

know—I understand. Your family will come? Wonderful."

Hanging up the telephone with a clack, Elsie fairly spluttered. "Those modern ladies of China!"

Turning to the other women, she said, "It's no use. You can't get those rich uptown women to join a parade in Chinatown. They think we are dirt or something." Elsie's voice was angry; then it softened. "But they will send about twenty girls for the street collection, Mrs. Yang told me. She is wonderful. She is doing the best she can. She may drag along some of her women friends, but in any case her own family will join the parade. Probably we can count on only twenty for the parade. Isn't it sad?"

"No," said Mrs. Chung, "you don't get those rich fashionable ladies to join in a street parade with laundrymen. They will come to a dance for war benefit at the Waldorf-Astoria, yes. But Chinatown is too common for them."

"Not for Mrs. Yang," said Elsie. Mrs. Yang could speak only mandarin, and it was usually through Elsie that the downtown office communicated with the uptown office. Elsie and Mrs. Yang had much fun together over the telephone although they had only met once.

"No, not Mrs. Yang. She's different. That family is different."

"What is all this business about being modern?" Elsie said. "High heels and permanent waves and a smattering of English!"

"It's this," Mrs. Chung replied in her big voice. "You are rich, your country means less to you. You are poor, your country means more to you. These rich ladies are too comfortable. Do they contribute a dirty cent or their time to the war relief? Not that I know of."

Tom stayed, listening and feeling something burning inside him.

When he left with Eva, he said to his sister, "Why did you laugh like that? It was embarrassing for Miss Tsai."

"I couldn't help it. You don't know how you looked and how Elsie looked letting you put the plaster on her temple."

"How did she look?"

"Why, she was embarrassed. She tried to look very serious, but her lips constantly dipped and moved. Tom, Tom," Eva sniggered.

"Eva, seriously, I think I ought to learn mandarin. I can exchange lessons with Miss Tsai. I can teach her Cantonese, or English if she likes."

When they reached home, Eva announced, "Mother, Tom thinks he ought to learn mandarin and exchange lessons with Miss Tsai." She broke into such loud laughter that she ran to the kitchen to laugh by herself.

From that day there was teasing in the family about Tom and Elsie.

Mother Fong thought well of Elsie. "That's the kind of decent girl I would like to have for my Tom," she said.

And so whenever Mother Fong and Flora went to Chinatown, they took special notice of Elsie and looked at her in a special light. These feminine suggestions worked on Tom, and it appeared more and more important to him that he should know mandarin and Chinese literature. He formed a new equation—Chinese literature was Elsie Tsai, and Elsie Tsai was Chinese literature.

3

The day of the Double Ten Festival came. At ten o'clock men and women began to gather in Chinatown. At eleven all the women met at the school to receive their instructions. Mrs. Yang arrived with her family, but there were no other Chinese from uptown.

"Hullo, Miss Tsai," said Mrs. Yang when she burst into the office with her children. "This is my Tengfei. This is my Shufei. And this is my Little Three. Shake hands with Miss Tsai, children."

Elsie was sitting at the large table that was covered with a pile of flags, sashes, and collection cans, and she was surrounded by girls on all sides. When she saw Mrs. Yang, she stood up. She had truly never in her life seen a woman like Mrs. Yang. Mrs. Yang brought something into the room wherever she went, an atmosphere of warmth and simplicity. She did not merely come into the room, she broke into it with a full smile and a hearty voice—a presence to be felt rather than described.

"Call me Elsie," replied Miss Tsai.

"Yes, I will call you Elsie. We had so much fun over the phone." Mrs. Yang had no reserve, no sophistication. Elsie felt the radiation from her, and all the women who knew her felt the same thing. She shook hands with everybody. She seemed so anxious to be nice to everybody, so desirous to please, so intensely interested in other people, so strong to do the right thing. Elsie remembered that her own mother had something of that quality, but she was not quite the warm, comforting, reassuring presence that Mrs. Yang was. "What a mother for her children!" Elsie thought. And she felt humble and close toward Mrs. Yang as she had not felt toward other women. The two made a wonderful team between the uptown and downtown offices.

Mrs. Yang plunged at once into business details, inseparably mixed with womanly gossip. That was what made her so irresistible to other women.

"Elsie, I feel you are like my daughter," she said with the unquestioned assumption that Elsie liked her, which automatically commanded the return of affection. "It is true," she added.

"I would be lucky to be your goddaughter."

"Of course, you can call me Mother."

And there, in the midst of all the busy preparations for the holiday parade, a new relationship was established.

Mother Fong and her entire family filed in. The men brought them to the schoolroom and then left, all except Tom. The room was crowded with people passing out and in. Mother Fong was introduced to Mrs. Yang. She shook hands with Mother Fong.

"Meet my daughter, Elsie," said Mrs. Yang.

Mother Fong was amazed. "Is she your daughter?"

"Adopted," said Mrs. Yang.

Mrs. Yang saw the Italian girl and went up to her. "I have not had the pleasure of meeting you."

"I'm Flora Fong."

"Glad to meet you, Flora."

In all the noisy confusion, arrangements for the parade went on. Some of the women went away for lunch, but Elsie was too busy to eat. Tom bought her some hot noodles from a nearby restaurant. Mother Fong sat and watched Elsie at work with an approving eye.

The parade was to start at one o'clock. A loud-speaker on the street announced the program. A hired brass band was ready, the streets were jammed, everybody was at his assigned position. Tom was to help hold the huge flag along with Eva and the other young girls. Mother Fong and Flora and Elsie and Mrs. Yang joined the women's group in the parade.

The women's group was to precede the men, while the huge flag was to bring up the rear. Other groups included the Chinese Athletic Club, the Cantonese Dramatic Club, the Chinese Boy Scouts, Chinese musicians, stilt walkers, a pantomime group in masks, and a lion dance. Each group of entertainers was contributed by one of the big Chinese guilds.

Ten minutes before one, Freddie appeared with Sing Toy, the latter in white boots, a bright red cape, and a majorette's cap tilted at an angle. Holding the majorette's baton, she took her station at the Bowery end where the brass band was.

Freddie and Sing Toy were in such a hurry that they did not see their family.

"Who is that thing walking with Freddie?" Mother Fong asked.

"That is Sing Toy," Flora whispered.

Mother Fong felt as if a red demon had opened the ground under her feet, gone through her body, and shot out again through her head, trailing a cloud of fire.

"Strike me blind! What is God doing to me? What have I done?" she exclaimed. The whole idea was so preposterous that it unnerved Mother Fong, although as a strong woman of over fifty she had seen most of the strange things in this life.

Freddie, after taking Sing Toy to her station, had gone by way of Worth Street to the City Hall to wait for the Mayor.

The band began to play. Marching in front of the band and heading the whole procession was no other than Sing Toy. They turned the corner and moved down Mott Street. The women's group was waiting at Port Arthur Restaurant to fall in behind the band and ahead of the other groups. These were variously stationed at the corners of Park, Bayard, Pell, and Mulberry Streets.

Sing Toy brandished her baton skillfully, stepped high and with great gusto, her white thighs showing below the tight shorts and her calves bulging above her white boots—an exact replica of an American majorette. A shout went up from the crowds standing on the sidewalks and peering down from the windows above. Sing Toy turned her eyes up and around and smiled to the crowd. Mother Fong covered her face with her fingers as if she could die of shame.

When the band passed, the women were to follow. The sight of Sing Toy upset Mother Fong so much that Flora had to pull her in line. "What is Heaven doing to me?" she mumbled. Walking along with her were Flora, Elsie, Mrs. Yang, and her daughters. Mother Fong looked around. The Chinese flag of red and blue with a white star flaunted from every shop and

171

tenement. On all sides, the windows and balconies were jammed with onlookers. The procession stopped more often than it moved, so that there was plenty of opportunity to talk and to observe. Mrs. Yang fell in line with Elsie and talked interminably. The Chinese drum of a theatrical unit was beating around the corner. The brass band played, and they marched again. When the band was not playing, the fife-and-drum corps of the Boy Scouts could be heard behind. There was nothing like drums and a good brass band for stirring a people to war enthusiasm.

Mother Fong was greatly moved. Little could she have guessed when she arrived five years ago that she would be marching with her American daughter-in-law, here in Chinatown, behind a brass band. She kept an eye on Elsie, another prospective daughter-in-law. Elsie wore a bluish green Chinese dress with the sleeves cut short near the shoulder. This was a little too modern for Mrs. Fong; she would not allow Eva to wear a gown with such short sleeves. Yet she knew it was the fashion in Shanghai. Elsie was a decent, responsible girl, and she looked almost like a picture. Would Tom be lucky enough to marry her?

Out in front she could see, when the band moved, Sing Toy's white-and-black baton moving up and down above the heads. The band was only three deep, and from time to time, she got a glimpse of the majorette's high-stepping thighs. Her happy frame of mind was disturbed again. Now what would Freddie do with such a girl for a wife? He went away from home when he was fourteen. Was it not strange that brothers from the same womb should be so different, that she should give birth to one like Freddie? That girl was sure to ruin him.

Each woman was holding a flag in her hand. Flora saw her father and mother on the sidewalk. They recognized her, and Flora raised her flag high, and they smiled happily in return. Mother Fong recognized some men she knew. Where was her own man? He would be in one of the Fong groups behind.

Two persons on stilts and a number of Boy Scouts were waiting at the corner of Pell to fall into their places.

"Do you think my Tom and Eva will be all right?" she asked Elsie.

"Oh, they will be all right. They cannot get lost marching with the flag."

"How long is this going to be?"

"Really only eight or ten blocks. Down Canal Street, then to City Hall square, back by the Bowery. But it will take quite some time. We have to stop for people to look at the shows and throw money into the flag."

"Do you speak English much?" Flora asked Elsie, who was on her left.

"Not much. I'm just learning. What I learned in China does not count. They pronounce words so differently from what I learned in college."

"Flora," said Mother Fong, "you change places with Elsie. I want to talk to her."

"Elsie," said Flora, "you come over here. I want to talk with Mrs. Yang."

"Elsie, how old are you?" Mother Fong asked.

"I am nineteen."

"You are a clever girl to be teaching Confucius' books. How does a girl learn to remember so many characters?"

Elsie smiled. "I learned them at home."

"Oh, I see. Nowadays, they don't teach Confucius at school. Are your parents living?"

"Yes."

"My Tom and Eva, they have forgotten all their Chinese books. Can they come and learn from you? Will you teach them?"

"I shall be glad to."

"Perhaps you want to learn English. My Tom is very good."

They had reached Canal Street now. All traffic was stopped for them to pass.

173

"Look at this parade," Mother Fong resumed. "Tom will be finishing high school next summer. I am planning to send him to college—I, a laundryman's wife. It is a good country, America, don't you think? Look at those policemen on horseback. Their uniforms are so clean. But Tom needs to learn Confucius' books."

"I shall be very glad to do it, Mrs. Fong," said Elsie with a smile.

At the corner of Mulberry and Canal, Mother Fong saw her brother, in a black suit, standing with a large group of merchants. Uncle Chan craned his neck and saw his sister and Flora and waved to them. Mother Fong and Flora waved back. On their side, Mrs. Yang and Flora walked silently and properly, only now and then exchanging remarks in English.

By the time they had gone around the City Hall and returned by way of the Bowery, it was nearly half past two. The procession broke up and the paraders scattered to the homes of their friends and relatives.

Mother Fong and Flora returned with their group to the school for a rest. Tom and Eva soon appeared.

"How much money did you collect on the flag?"

"I don't know," said Eva. "Everybody threw something into it, and quite a few threw dollar bills. Even the Americans gave. Someone threw an old bronze vase from a top floor. There were ever so many dimes and quarters. They are counting them now."

After a while, Eva rose. "I want a can. There is such a crowd outside today."

"Are you not tired?"

"No."

Elsie registered the can and gave it to Eva, and Eva disappeared.

"Did you see your father?" the mother asked Tom.

"Yes, we met him. He said he was going to Uncle's shop."

The women rested and had a cup of tea while Elsie and

Mrs. Yang kept track as each girl came in with a can full of coins and handed it to Elsie. Mother Fong said she wanted to go to Uncle's shop.

"Don't go yet. Mayor La Guardia is coming to give a speech at half past three," said Flora.

The hall began to fill again. There was no proper assembly hall for a meeting of this kind, and the school seated only two hundred. Soon they heard motorcycles announcing the arrival of the Mayor. The elders of Chinatown were all gathered. The Chinatown people had voted for La Guardia, who always stood for China.

In came Freddie with a red carnation in his buttonhole, making way for the Mayor. The hall was all noise and confusion. A public-address system was hooked up to a loud-speaker on the street, and a tense crowd stood outside to listen. The Chinese national anthem was sung. After an introduction by the president of the Consolidated Benevolence Association, La Guardia made his speech.

The members of the Women's Committee sat on a front bench. The Mayor was dramatic. He grimaced, gesticulated, chewed the bows of his spectacles, bent his head to one side, threw up his stubby hands, and thumped them down on the table. All Mother Fong saw was his tongue when he opened his mouth wide and threw it out at the end of a sentence. His speech was highly effective. His sentences were short, and he had a gift for striking phrases. What he said was always to the point, clear, forcible. He pronounced his words slowly and clearly, with marked modulation, lending emphasis at the proper place, and not wasting a single word.

"Americans say to the Chinese people, 'We love you.'" He made a wide gesture of embrace.

"But Confucius says to the people of the United States, 'Give us guns.'" He clasped his hands before his chest in an attitude of prayer. This brought the house down.

As soon as he finished, he stepped down from the platform.

He shook hands with the elders and touched some children's cheeks.

Freddie was in his element. He went up and shook hands with the Mayor, and at that exact moment there was the flash of a photographer's bulb.

"Allow me, Mayor, I want to introduce you to my sister-in-law. She is an Italian girl married to a Chinese."

"Well, that's great. Too bad Marco Polo didn't marry one of your pretty Chinese girls and bring her back to Venice."

Freddie waved to Flora, and Flora was delighted to come up and shake the Mayor's hand.

"What's your name?"

"Flora, Flora Maggio."

"Where is your father?"

"He lives across Canal Street."

"Well, Flora, you've got a good name. Stick to it, and don't let anybody change it to Fiorella. I am sick of the Little Flower business. And don't forget," he grimaced again, "when you have a Chinese child, call him Marco Polo and send him back to China to write another great book about China for us. We know too darn little about that ancient country."

Chapter 14

IN A WAY ELSIE TSAI WAS HAPPY AND IN
a way she was disappointed at her work in the Chinatown
school. The conditions of her appointment were that she
should be able to teach mandarin and "understand the Four
Books and the Five Classics." This was the elders' way of putting it, meaning merely that she should be good in classical
Chinese. But as they worded it, it was a very stern requirement,
one that modern Chinese college graduates in general could
rarely meet. Elsie had come with the idea that she was to teach
the classics. She found the standards of the children so low in
Chinese that she could teach nothing but grade work. She
could not even make them study the most elementary volume,
called *Three Hundred Tang Poems*. The boys were of all ages,
and when they came to class, they had already been to school
all day and were listless or tired or uninterested. After a while,
she ceased to entertain any idea of a more advanced teaching
program and sat back at ease with her routine. There was really
no classwork for her to prepare.

She occupied a good well-lighted room on the top floor of
the school building. She had no relatives and knew almost nobody in Chinatown. All around her people talked in Cantonese
and Cantonese only. She had spent four months in reconnoiter-

ing New York and learning English and Cantonese. Like most Chinese young people who come over to this country to study, she felt very homesick for China in the first months, and at night when she returned to her room, she felt lonely and lost and often cried herself to sleep, thinking of her parents and sister in faraway China.

Luckily the war changed her life and filled it. The war suddenly threw everybody together, at least those who were like minded and devoted to the same cause. Then Elsie forgot her troubles.

When she first met Tom, she was not thinking of marriage. She was young, she was saving money to do more college work. But she had an enormous reserve of time on her hands. Tom had good features and looked like any other healthy Chinese young man. The only thing that set him apart from others was the intelligent but shy meditative look in his eyes. She remembered the way he threw the remark "I'm a laundryman" at her by way of introduction.

That day of the little accident had brought Tom suddenly very close to her. She had seen a special look in his eyes when he asked, "Are you hurt?" Eva's giggles and the other women's smiles when Tom stood so close applying the plaster to her temple made her conscious of a special relationship. It was as if all the women except herself expected them to fall in love.

During the busy week before the celebration she had seen Tom at close range. She saw his entire family, and she noticed that he was not at all shy or reticent in the inner circle of his family. What did Flora mean by asking during the parade if she wanted to learn English, and what did Mother Fong mean by asking if she would teach Tom the classics in exchange for lessons in English? Were the women plotting behind her back to bring them together? She thought of Mrs. Yang who said she could be her adopted daughter. Was that a joke? Life in New York was becoming interesting for her.

Tom could come in the afternoons, but she would be having

classes. Would she want him to come when the classes were on? No. Could he come in the evenings when she was free? That would be too intimate, too interesting, she thought. What did she know about him? No, she would not fall into a romantic trap. Tom could come on Saturdays. What was wrong with Saturdays? Nothing was wrong with Saturdays.

"What is wrong with Sundays, Miss Tsai?" Tom asked.

"You don't want to work Sundays," Elsie replied.

"Miss Tsai, you teach me mandarin Saturdays, and I'll teach you English Sundays. I'll take you out Sundays. You don't know New York and America, and I do. I'll teach you English until your ears tingle. We'll jabber, jabber, jabber all day. It will be such fun."

"Why, it is a wonderful idea," responded Elsie immediately, as the idea of having a young man take her out on Sundays loomed on her horizon. "What do you mean jabber—jabber—jabber?"

"You see, I'm teaching you already. Jabber, jabber, jabber. I'll make you learn the most dramatic English words. But you say it all wrong. Jabber is a quick sound. Don't say jabber—jabber—jabber as if you are holding a jade bowl full of water and afraid of spilling it."

Elsie laughed.

"May I call you Elsie?"

"I don't see why not. All your family call me Elsie anyway."

"That's right. We spoke of you at home as Elsie, and it is strange for me to call you Miss Tsai when I see you."

"Does your family speak of me at home?"

"All the time. Especially Eva."

"Why?"

"You know why."

There was that telltale look on Tom's face again. A faint color crept into Elsie's face.

When she woke up the next Sunday morning Elsie was happy in spite of herself. It was her first Sunday with a young man to take her out. Her first lesson in the classics with Tom the day before had been a discovery. Tom really meant to learn. He had a burning shame about his ignorance. He listened so intently when she spoke of Chinese history.

At ten o'clock Tom came for her.

"Where are we going?"

"Let's walk over the Manhattan Bridge."

"Can we?"

"Sure we can."

It was a late October day. Tom was in his open-collar blue sweater.

"Why don't you wear slacks? They are better for walking."

"What are slacks?"

"Trousers that women wear for country walks. Have you got any?"

"Yes, I got some for the sea voyage."

"Slacks are the thing."

"I'll change, then. You wait here."

She came down a few moments later in navy-blue slacks and a pink sweater.

"Is this all right?"

Tom looked hard. He could hardly recognize her. She tried to turn about in the way of American models but ended in the most Chinese fashion, her arms bent before her chest and her tapering fingers turned inwards.

"Come on. Let's go."

"Haven't you a hat?" Elsie asked.

"I never wear one." His tone was very final.

Elsie's Western dress seemed bizarre in Tom's eyes, but the combination of the modern look and the thin-spun cobwebby delicacy of her Oriental accent and gestures fascinated him.

They went across the bridge, the sun shining in their faces. On their right columns of black smoke from the ships of the Navy Yard darkened half the harbor. Tom walked beside her, a volume of Whitman's "Leaves of Grass" in his pocket.

"Afoot and light-hearted I take to the open road,
  Healthy, free, the world before me,
  The long brown path before me leading wherever I choose."

"Tom, what you mumbling? Are you a bookworm?"
"I'm reciting a poem I like."
"What is it?"
"Walt Whitman's *Song of the Open Road*. I've got it with me. I know a place where we can sit on the other side."
In the middle of the bridge, they stopped to look at the scene. The harbor was enjoying an idle Sunday, too, and only a few tugboats were moving lazily up the river. In the distance was Governor's Island, and still further, barely discernible in the foggy atmosphere, was the Statue of Liberty.
"What is that?" Elsie pointed to a boat crowded with passengers.
"That is a pleasure boat that takes people for a trip around the island."
"What island?"
"Manhattan. Manhattan is an island, you know. Some Sunday we will take the boat trip and see Manhattan from the water. You like the water, don't you?"
"Not particularly. Why?"
"Well, New York is a port. People ought to see it as a seaport, with the bridges, the ships coming and going, the ferry crossings. We are right on the Atlantic Ocean. Out that way is Coney Island, the beach. When I first came, I didn't see the beauty of it."
"Tom, what are you going to do with yourself?"
"I don't know. I can't decide. Mother is determined that I

shall go to college. But no Harvard or Princeton for me. I'll find some city college nearby. If I board at home, it won't cost much."

"What would you like to study?"

"It must be science for me. Perhaps I shall take engineering. Look at those bridges, aren't they the most inspiring things in the world?"

On the opposite bank they roamed the streets until they found a shady bench in a square where, each with a hot dog in hand, Tom said he was going to give her lessons in English. Elsie had learned to read English and had gone through *A Tale of Two Cities* in her freshman year in Shanghai. The chief trouble was with her pronunciation. Tom opened the book to the *Song of the Open Road*.

> You flagg'd walks of the cities! You strong curbs
>   at the edges!
> You ferries! You planks and posts of wharves! You
>   timberlined sides! You distant ships!
> You rows of houses! You window-pierc'd facades!
>   You roofs!

"I thought this was the right place to study this passage," said Tom.

"The words are good," Elsie said. "But do you call this poetry?"

"No, not this passage in itself. You have to read the poem as a whole."

They chose another passage. The trouble with Elsie was that she seemed to be reciting her lines, dwelling on each word in a dead monotony of unchanging sweetness. It usually took her a full second to say and complete the word "hand."

"What are you doing? Chinese embroidery?"

Elsie smiled in embarrassment, but she understood.

"You know," said Tom. "They never teach English correctly in China. They teach you words and not sentences. The students try to recognize words and not sentences. I know a way."

"What is that?"

"You learn only three sentences a day, but you learn them perfectly, as a whole. Say them the way they are said by Americans. Never mind the individual words, or the grammatical structure. You'll be surprised."

"I'll try."

Tom picked two lines for her to repeat. They were:

Allons! Whoever you are come travel with me!
Traveling with me you find what never tires.

"Say this line after me," Tom said.

" 'Come travel with me. Traveling with me you find what never tires,' " recited Elsie after him.

"Do you know what that means?"

Elsie looked at Tom. "I understand what that means," she said with a knowing smile. "Tom, what do you do when you have free time? What do you do for relaxation?"

"I? You mean when I am not studying? I deliver laundry. After that, if I have time, I go to the East River and watch the river traffic. I go to the movies. I do all sorts of things. I roam over the whole town. I have good legs."

"You must be a happy man. You have your family with you here."

"Yes. Do you have any relatives here?"

"No."

"You must be lonely in your free hours."

"I am."

"Why don't you sometimes come to my home and spend an evening there?"

"I'm afraid I'd be in the way. Do they approve of your coming out with me this way?"

"Of course they do. There are always things going on in my home. Since I met you, I have often wondered at night what you are doing alone in your room. I lie at night thinking of you."

Elsie shot a look at him. "Do you?"

"I do. . . . Elsie."

"What?"

"Only two weeks ago I was afraid of you. I am still a little afraid of you now."

She laughed. "What do you mean?"

"I don't know how to explain it. There is so much of you that is new and exciting to me. You know so much that I do not know about ancient China, the classics, literature. Will you teach me, really?"

Her eyes looked absorbed for a moment before she said, "I will teach you what I know. I know so little myself."

They sat there in the October sun for a while, then Tom said, "Shall we go?"

Elsie rose, her body feeling a little limp.

"Can you walk back? I'd love to walk back."

"Let's take a streetcar, please."

It was the first time Elsie realized that Tom indeed had good legs.

Elsie was yet to discover, on the following Sundays, how mercilessly Tom could walk and how like him it was to forget whom he was walking with. Sometimes in the quiet of a Sunday morning they prowled together through the dark shadows of Wall Street. Sometimes they sat on the wharves looking at the incoming ships. They took boat rides, which Elsie enjoyed better. They took Fifth Avenue bus rides, going back and forth. One cold November morning Tom took her by subway to Coney Island to look at the winter sea. When it became too cold he gave her English lessons in a movie theater.

But the evenings in Tom's home were the best. When she found it unbearably lonely, she would telephone him to ask if she could come up and he would always be at the Eighty-fourth Street station waiting for her.

3

Flora's confinement was drawing near. Mother Fong was sure it was a boy. She talked herself into believing this sincerely, claiming that she could tell from the shape of the mother's body. Flora had agreed to take Mayor La Guardia's suggestion to call the child Marco if a boy, but despite his advice, she would call her child Fiorella if it was a girl. When Mother Fong was told that "Fiorella" meant the Little Flower (Shiu Far), she approved. As for Marco Polo it took her a long time to believe that what Flora and Tom told her was a true story.

One Saturday evening in January Uncle Chan came to dinner. Soon after dinner, Flora said she felt spasms. It could not be, for the child was not expected until the end of February. Flora's doctor was sure of that. Toward ten o'clock, the pains came again, this time more serious. It could be, Flora thought. She had been leaning against the banister for breath, coming up the dark staircase that afternoon, when a child brushed past her, and she turned and sat down on the staircase. She did not think at the time the shock was serious. She called up her doctor but there was no answer, and she was desperate.

"Well, if the doctor says it is in February, then it is early yet," said Uncle Chan. "Perhaps she has eaten something that disagrees with her. I can run over and get some medicine to protect the embryo. What do you say, Sister?"

They did not know what to think. They tried to call the doctor again, but he was away for the week end.

"What hospital are you going to?"

"Women's Hospital, on Hundred Tenth."

"Well," said the uncle, "Since the doctor is away, the best thing is to take medicine for easing the spasms and protecting the embryo. It will do no harm, at least."

Uncle Chan went away and in an hour or so came back with a package of Chinese medicine. After it was taken, they sat and watched. Spasms of pain came and went. They could not tell whether the pains were increasing or going away.

"She will be all right. It takes a little time for the medicine to work," said Uncle Chan, and he fell asleep on Tom's bed, snoring. Loy and his parents kept watch.

Toward half past three in the morning, Flora felt an onrush of pain. She could not stand it any longer. The whole household was waked up.

"Call the cops," said Flora between her cries of anguish.

Mother Fong could not understand this. "Call the cops," Flora insisted. Loy went down to the shop and rang up the police.

In a short time a policeman arrived, and said he was taking Flora away. It took some time for Loy to get a taxi, and when he got the taxi, there was yet some more delay. A small suitcase was hurriedly got ready, and Flora was taken as she was. It was a cold night, and they brought a blanket to wrap Flora in.

The policeman and Loy carried Flora down the stairs. Mother Fong insisted on going along. Outside the driver had started the motor. Flora screamed and groaned, and neighbors peered out of their windows to see what was going on. Loy got in the back seat first and arranged for Flora to sit leaning on him, while they carefully wrapped her up in the blanket. The policeman and the mother sat in the front seat. Flora's groans mingled with the rumble of the car.

"Step on it. Drive as fast as you safely can," said the policeman to the driver. It was four o'clock, and the road was clear in the small hours of the morning. But Flora's cries grew louder and louder. Mother Fong turned round and held Flora's hands.

There was a loud cry. Mother Fong felt round Flora's body. "Heavens, I think the baby is coming out." The blanket was wet.

The policeman and the driver kept strict watch on the road. "Slow down," said Loy. "The car is shaking too much."

The car slowed. Flora could not stand it any longer and clutched wildly at both Loy and the mother. There was a last cry of anguish.

"Stop the car," said the mother. "I think the baby has come."

The driver drew the car up to the curb and stopped the motor. They were only a few long blocks from the hospital.

All was quiet. Flora's groans had ceased. Mother Fong felt the wet, warm limbs of a baby, and the blanket was a wet wad. The driver turned and said, "Jesus! Would you believe it, officer? This is the second time a baby was born in my cab."

"Good luck never comes singly," said the policeman. "This is my first."

"I've kids, too, at home, five of them. The trouble with women expecting a baby is that they will wait till the last minute. I always tell my wife to go to the hospital at the first sign."

Mother Fong took off her coat and wrapped the baby up carefully with the lining next to it and waited for the cord to come out. She lost no time in groping over the baby.

"It's a Marco," she whispered to Loy. "Congratulations, Flora."

"Congratulations, Mother," said Loy. Turning to the policeman, he said, "It's a Marco Polo."

"What do you mean Marco Polo?"

"It's a boy," Loy said proudly. "My wife is an Italian."

The car started again and proceeded slowly toward the hospital.

The next day the evening paper reported that Sergeant O'Toole had delivered a Sino-Italian baby named Marco Polo in a taxicab. There was a picture of the mother and the baby. The following morning Flora received a telegram of congratulations from Mayor La Guardia.

Chapter 15

❦❦❦❦❦❦❦❦❦

I

FLORA CAME OUT OF THE HOSPITAL AFTER
ten days. Mother Fong had sent a gift of ten dollars to Sergeant O'Toole as a way of expressing gratitude for his help, but the policeman would not accept it. Even then the childbirth alone had cost them over a hundred dollars. Every day Loy had taken Flora chicken soup, cooked with slices of black leek, as the hospital said she could eat anything she liked. The black leek was good for the mother's milk. Now Loy had gone to the hospital to bring his wife and baby home. A good pot of chicken soup was standing ready on the range. Flora's bed had been made, and the father and mother were ready for the reception.

The father could not help but be happy. He had broadcast the news to all his friends in Chinatown, and everybody had congratulated him on becoming a grandfather. In that society, it sounded like having made a million dollars and was certainly better than having completed a new house. It was the achievement of one of the grand purposes of human life, the attainment of an honor to which all men aspired but in which not all succeeded. A man toils and sweats; life is for the most part a sordid and risky affair, and many fall by the wayside. It is like crossing the mythical bridge of a hundred spans end-

189

ing in a fog of nowhere. Some drop out early, some reach the fortieth span, some the fiftieth, a few reach the seventieth, and very few the eightieth. He must be a lucky man to have lasted so long. People called him blessed.

The day before Flora's homecoming, he had gone to Chinatown and bought a pair of red candles two feet high with golden characters on them, indicating a combination of all earthly happiness, "luck, honor, and longevity." Wealth was not included. These were Chinese candles, for the American candles were not good enough, the form and color were not just right, and there were no golden characters on them. American candles did not have the proper shade of deep red, they tapered upward instead of downward, and the wick did not splutter and crackle now and then as candles should for good luck.

Tom Fong, Sr., wanted the occasion to be solemn. He had put on a coat and a tie and his best pair of shoes. Mother Fong wore a gold pin and a fresh deep-red carnation in her hair. She had been to the hospital to see Marco several times, and Father Fong once, after he had resisted the temptation long enough. But this was to be the formal affair. The red candles were lit below the grandfather's portrait, and the father and mother sat erect in the hard chairs on the right and left of the candles, waiting for Flora.

"I gave Loy a hundred and fifty dollars to take along," said the father, looking out through the window into the upper floors of the houses across the street. "I think he said it would cost ten dollars a day. It is lucky there are no operation charges. Mother, when will it be that we can sell this laundry and set up a restaurant?"

"It will be four or five years yet. It is not right for you, a grandfather now, to be working like this. But we will wait. You are not tired of this work, are you?"

The father's face was wrinkled. "When I see old Leong sitting at the cashier's desk smoking his pipe, I wish I could stop working. I have worked and ironed for over thirty years now. But I have to keep on working till we save up enough. That war contribution put us back three hundred dollars. This grandson of ours will cost us another two hundred, I am afraid. And we shall have to celebrate when our grandson is one month old."

"Yes, and there is the fifty dollars I promised the goddess if she gave us a boy, and now she has given us a boy," the mother said, also looking straight out through the front window.

"I suppose a hundred dollars for the feast will do. People give gifts, you know. That and the pledge to the church will make it a hundred and fifty. The hospital one hundred. I don't know what the doctor will charge. He did not deliver the child."

"Now that I think of it," said the mother, "I can never understand what American policeman do. Are they supposed to deliver babies? I thought policemen were only for catching thieves." She laughed. "When Flora said, 'Call the cops,' I thought a thief had got into our house. This is really a strange country, where you can call a policeman at night and ask him to come out in the cold like a house servant and take someone to the hospital for you. He is an official, isn't he?"

"That is America. It is their custom. They are not afraid of their officials."

"It is certainly different from ours. I must say it is not a bad custom." The mother shook her head in amazement.

They heard a car stop below and ran to the window. There was Flora, beautifully dressed in black, and Loy holding the baby, wrapped in a tiny bundle of white.

"Flora! Loy!" the mother shouted from the window.

Flora looked up, all smiles.

The mother went out to turn on the light on the staircase. When they came up, she said, "Flora, you hold the baby. Your father is in there in the sitting room."

They walked straight in, and Flora handed the white bundle to the grandfather, sitting straight in his chair to receive his first grandson. Loy and Flora stood by. To Flora the lighted candles were a surprise.

Tom Fong, Sr., took the baby and heaved a deep sigh. He held the baby tightly, preciously, and examined it carefully. There were tears in his old eyes. This was the great consolation of his old age.

"Is it to be called Marco?"

"Yes, Marco," replied Flora.

"Flora, you are a good daughter to me, and I am thankful to Heaven. And, Loy, you are a good son."

He dropped a small red paper package into the daughter's hand. It held the "string money" of two silver dollars. Flora did not understand, and Loy explained that was the grandfather's gift for speeding up the growth of the child.

"Now may I have him?" said the grandmother, sitting in the other chair.

The grandfather stood up and handed over the baby to the grandmother. The child had conferred upon him an honor that neither king nor president could bestow, promoting him to grandfather and his wife to grandmother. The grandmother dug into her pocket and thrust a similar red-paper package into the baby's tiny hands.

"May you grow up fast and strong, Marco, my grandson."

"Isn't he an adorable baby?" said Flora, exultant.

"Yes, he is a pretty child."

"We must ask that girl teacher at the school—what's her name?" said the father.

"Elsie Tsai," said Flora.

"We must ask Elsie Tsai to write the child's name in Chinese. Ask her to choose some nice characters. Well, you had better go to bed. There is chicken soup in the kitchen for you. I'll hold Marco until you are ready."

Only a few days later, the family was already planning the celebration of the baby's completion of his first month, according to custom. It was a busy time for Loy, and his family and Freddie and Uncle Chan were a great help. No prominent leader of Chinatown must be overlooked, and no distant relative must be missed in the invitations. Elsie Tsai had to think fast, for the invitations had to go out in Chinese. The customary translation of Marco Polo's name, meaning "horses can," evidently would not do. But Elsie was ingenious; she thought of the two characters for Ink Brother, which sounded the same as Marco. It was in fact lovingly poetic in a teasing sort of way, since ink represents the writer's profession, and the "brother dealing in ink" constituted a pious wish that the child might grow up to be a scholar.

"Well," said the grandfather contentedly. "If he drinks enough ink, he will not have to sweat like his grandfather."

Flora thought the name funny. "Is that a fair translation?" she asked Tom. "Marco Polo was a trader, a commercial man."

"Yes," said Tom, "he was a trader. But the only thing he ever sold to us was his book."

The invitations went out to distant relatives in Boston, Detroit, and San Francisco, for the Fongs were widespread in the country, and even to their village in China. Friends and early associates whom Tom Fong, Sr., had forgotten for ten or fifteen years were brought to mind. For the birth of a grandson under these happy conditions was a crowning symbol of his successful life, a reminder to all his friends that Tom Fong had arrived. Wrapped in his swaddling clothes, little Marco was totally unaware how important he was, how much his arrival meant to his parents and grandparents.

"Flora," said the father, "ask your parents to come, for it is your day. We shall send them an invitation, but persuade them to come."

And they did not forget Sergeant O'Toole.

It was decided that the dinner was to be held at the Port Arthur Restaurant. For Tom Fong was able to persuade his friend Old Tuck to appear in honor of this occasion, and the restaurant was selected for Old Tuck's convenience. Freddie brought Sing Toy and a local judge. Freddie was useful for he gave the family much face. Of the prominent leaders of Chinatown, those whom Freddie knew were invited, and those who were invited came, for no one wanted to make Tom Fong lose face. Mother Fong's friends and acquaintances on the Women's Committee were invited. Mrs. Yang had a special invitation through Elsie, and she came.

When all were seated, the guests occupied four round tables, and Tom and Eva and the other members of the family were distributed at the different tables to serve as hosts. The guest of honor was Marco, carefully washed and powdered and bonneted and tied with a new blue ribbon, and held proudly on his mother's breast. Prominently displayed on each table were dishes of boiled red eggs, symbols of the occasion. The Chinatown leaders and Flora's mother were at the table of honor with Flora, where sat also Father Fong, Uncle Chan, and Old Tuck. Mother Fong made Elsie sit next to her at another table with Tom and Mrs. Yang. Loy, as the father, presided at a third table where Eva had to sit with Sing Toy, while Freddie acted as host at another table with the American judge. Sing Toy was easily the most strikingly dressed figure and she drew much admiration.

During the dinner, Flora was studying Sing Toy, Sing Toy was studying Mother Fong, Mother Fong was studying Elsie, and Elsie was studying Flora. Tom was studying Granduncle Tuck.

But Mother Fong was also studying the cost of the dinner and how much the restaurant would make from a party like this. The restaurant would probably make from such a birthday as much as the washing and ironing of five families' laundry for a week.

Before the dinner, the guests were served with a bowl of chicken broth with wine and a bowl of pigs' knuckles cooked with peanuts. These were identical with the dishes Flora ate during the month after the baby's birth, to help her breast feeding, and were now given to the guests to symbolize the occasion. The dinner, if not extravagant according to Chinese standards, was sumptuous for the American judge, and it was decent and appropriate for the Chinese guests. It opened with the "fairies' chicken," preceded by a toast to the parents and grandparents. It disdained the Moo Goo Gai Pan but followed with fried chicken livers, bamboo-flavored shrimp balls fried with tree fungus, fried slices of white chicken meat coated with albumen, climaxed in the middle with sharks' fins, viscid and smoothing to the throat, with the essence of distilled chicken soup and flavored with finely chopped ham. When the palate somewhat palled, it was resuscitated with small bowls of soup of sweet lotus seeds, tickled by bits of carrot balls lending flavor to soft strands of ligaments of scallops, seduced with slices of crisp-skin fish, and urged with thin hard sticks of peppery fried beef and parsley, and finally soothed with long strings of Yangchow noodles for good luck.

Toasts were drunk throughout the dinner. In the middle of the dinner, Mother Fong had relieved Flora of the baby so that the mother could eat. On such an occasion, the mother's family took precedence over the father's family. Old Mrs. Maggio was happy when she saw Flora so happy. She did not know that she was so important. Father Fong asked Old Maggio to make a speech, and he stood up and said he could not make a speech but that Loy was a good son-in-law and the Chinese were *simpatico* and that he was very happy to see this day.

Tom kept his eyes on Granduncle Tuck. The old man was

indeed very old, but when he spoke, his mind was perfectly clear though his voice was small.

"Who is he?" whispered Elsie.

"Granduncle Tuck, the oldest man in Chinatown," said Tom.

Old Tuck stood up. A hush went over the whole room. He shot his glass eye over the tables of guests. He still commanded awe from the audience, but he was evidently in a happy frame of mind and smiled placidly.

"Tom Fong, congratulations," he said. "Today I drink to the success of my friend Tom Fong. We were good and close friends in the Klondike days. He and I and another man, we were the only three Chinamen in town. When you spend a whole winter in the Klondike with a man, after you have dug in for the season, you know him pretty well. Tom Fong was in his twenties, and he was strong, and he was thinking of his wife. [Laughter.] We made candles out of the bears' fat, and we ate bears' paws, which were delicious. Well, after we had digested the fourth cub we had trapped, Tom was rather sick of it all. He didn't want any gold, he wanted his wife. [Roars of laughter.] So the next spring he took a boat and went back to his wife. Then after a while he came back. We had some tough times, then. I was back in Portland then, and one day I met Tom in a bar. I asked him what he wanted to do, and he said he didn't want to go up North any more, he just wanted to make an honest living with his pair of hands. 'America is a big place,' he said. 'There must be some way for a man to make an honest living with his hands.' Well, Tom was right. He took to washing, and he has been washing for the last thirty or forty years. But Tom Fong was smart. He went back to his wife a second time, and there was Loy. He went back again and there was Freddie. He went back to his wife every five or six years while I stayed. There he was smart. Now you see the difference. Tom always made me think of those eels that travel a thousand miles half across the Atlantic Ocean to lay their spawn. The great mistake in my life, was that I did not follow the instinct of the eel. And now look at him, a grandfather. Look at Loy and Freddie and Tom junior. Tom Fong in all his life as I knew him was an honest man. I drink to my great old friend, Tom Fong, an honest man."

Tom Fong stood up, inwardly happy without showing it, and drank in response to his friend.

When the dinner was almost over, Old Tuck took a red egg and rolled it over Marco's head. Then the tray of red eggs was passed around the table, and each guest as he took an egg threw into the tray his "red package," a gift of cash.

Mother Fong stood up and drank a cup to thank everybody, and the dinner was over. When the bill was presented, it was one hundred and thirty-seven dollars. The greater part, however, was covered by the gifts.

Late in the evening, at home, Tom Fong said to his wife, "I've never spent so much money on a dinner. But it was worth it."

3

Flora had consulted Father Bosco and he had said, "Of course he is to be baptized a Catholic. You know what the Church's instructions are as to the duty of parents. It is for the soul of your child."

"This is a Chinese family. Should I not tell the parents of my husband?"

"Usually it is the pledge of the father and the mother together that their child shall be brought up in the true Faith. It would be much better if it did not have to be a secret. I would advise you strongly to have a serious talk with your husband and prevail upon him. Your duty as the child's mother is all the greater because you know the truth."

"Loy will be easy; he is my husband. But I shouldn't like to do anything about their grandson that the grandparents didn't know. In a Chinese family the old parents are so important."

"Well, you might try. No doubt your mother-in-law is well disposed toward the Church now that she has had her prayer granted. Tell them your son won't be the first Chinese to become a Catholic. Do you realize that there are nearly four million Chinese Catholics?"

Flora was truly surprised. Of the two American institutions in the heart of Chinatown, the church and the rescue home for the unemployed, neither was able to claim a Chinese. Father Bosco saw her look and went on.

"Yes, the Catholic mission in China dates back to the thirteenth century, and the first missionary to China was an Italian. There are Catholics in every province of the country. We have a great university and a famous observatory in Shanghai. Flora, you are an intelligent girl. You ought to do what Matteo Ricci did. Did you ever hear of the great Italian missionary Matteo Ricci?"

"No."

"Well, Matteo Ricci went to China in the late sixteenth century. He was a great mathematician and taught the Chinese astronomy. But he was a very intelligent man. He first made himself a scholar of Chinese literature, and he was able to present the Catholic religion in the light of the Chinese mind, and he won many friends at the Emperor's court."

"Father, you know I'm not a learned girl."

"What I mean is, the Catholic Church is a universal religion. It teaches universal truth. But truth has different colors in different countries. The Americans like certain aspects of it, the Chinese some other aspects. Do you see what I mean? I don't know much about the Chinese except that they have great respect for the past and for their families. Perhaps you know better. God will show you the light."

"Father, did you say there were many Chinese in the past who were Catholics?"

"Yes, in Matteo Ricci's time, there were three hundred

princes and members of their families who were Catholics. And the Catholics were in charge of the Imperial Board of Astronomy for two centuries. Right now, there is a great Chinese scholar, Lu Cheng-hsiang, formerly premier and chief Chinese Delegate to the Versailles Conference, who is now a Benedictine monk in Belgium."

But it was a very difficult subject for Flora, and she spoke of it to Loy.

"What does it mean?" Loy asked.

"It means that we promise to bring up Marco to be a Catholic as far as we as parents are concerned."

Loy thought a long time and then said, "Do you want it very much?"

"Yes, I want it very much."

"It is all right with me, but we have to consult my parents. It does not make me a Catholic, does it?"

"No, Loy. But I do want Marco to grow up and believe in what I believe in."

When Loy spoke to his father, the father said, "Well, that comes of your marrying an American. If Marco is to grow up to be an American, you might as well make him believe what Americans believe in. To make Flora happy, you had better accept it."

Flora was surprised when Loy told her his father's judgment.

"I thought Father was a Buddhist."

"Buddhist nothing."

"Confucianist?"

"Flora, you don't understand. Confucianism is not a church."

"But what about the Buddhist priests? Wouldn't they object?"

Loy laughed out loud. "I never heard of such a thing. The Buddhist priests do not organize a parish. If we like, we go to them. Nobody cares. Nobody bothers you in China. You can be Buddhist, Confucianist, and Taoist all at the same time."

"The Chinese don't take religion seriously, then."

"Some do and some don't. Most people don't."

So when Flora spoke to Mother Fong she was more confident and less afraid.

"Mother, I have arranged with the priest and have told him you want to redeem your promise. Mother, I want very much to have my child grow up a Catholic, like myself. I want him baptized."

Mother Fong was stirring the pot.

"What is that?"

"The priest will sprinkle some water on his head. It won't hurt him. It is a symbol. Mother, the priest told me that a great many Chinese ancestors in the past were Catholics."

"Well, the longer one lives, the more one learns. Since that baby was born, I have never ceased to hear about that Italian in China hundreds of years ago. I didn't know whether to believe this Marco Polo story or not until Elsie told me it is true. Now you tell me there were many Catholics in China several hundred years ago. Were they Italians, too?"

"No, they were Chinese ancestors. The priest told me the Catholic Church is very old in China."

"How old is it? As old as Confucius?"

"It is almost two thousand years old."

Mother Fong looked at her daughter-in-law and said, "Well, if it is that old, it must be good. Otherwise people would not have believed it for so long."

"You agree, then, Mother?" cried Flora. Her heart beat hard.

"Well, Flora, I have long been watching you. Your mother has taught you good manners, and you help my son. I tell you that in China we never liked the Christians because of their gunboats."

"But we don't have gunboats here."

"Yes, there are no gunboats here to put my grandson up against me. I suppose that makes a difference," she said as she laid aside the ladle and wiped her hand on her apron.

"The priest told me there were more than three hundred

princes and princesses in China who were Catholics. It is true. The priest cannot lie."

Mother Fong looked at Flora, and she said, "Flora, Marco is your child. He is born an American, and I want him to grow up like an American. So long as it does not set him apart, like the Christians in China, I don't mind. But I want to ask you: does the Catholic Church teach sons to obey their parents?"

"It does. Most certainly."

"And to be honest and thrifty?"

Flora was not sure about the doctrine of thriftiness, and she answered hesitantly, "yes." But she was quite sure about the teaching of honesty.

"What I mean is, does the Church teach a boy to be a good son to his parents?"

"Most certainly yes."

"Then why didn't you say so in the first place? Can a person object to that?"

"You will give your consent, Mother?"

"You don't have to ask."

Flora was overjoyed. She arranged with the priest, and when the date came, all the family put on their best clothes and went to the church. Flora was warmly happy that the family was doing this all for her.

After the ceremony the priest shook hands with all the family, and they gathered round him while he explained kindly and simply the deep meaning of baptism. Mother Fong lighted some candles and knelt before the image of the Virgin, putting her palms together in the Buddhist attitude of prayer, and gave the priest an envelope that held fifty dollars, as a donation to the church.

Chapter 16

✂✂✂✂✂✂✂✂

I

TOM FONG TOOK ACCOUNT OF HIS FINAN-
cial standing. He had been able to save only two thousand
dollars in the past six years. How long was it yet to be? He
was thankful that he was in good health and able to work for
some more years, although he was past sixty. The gods had
been kind to him and had recompensed him well.

One night in May, he said to Tom, "You will graduate this
spring. Your mother and I want you to be a learned man, not
like me. You must find out where you can learn a profession
and get out of this laundry business. Daiko has worked for you
to go to school. When you are successful, don't forget what he
has done for you."

He went then to Chinatown to a meeting of the elders of
the guild to which he had recently been elected. It was his first
meeting, and he was feeling happy. He said good-by to his
wife and said he would be home late, and he took a second
look at Tom as he went away. It was the look of the old
father, full of hope and confidence in him.

Then the tragedy struck. By eleven o'clock the father had not
returned. The family remembered that he had said he would
be late. At quarter of twelve the telephone rang. The call was
from the Bellevue Hospital. There had been an accident; the
family was to come immediately.

The hospital did not give any more information. In the hour of crisis, Mother Fong did not show any fear. Flora had to stay with the baby, but all the rest of the family went.

They arrived at the hospital to find Tom Fong in a state of unconsciousness. He had been struck by a motor car near the ramp of the Manhattan Bridge, and his skull was fractured. Tom and Eva and Loy wept, but there was not a tear in Mother Fong's eyes. They were permitted to stay near the injured father, hoping that he would say some words to them. Mother Fong sat like a statue, in a daze but now and then calling to her husband. Tom Fong, Sr., never regained consciousness. An hour passed, like an eternity to the family, and then he died. Only then did Mother Fong break down.

Loy had gone out to learn what had happened. A car coming down from the bridge fast had collided with a truck. The truck in trying to avoid it swerved violently to the curb and knocked down the father, throwing him several feet. The man in the car had been killed instantly. When the police came, they found Tom Fong lying in a pool of blood, dying a typically American death.

The family filed silently away from the dead man's bedside. They called up Freddie, who was not at home, and then they called Uncle Chan's shop. In ten minutes the uncle arrived. The necessary papers were signed, and the uncle decided with them that the body was to be sent to a "longevity parlor" in Chinatown.

Late in the night they left the hospital and took a taxi to the uncle's shop. Passing the place of the accident, they saw the truck and the smashed car still there. They stayed at the uncle's shop, and no one slept that night. They reached Freddie at two o'clock in the morning. He found the mother wailing, Tom and Eva stricken, and he could bring them little comfort. When the news struck, they were too dazed to cry, but now the neighbors near Uncle Chan's shop heard the deep wailing that night.

The whole guild came to help in the busy week that followed. Tom Fong, Sr., was buried with honors. Wreaths and scrolls filled the hall of the longevity parlor where, according to custom, an enlarged portrait of the deceased was hung. A great many of their friends came to the funeral, and the coffin was followed by Tom Fong's wife, his three sons, and his daughter and his daughter-in-law and the uncle, the women in black and the men merely wearing black arm bands following American custom. The black was dismal and depressing, and the women wept bitterly. Onlookers on the street who saw the dead man followed by so many sons and daughters called him blessed. And everybody who knew him said, "He was a good and honest man."

Freddie came home to stay with his mother for a week. The expenses of the funeral had been great, but Freddie was able to borrow two hundred dollars and the uncle helped with one hundred, and the gifts from friends also totaled over two hundred, so that their finances were not too badly damaged. Luckily, they had been able to save for such an emergency.

The family remained in deep mourning. The father's portrait enlargement, which they had hastily ordered for the ceremonies at the longevity parlor, was now hung up where the grandfather's portrait had been, and the latter was moved up above it, almost as if they were arranging ancestral tablets. White candles were lit before it. After weeks had passed, the family held council. Loy and Flora were for carrying on the laundry. They would be one hand short, but Tom would be graduating next month. They had now barely over fifteen hundred dollars in their savings, and they were a long way from their dream of a restaurant. Freddie talked a great deal about his father's refusal to be insured. Tom Fong had never made a will as men do in America. Flora was for claiming damages. Mother Fong did not know what this meant.

"In America," Flora said, "if a flowerpot falls off a window sill and injures a person, the person collects damages for his hospital bills. If a bad staircase causes an injury, you sue the landlord for damages, and if a grandstand collapses and somebody is injured, he sues the management of the grandstand for damages."

Mother Fong knew that they were entitled to compensation of some sort, as in China, but she did not know that it was so legal and so clearcut as all this. In China one arranges; one does not go to the lawyer and sue under the law. Freddie and Loy were of the same opinion as Flora, and Freddie was instructed to take legal procedure.

"How much can we claim?" the mother whispered to Loy in a tone that suggested the subject was indecent.

"Five thousand dollars at least."

"Five thousand!" Mother Fong was amazed. She dared not smile.

"Certainly not less."

During the days that followed, in which Tom was graduated from his school, great plans for the future were shaping in Mother Fong's head as she thought of the sum she might receive.

One day a check came from the insurance company. It was for five thousand dollars. The money that Tom Fong had slaved all his life to save lay now in Mother Fong's hand.

Then a woman came to call on the Fong family. Tom opened the door. The woman was in her fifties. She wore a formal-looking hat, a black dress trimmed with a white lace collar, and black gloves coming halfway up her arms. She stood very erect, looking at them with very small but bright eyes. She looked as if she were in deep trouble. Her pale lips moved.

"May I come in?"

When Tom let her in, she chose a seat and sat silently for a moment before she asked to see the mother.

"What is it you want?" asked Tom.

"I want to see your mother, please."

When Mother Fong came in, the woman rose.

"I have come to see you because I must," she said. "I felt very badly when I heard that your husband was killed. It was my son who was driving the car. I hope you are not angry with me for what my boy did. You know that he was killed, too." She took out a handkerchief and blew her nose; her voice was thin and tired.

Mother Fong sat and listened and knew that this was a good woman. "I am so sorry you lost your son."

"He was my only son, and I am left alone. But that is not what I came to talk about. I hope you have received a check from the insurance company."

"Yes, I have. Thank you."

"Do not thank me. The insurance company paid it. I hope it will compensate you a little, just a little. I thought I ought to wait until it was paid before I came to visit you."

Mother Fong was embarrassed before this well-dressed woman who began to ask about the family. Flora appeared from the kitchen when she heard what was going on in the sitting room, and she was introduced. The woman began to smile more easily as she learned that Tom had graduated from senior high school and that his sister was still in school. She looked at Tom and asked him what he was planning to do.

"I'll help my brother now."

"Is that your brother working down in the laundry?"

"Yes. He is Flora's husband."

The woman turned to the mother. "Are you planning for your son to go on with his studies?"

"He wants to do more studies. I believe he can now."

The woman thought for a while, then slowly opened her handbag, took out a fountain pen, and wrote a check.

"Mrs. Fong, will you accept this from me?"

"No," said the mother. "We are paid already."

The woman still held out the check. "Money means very

little to me now, Mrs. Fong. You are a mother, and you know what the loss of my son has meant to me. I can see you have a good family. I would feel better if you would let me help a little, perhaps for your son's education. Do with it what you like and forget about me."

She rose and pressed the check in the mother's hand and said good-by. Mother Fong took the check and held it in her hand as she saw the sad rich woman to her door. As soon as the woman was gone, all three looked at the check. It was for two thousand dollars. The mother collapsed into a chair. Tom and Flora jumped to look out of the window and saw the strange woman enter a black limousine. They looked again at the check and could not even read the signature.

"Tom," said the mother, "this is for your education. The Americans are so kindhearted when people are in trouble. I don't understand it. But you ought to remember your benefactress."

"She did not even leave her name," said Tom.

"Of course we could find it out from the insurance company," said Flora. "But I think this was the last she would want us to see of her."

3

So many things happen to our lives without our control. The wisest man on earth does not know what is going to happen to him the next day or next month. Tom Fong's death by accident had an irony about it, for it changed the whole life of his family.

Loy was the eldest son and the head of the family since he was now its support. Mother Fong depended on him and consulted with him and Flora on all their plans. Now that they had the capital for the restaurant of which they had dreamed, they were hesitant to venture out and leave the laundry, which was bringing them a dependable income. With the five thousand dollars and the woman's gift for Tom and their own savings, they had more than eight thousand dollars in cash. The mother was firm that the woman's gift was to be kept for Tom's education, yet it would be good to have that reserve. Mother Fong was quite decided that they should not spend more than five thousand dollars on the restaurant and should keep the rest of the money.

She called in her brother, who agreed with her about starting with a small restaurant. Any number of persons in Chinatown could give advice on the details of running a restaurant. Supplies could be obtained on credit from the butchers and poultry yards and the stores. If Loy was willing to give up the laundry and manage the restaurant, the uncle would help to arrange credit through his own store.

Loy was a cautious person and was not so sure he should give up the laundry, but Flora and the mother and the rest of the family were firm. They would have to advertise and find someone to take over the laundry. They must look for a good place for the restaurant. The big question was whether it was to be in a basement or on the street level. Rent in Chinatown was unbelievably high. A corner shop in a good location would rent for three to four hundred dollars a month. A great many restaurants were doing a good business in basements. This would be a saving of at least a hundred dollars a month. Mother Fong was for saving the hundred a month, or twelve hundred a year. Besides, there happened to be a basement available on Doyer Street. But on this question the family was sentimental.

"We ought to be thankful that we are able to start a restaurant at all now," said the mother. "If your father were living . . ." She left the sentence unfinished.

But the rest of the family was unanimous, Loy, Flora, Tom, Eva, and Freddie.

"Mother," said Eva, "you don't want to look up from the window and see people's legs passing high up over your head."

This was also Tom's sentiment and Flora's sentiment. So they let the basement location go, willing to wait a few months.

Now that it was decided that they were to move to Chinatown, they were a little sad to leave the house in the Eighties where they had had so many happy years and where so much had happened. Tom and Eva were particularly sorry to leave the place that had been home to them since they came as children—the familiar sitting room where Tom had lain and thought of many things at night, the kitchen where the family ate, the yard behind, the roof above, the dark staircase had become familiar parts of themselves. And it was not only the house, it was the neighborhood, the sights and smells of the street, the children playing and the housewives sitting on doorsteps in the hours before and after supper. It was the sound of the Third Avenue El, the people in the shops, the grocer, the Czech shoemaker, and the Italian vendor, who wore a black suit winter and summer, from whose cart they bought their fruit and vegetables. Tom felt that this was his home, the sidewalks on which he had played when he was a boy, that he traveled every day when he went to school. He lay in his bed and looked out to the jagged roofs on the avenue and the El passing by, and he thought of his first night in New York. New York had been kind to him, and he was a young man, and now he was given a chance.

Chapter 17

❦❦❦❦❦❦❦❦❦❦

I

DURING THE SUMMER, WHILE THEY WERE looking for a place for the restaurant, Freddie was unusually good to his mother. He came often to see her and was even affectionate. He told her that he was doing well and had been lucky in selling several policies lately.

"Ah-Tong, you were always able to take care of yourself," she said, "but now that your father is dead you must be especially careful."

"Don't worry, Mother. I can always look after myself."

Then one day late in September he appeared looking very serious. Tom and Eva and Loy and Flora were all in the room when he came in. He glanced round at them and then turned to his mother and said, "Mother, I have always helped the family when you needed help, haven't I?"

"Yes, Ah-Tong, you have."

"I gave Father the money for you and Tom and Eva to come to this country, and I helped with his funeral, and I helped with the claim from the insurance company."

"Yes, you did, my son. Why do you speak of these things now?"

"Mother, I am going to get married."

Tom and Eva cried out in surprise.

"Shame on you!" said the mother. "Your father died only four months ago! Whatever put the idea into your head that you must get married now? What will people say?"

"Why, Mother, in this country it is perfectly all right."

"Have you no respect for your father? Have you the face to hold a wedding so soon after his funeral and let all Chinatown talk about it?"

"Mother, you don't understand how it is in America. If you don't want people to know, then we won't have any marriage celebration."

"Can't you wait a little?" said Loy. "Wait another six months. It will look better."

"I have to be married now," said Freddie.

"Why do you have to?" Loy asked, but Freddie did not reply.

"Mother," he began again, "I am not coming to you just because I know you have the money. But I really need a thousand dollars right now."

"A thousand dollars!" she exclaimed. "No, you are not going to touch that money."

Tom could see that Flora was simmering. Her eyes flashed at her husband, and he said, "You know that five thousand dollars is for the restaurant."

"Yes," said the mother. "We've been planning for it, working for it for years. Your father and Loy slaved and sweated to save."

"It is Father's money, isn't it?" Freddie looked at Loy a little angrily. "And I am as good a son as Loy."

"Ah-Tong, you are my son, just like Loy and Tom. But we all have planned and worked to have a restaurant. Now we are just ready to start it. You can come and help us run it if you like. It is not as if your father had left property to divide among his sons. This is our 'blood capital' to open a restaurant, and I am not going to touch a cent of it."

"Mother, you are being unfair to me," said Freddie. "What about the two thousand dollars that the woman gave?"

"Why do you need this money?"

"I will tell you. I'm going to get married, and I have to furnish a new apartment. And besides, there are two men to whom I have sold policies. They are after me."

"Why are they after you?" asked Flora.

"Because they paid me the money, and I haven't delivered the policies yet."

Loy looked stern. "Did you spend it?"

"Yes. Part of it was for the funeral. You remember I used two hundred dollars for the funeral."

"Did you gamble the rest of it?" Loy asked.

"No, I didn't gamble any of it. But I spent it. It is five or six months since I sold the policies, and I kept putting them off. Mother, I'll be in trouble if they go to the company. I'll lose my job."

The mother looked very troubled.

"They can sue me if I don't give them the policies," said Freddie, pressing his point.

"How much do you owe for these policies?" she asked sadly.

"Five hundred dollars. And besides, I'm going to get married. I won't spend any money on the wedding, but I need some to fix up a flat. It all happens at the same time, you see?"

"Can't you wait and not marry now?"

"No. We will go to a justice of the peace. The people in Chinatown need not know."

Mother Fong understood and did not ask more.

"That other money," she said to Freddie, "is to be kept for Tom's education. The woman said so. But I do not want you to lose your job. Do you really need a thousand dollars?"

"I would not ask for it if I didn't need it, Mother."

"All right, then. I shall let you have the money, but you must pay it back for Tom when you are able."

"I will, Mother, you can depend on it."

"And now, about this Sing Toy," said the mother.

Freddie hesitated. "I know you don't approve of her, Mother."

"You may be sure I do not."

"None of you understand her. She is a Broadway star, and she does us a favor to marry into our family, and yet all of you act as if you do not welcome her. That is why I have not brought her home."

"I am only warning you," said Mother Fong, "and I say nothing more. You chose her, and you are going to live with her, and I cannot stop you. But I do not approve."

"Well, say what you will, Mother. I'm in love with her. Mother, you don't know what it is to love a person."

"You tell me that I don't know what it is to love! My son, you have lost your head. That is all."

2

Freddie did not let his family know when he was to be married. But late one afternoon, when all the family were at home, he drove up in a green car that looked like new and brought Sing Toy up the stairs, his arm around her waist.

"Mother, here is your second daughter-in-law," he announced. "We got married last night."

They all exclaimed and smiled and gave their congratulations. "Here! I've brought a bottle of champagne to celebrate with the family," said Freddie. He unwrapped the bottle, and Eva ran to bring glasses, and everybody drank and tried to put the best face on the matter. The women indulged in cutting compliments whose sublety eluded Tom for a time. It is an art, born in women, but which no men practice except brilliant diplomats, as a sex aberration, and which even then they do not do half so well as any normal woman.

214

"I don't know how I should address you now," Flora said to the bride. "Is Sing Toy your stage name?"

"Yes. Call me Sing." Certain vibrations in the air told her that she was in hostile territory.

"It is such a sweet name, and appropriate, too."

"Now, Tom and Eva," said the mother, "you must call her Yisow."

Eva joined in the delicious game. "Remember the parade last year, Yisow? How did you learn to brandish the majorette's baton so expertly?"

"Oh, it's easy after you practice it a few times."

"Not for me," said Flora. "I would be so embarrassed. I just couldn't. We admired you so from behind in that parade. But of course, darling, you are used to the admiration of men."

Freddie was happy to see his wife apparently getting on so well with her sister-in-law. "Sure, Flora, she is a cute baby. Baby, now you see what a loving family I've got. Come on, dance with me to celebrate."

Freddie turned on the radio and tried to pull Sing Toy up from her chair.

"No, Freddie," she said. "Not now. I'm in your mother's house for the first time."

"Come on, everybody give her a hand!" Freddie said and clapped his hands.

"Please," cried Eva and clapped hard.

"Do a jitterbug with me. Come on!"

"Freddie, please, not now."

But Freddie dragged her to her feet. "Obey your husband, remember? You promised only yesterday."

Sing Toy reluctantly did a few steps with him. The room was noisy and full of gaiety, and Freddie and Sing Toy laughed together as she returned to her seat.

"Darling," said Flora, "your mascara is dripping."

Sing Toy took a little mirror from her bag and wiped her eyes lightly, expertly.

Then Loy said, "Ah-Tong, is that your car down there?"

"Yes, we paid eight hundred and fifty for it. Isn't it a dandy?"

"It is a beautiful expensive car," said Flora with emphasis.

"Oh, you mustn't misunderstand," said Freddie. "It was Sing's money."

"Oh, I see!"

"Can you let us use the car some Sundays?" Eva asked.

"Why certainly," Sing Toy answered. "Now that I have a car, I wouldn't know how to get around without it. Come down and take a look at it."

They trooped noisily down to the street, all except Freddie and his mother, who held him back. When they were alone, she asked, "Well, when is it to be?"

"When is what going to be?" her son asked in surprise.

"No, no," said the mother, shaking her head and looking up at her tall son, "you don't fool your own mother. How old is it?"

"What do you mean, Mother?"

"You had to get married quick, didn't you? How old is the baby in the bride's stomach?"

Freddie blushed. "Mother, how did you guess? Mother, please, do they all know?"

"We all guessed it."

"Will you please keep it from Tom and Eva?"

"Keep it! Can't they count the months when the baby arrives?"

"Mother, I am in love with her. Please don't speak about it. When the time comes, we can tell people it was born early. They don't even have to know when we got married."

When the others came up from the street, nobody noticed anything unusual in the mother's face or in Freddie's.

When the bride and groom left, the family looked down from the window and watched them drive off in the flashy green car.

"Mother!" cried Tom. "I am sure he used the thousand dollars to buy that car."

"If he didn't, he can chop my head off," said Loy.

"And when we borrow that car, we'll have to thank Sing Toy for it!" said Flora.

"Well, there is your old mother," said Mother Fong. "Fooled by her own son. I'll never believe another word of what he says."

"Remember that contribution game he played on Father?" said Tom. "Will I ever get that money back for my education?"

"He promised to return it. But I don't know what to believe now," said the mother sadly.

3

They at last found a place on Pell Street for the restaurant. It was a long narrow room with space for only ten or twelve tables, and a kitchen at the back. About the painting and furnishing Tom and Eva had a great deal to say. They had seen modern restaurant interiors and knew how they ought to look. The old floor had to be covered with linoleum, concealed lights had to be put in, and the walls must be redecorated. Eva had been long enough in America to have definite ideas of her own, and her ideas clashed with those of her mother. Mother Fong agreed that they should have linoleum, but she did not see why they should have concealed lighting. She approved of a new coat of paint and new tables, because she wanted this to be the cleanest restaurant in Chinatown. But she wanted all kinds of pictures on the walls. Eva was insistent on bare walls and Eva won. She insisted that it would not cost any more to have the place modern than to have it furnished in antiquated style, "packed with junk," as she said. So when the interior was finished, it had an ultramodern look, with its bare walls, indirect lighting, laminated bakelite table tops, and aluminum chairs with red leatherette seats.

Loy and Flora were happy. Their days of slaving and pinching and skimping were rewarded. The family had to take a flat on the fifth floor above the restaurant. It had only two and a half rooms, much smaller than the one they had uptown, but they were satisfied. Flora brought her parents to see the new restaurant and felt proud.

The family decided that they must hire a cook. That was the only help they were going to have, and even that was to be only temporary until Loy could learn to cook.

"Loy, you stay in the kitchen and watch," said the mother. "You should be a good cook in four months."

"I a cook?"

"Where do you think they get all the cooks in Chinese restaurants here? How many of them were cooks when they came to this country? I shall be in the kitchen, too, and I shall watch. Flora, you will be the head waitress and cashier, and Tom and Eva, you will help. We shall have no outside help except the cook, and after four months, no help at all."

And so the restaurant was opened with a special party for invited friends. Tom had thought of the name for the restaurant, "Marco's Cathay." Mother Fong rigged up a play pen for Marco in a corner of the kitchen and watched over him, and now and then Flora would come in to feed him or play with him. When nobody was with him and he was bored with watching the kitchen world, Marco would fall asleep in his pen. Strange that a mother's ears could hear through walls! Sometimes when Marco cried even a little in the kitchen, customers were surprised to see the Italian girl leave the cashier's desk and dash to the back, even when they were waiting to pay their checks. During the hours when Mother Fong and Eva were busy, Flora could be seen sitting at the cashier's desk hugging her baby and looking out on the street.

Father and Mother Maggio came often and began to like

Chinese food. Mother Fong did not want them to pay, but Mother Maggio insisted that otherwise she would not come again, and so Flora struck a compromise and let them pay the cost price of the meal. The cost of the material for a meal, not counting labor and overhead, was usually forty per cent.

Tom and Eva walked the floor of the restaurant, blissful with a secret happiness. They were on the street level at last. It was a strange feeling, like walking on stilts. Merely looking down on the people passing on the street was an enjoyable sensation. When the shop was first opened, there were moments when Tom caught himself looking up through the top of the window, expecting to see the feet of people on the street passing above his head. Now it was as if the whole street had become lowered to their level, or their shop had been bodily lifted upwards. Flora and Eva and the mother sat in front of the restaurant at idle times and watched and agreed that it was good.

Loy was still very silent, almost lost with the strange feeling that he did not have to work always with his hands.

"You might put on a coat," said his wife.

"I can't stand it. It makes me feel idle," he said.

And so he still went about in his shirt with open collar. But Flora bought herself pretty white aprons and bonnets.

Tom was lost. He could not cater to the customers, could not serve as an attentive waiter, could not really understand this whole business of opening a restaurant and making money. Physical work he could understand. "Let me clean the tables and wash the dishes," he said.

He washed dishes sometimes very fast and sometimes very slowly.

"Tom, haven't you finished?" said Eva coming into the kitchen with a tray of soiled dishes. "What are you doing? Oh, Tom!"

"You mind your own business. How is it out there?"

"A little slow. Wait till Saturday and Sunday."

Then suddenly Tom speeded up and cleaned all the dishes in five minutes. "Eva, come in," he said from the kitchen door.

"What is it?"

"Come and look. Who can wash dishes faster than I do?"

"Oh, you! You broke a glass. See, it is cracked."

"Is it? I don't see why people don't make glasses unbreakable."

"If they did, they wouldn't be able to sell any more because people wouldn't need to replace them."

Tom was lost in thought again. The result of his philosophic occupation was soon seen in action. The next day Eva found him working with two big wire trays and some metal strips.

"Now, what are you doing?"

"This is a dishwashing machine. It's only a makeshift."

"Tom, you will break all the dishes," said the mother.

"Please let me try. I shan't break a single one."

"You are still a child," said his mother fondly. "Do you think you are a mechanic?"

"Mother, I fixed that long water pipe for you. It works, doesn't it?"

It was true that Tom had connected up a pipe extension and led it around the wall to the sink. After he had given it a coat of aluminum paint, it was quite beautiful. He was a frequenter of hardware stores and had a complete kit of wrenches, pliers, drills, and other tools.

Now, as he said, he was working on a makeshift dishwasher. He clamped the two wire trays together, and after he had put some experimental dishes in, clamped them together. He turned on the rubber spray attachment of the faucet and sprayed the dishes. Then he turned the tray upside down, very carefully, for his mother was watching, and sprayed again.

"There, they are all clean," he exclaimed.

"It scares me to see you turn those dishes upside down," said the mother.

220

"You don't wash many dishes that way," said Flora.

Tom puckered his brow. "I'll work out something better. Please, let me try."

He analyzed the problem. The important matter in dishwashing was stacking and drying. "There is plenty of hot water. If the dishes are stacked properly, they will dry by themselves. That is the great idea," he told Eva.

The next days she saw Tom working with a bundle of heavy chicken wire and a pair of shears. His fingers were cut and bruised, but after two weeks he produced something that excited the family. It was a chicken-wire drum cut in half lengthwise, more than three feet long, fitting into the wide sink. It had sections for stacking plates, cups, bowls, spoons, and chopsticks. Above it he attached a two-foot hose with a spray attachment, which could be moved about freely to spray the dishes from all angles. After that, they were simply left to dry. He did not have to move a thing.

"It's handy," Loy said. "Tom, you ought to be a mechanic."

"I think I will be," said Tom.

Inevitably there were other improvements. Tom strung two long wires along the floor of the restaurant against the wall. This was for signals between Tom and Eva. A red light over the sink blinked when Tom or the mother was needed outside. A green light meant that a handsome customer had walked in.

"It is silly," said the mother, but she did not forbid it.

"I want to have three wires," he said.

"What next?"

"You see, with three lights, red, green, and blue, I can have seven kinds of signals."

"What do you want seven signals for?"

"I will write it down for you." Tom showed his mother a pad of paper, on which he had written down

A—red
B—green
C—blue

A   Loy wanted
B   Mother wanted
C   Tom wanted
AB   Something exciting in the street
AC   A handsome customer
BC   A beautiful girl
ABC   Something *very* exciting

So it turned out that when Elsie was seen passing in the street, Eva at the front of the restaurant flashed AB. But when Elsie walked into the restaurant, Eva flashed all three lights.

Chapter 18

❧❧❧❧❧❧❧❧❧❧

I

BECAUSE THERE WERE ONLY TWO BED-
rooms upstairs, one occupied by Flora and her husband, and
the other by the mother and Eva, Tom slept in the restaurant.
It was usually after eleven o'clock when the last customer was
gone and the place cleaned up, and he could get out his roll
of bedding and spread it on a camp cot.

When the family had gone upstairs and he was all alone, he
clicked on his bed lamp and read. His reading was promiscu-
ous and haphazard, from a manual of electricity to Chinese
history. He still could not form in his mind any impression of
Confucius. The Emperors Yao and Shun had lived four thousand years ago, Confucius two thousand. They all seemed very
remote. The Bronx Zoo was infinitely closer to him. He read
English and Chinese, but he always ended, before he went to
sleep, with thoughts of Elsie and what she had said to him that
afternoon.

Elsie was near him now, living in the very next block, and
the change meant much to him. He was no longer able to take
her out for walks except on some weekday afternoons. On
Saturdays and Sundays he was always busy, and so he was on
weekdays from four o'clock until the late evening. Between two
and four o'clock he was always free, but sometimes Elsie was
not.

"I am glad I can see you so often," he said to her one day. "But I miss our outings on Sundays."

"If we can't go, then we can't go," said Elsie without even a slight suggestion of regret.

"Aren't you disappointed?"

"If we can't, we can't. Why be disappointed?"

"Didn't you enjoy the outings we had? You act as if you didn't care."

"Tom, you are too American! Why be upset about what we cannot help?" Her tone was sure and calm.

"How am I too American?"

"You always want to do this and do that, go to the beach, to Ossining, to the Bronx. Tom, why can't you keep still? Always walking, walking, walking. Remember last time how you dragged me all through Van Cortlandt Park in the rain until I had to take a streetcar on Gunhill Road?"

"Wasn't that a wonderful walk?"

"Yes, but I could hardly move my legs all Monday and Tuesday, and I got blisters on my feet."

"Didn't I tell you to wear low-heeled shoes? Elsie, I love the tune you whistled that day in Van Cortlandt Park. It haunts my ears. Come, teach it to me."

They hummed the song, "There's a Long, Long Trail A-winding." It was a kind of marching song, but it was soft and slow and suited Elsie's soft low humming very well.

There's a long, long night of waiting
Until my dreams all come true;
Till the day when I'll be going down
That long, long trail with you.

Then they whistled the tune together and laughed.

"When I hear that tune, I always think of you wandering in the woods that day with a stick in your hand."

"Tom, you are funny."

224

"Why?"

"That time you dragged me out to Coney Island beach in the winter to look at the sea. Why are you so restless?"

Yes, why was he so restless? Nobody but Elsie had ever told him he was "too American."

"I'm just impatient by nature. I love to walk in the rain. How can I explain that? What I started to say was that I can't go on Sundays any more, and you talk as if you didn't care."

"It isn't that I don't care. I love to go out with you. Can't we go on some other day?"

"I'm sure we can."

"Then we go on some other day."

Her words were again clear, brief, devoid of emotion.

"And if we can't go out at all?"

"Then we don't go out at all. Why fuss about it?"

Tom was quite struck with this. Eva had had a little bit of this leave-it-to-heaven imperturbability, but Eva had greatly changed. Now she was active and wanted to do things. Here was Elsie, far away from home, living alone, but quite content to stay in if she could not go out. What was her point of view?

"Elsie," he said slowly, "I think you are too Chinese."

"Why?"

"You are never upset about anything."

Now Elsie was surprised. She was a modern girl, or thought she was. Didn't she cry? Didn't she laugh? But to sit quietly, to wait patiently, to take what came along was the natural thing, the sensible thing to do. She was not aware that this was particularly Chinese. All Chinese are like that.

"Now," said Tom, "don't call me an American any more. Shall we go out together some day next week? I can arrange it with my mother. Monday is a good day when everybody goes back uptown."

"Okay," Elsie said in English. Tom, watching, saw a sweet

look in her face and knew that she really wanted to go out with him.

He went home newly conscious of a certain stability and reserve power in Elsie. He had not known any other girl like that. Elsie could suffer if she had to, but because she had that strength in her, she would suffer less. His sister, by comparison, was a bouncing rubber ball. He felt that this was Elsie's Chinese training, perhaps because she had read so much Chinese literature. He called it Elsie's point of view.

2

The following Monday, Tom expected Elsie to come to the restaurant. But she did not come. He waited for half an hour and then lost patience and went to the schoolhouse.

"Elsie!" he called from downstairs.

There was no answer. He called again and again. What had happened?

He hurried up the stairs and knocked at her door.

"Who is it?" He heard her voice shake.

"It's me, Tom. What's the matter? Aren't you coming?"

"Come in, Tom. The door is not locked."

Elsie was lying on the bed, her face wet with tears.

"Are you ill?"

"No. Come in and sit down."

"Elsie, why you are crying!"

She sat up, leaning against her pillow, but did not answer—Elsie, who had always looked so calm.

"What's the trouble?" he urged.

"My father died. Here is my mother's letter." She held up the letter clutched in her hand and broke into crying. Tom sat miserably silent until after a while she said, "Come, sit over here. I want to talk to you."

Through her tears, she told him that she had got the letter

this morning, that her mother had written from Chungking, that her father had been killed by a machine-gun bullet, while on a boat fleeing from Hankow, when the Japanese strafed the refugees from the air, and that her mother had escaped with a surface injury in her left arm. Her family had left Shanghai for Hankow the previous winter, just before the Japanese capture of Nanking, and was again moving up the Yangtse River into the recesses of faraway Szechuen.

"Tom, I must go home. My mother is all alone."

The news struck Tom like another bullet. Not until then had he realized how dear and how necessary she was to him. "Elsie, I can't let you go. Does your mother tell you to go home?"

"No, she tells me to stay and study here. But I must go to her, I must."

"Does she have nobody there with her?"

"I have a married sister. Her husband is working somewhere in the interior, I never know where. They are moving about all the time."

Tom ached to comfort her.

She handed him her mother's letter, and Tom scanned it for a moment. "She writes a beautiful hand," he said.

"She taught me almost all the Chinese I know. I was very close to my parents. My sister is ten years older, and she was married long ago. So I am practically the only child."

Tom looked at her earnestly. "Your mother must be a wonderful woman to bring up a girl like you. Elsie, you are very beautiful."

"No," she said quickly, "it is my mother who is beautiful. She was a very great beauty in her youth. My father depended so much on her. Really it would have been a worse tragedy if my mother had died first. My father would have been lost without her. They were very much attached to each other. I tell you, Tom, there is a Chinese woman here who is very much like my mother."

"Who?"

227

"Mrs. Yang. Tom, I never left my mother before, and now she is alone, and I want to go back to her."

He touched her hand as it rested on the bed. "Elsie, don't leave me. If your mother is like Mrs. Yang, she must have friends everywhere. Elsie, I know this news is a terrible shock to you. Why don't you wait to hear more? Perhaps your mother will be all right."

"I can't wait."

"Now, Elsie, there you are wrong. I was just learning something from you. The other day you told me I was too American and too impatient. You wait a month, and things may look different to you."

But she said she could not talk of it any more now. So Tom went home and told his family what had happened, and Mother Fong and Flora and Eva all went at once to see Elsie.

"Poor child, she is all alone in New York," Mother Fong said when she came back.

The next day Tom went very early to the school, knowing that Elsie would be alone and thinking of her family. They did not speak of her wish to go to China, but they sat and talked for a long time, and Elsie spoke of her father, how he was always a selfless man, how he was a poor scholar and did not want to contend with anybody, how without the mother he would have been taken advantage of by everybody. He did not believe in contention, and he was always contented. "He used to let mosquitoes bite him," Elsie said. "When I was a child and scratched till my arms bled, he said, 'If you conquer the itch, you conquer the mosquito.' That was Father. He taught me that an itch is a feeling that comes from your mind. If you have the power of concentration to shut it out of your mind, it goes away."

"Do you really believe this?"

"I do. My father was a great admirer of Laotse."

"Of whom?"

"Of Laotse. Have you never heard of him?"

228

Tom had another of his embarrassing moments.

"My father used to quote him often. 'The honest men you believe; the liars you also believe. The good men I declare good, the bad ones I also declare good. The sage rejects no man, and for that reason there are no rejected men.' Things like that."

"Who is this Laotse?"

Elsie wrote the name down for him in Chinese characters. They meant the Old Boy, or something very nearly like it.

"Oh, Lotsi!" Tom exclaimed in Cantonese.

"So you have heard of him?"

"I have heard there was such a person."

"I'll read his book with you, if you like. It is not hard to read at all."

"Is this the book that taught you all that calm?"

Elsie smiled. "Why, you saw me crying so hard yesterday, and now you say I am calm. But it is true that reading this book is likely to change a person."

"Is he better than Confucius? I really could not get anywhere with Confucius."

"He's much better. He changes your whole view of life and everything by a few words. Tom, I like you when you are gentle as you are now, not tearing about to get something you don't really want."

"What does Laotse say about bringing you some noodle soup?"

"I shall be all right, Tom."

"No, let me bring it to you."

Tom went out with tremendous inner excitement. He had learned a great deal about Elsie's family in the last day, the family that had produced this exquisite jewel. He felt that in discovering Elsie, he had discovered a vast new continent which made her what she was. "The liars you also believe." He had never heard a moral teaching quite as extraordinary as that. Laotse was not dull like Confucius.

He brought back a bowl of noodle soup with shrimp and

mushroom in it, and Elsie was grateful for his attention. She began to doubt whether she should leave Tom to go home to her mother.

During this period of Elsie's sorrow, Tom came regularly to see her. But as the weeks passed, he thought he saw a remote look in her face. She was happy with him at times, and not happy at others. He felt an elusive barrier somewhere between them. He urged her to stay in America, for here was her chance to learn English and get a modern education. But he felt that she was torn between him and her love for her mother, and he knew that she could not yet decide whether she should go.

<h1 style="text-align:center">3</h1>

Laotse was a dazzling light, so blinding that it took some time for Tom's mind to adjust itself to him. You either have read Laotse or you haven't; if you have read and understood him, you are a changed man. "When the highest type of men hear the Tao, they try hard to live in accordance with it; when the mediocre men hear the Tao, they seem to be aware and yet unaware of it; when the lowest type hear the Tao, they break into loud laughter. If it were not laughed at, it would not be Tao." Actually no one ever reads the book of Laotse without laughing at first, and many end by laughing at their own laughter. So it was with Tom. Furthermore, Laotse helped him to understand Elsie better.

She knew the book well. The first time they sat for an hour over the small paper-bound volume. It was probably the most exciting hour Tom had ever spent with her.

"Tom," she said, pointing to a page of the book, "this is just like you. 'He who stands on tiptoe does not stand firm; he who strains his strides does not walk well.'"

"Don't I walk very well?"

"You do. But you don't always get there first."

"I'm afraid I don't follow. But you don't get there by sitting still, either."

"Yes, you do."

"Elsie, either you are fooling me, or I am very stupid. This is all paradox."

"No, it isn't. It's just good sense."

He looked into her eyes, turned upon him from the shaded corner. She seemed one who heard all, knew all, absorbed all, but spoke no more than was necessary. Again he felt tremendous power in her reserve; it was new and exciting, almost frightening.

"Elsie, you are so calm."

"What do you mean?"

"I mean your point of view. You look at things differently from Eva, from Flora, from all the girls I know. You are so—relaxed."

"Relaxed?" That was all she said, as she held up the book again. After a few minutes they came to three lines that held Tom's attention:

Movement overcomes cold.
But keeping still overcomes heat.
Who is calm and quiet becomes the guide of the universe.

"There it is! That is what I mean!" exclaimed Tom.

"That is not paradox, is it?" asked Elsie sweetly. Suddenly she smiled. "I must tell you what my father always said."

"What did he say?"

"He said that Laotse was for women and Confucius was for men. 'Know the male, but keep to the female,' was his favorite line. I'll show it to you."

Elsie rustled the pages of the well-thumbed volume until she found the passage:

The Spirit of the Valley never dies.
It is called the Mystic Female.

231

The Door of the Mystic Female
Is the root of heaven and earth.

"There, you see! 'The Female overcomes the Male by quietude.'"

"Is that why women always seem to yield and always win?"

Elsie smiled again. "Father used to tell me that Laotse called
Tao the mother and not the father of heaven and earth. You
take the book home with you. You see it is not too difficult. I
know you will like it."

As Tom went home with the small volume rolled up in his
hand, he felt as if he had met a new friend. That night after
everybody had left and the restaurant was closed he took out
the small volume and read in bed. Some passages caught his
immediate attention.

> When the world lives in accord with Tao
> Racing horses are turned back to haul refuse carts.
> When the world lives not in accord with Tao
> Cavalry abounds in the countryside.

Laotse kept on turning out paradoxes for him. It was almost
the philosopher's habit of speech.

Because he does not contend, therefore none can contend with him.
He does nothing, and through him everything is done.

Even in victory, there is no beauty,
And who calls it beautiful
Is one who delights in slaughter.
The slaying of multitudes should be mourned with sorrow.
A victory should be celebrated with the Funeral Rite.
Therefore when two equally matched armies meet
It is the man of sorrow who wins.

All the world says my teaching resembles great folly
Because it is great; therefore it resembles folly.

If it did not resemble folly
It would have long ago become petty indeed.

My teachings are very easy to understand and very easy to practice,
But no one can understand them and no one can practice them.
In my words there is a principle;
In the affairs of men there is a system.
Because they know not these,
They also know me not.
Since there are few that know me
Therefore I am distinguished.

Late in the night as Tom clicked off the light, he softly cried, "Hurray!" for the Old Boy. This was the most exciting discovery of his life.

Chapter 19

EVEN THE KNOWLEDGE OF LAOTSE COULD not keep Tom from going clamming. A springtime holiday was coming, and Tom said, "Mother, clams cost seventy cents a dozen at restaurants in New York. I know a place where I can pick clams from the sea, just from the sea, for nothing. To-morrow the shop will be closed, and I want to pick four or five dollars right out of the sea for you. Eva wants to go, too. And Elsie."

"Where?"

"Out on Long Island in Hampton Bays. We can borrow Yiko's car."

The arrangement was made. Freddie was glad enough to go along and drive the car. Sing Toy's baby had been born in March. It was only a girl, and the family had paid very little heed to the event. Indeed, the less said about it the better, Mother Fong remarked, except to explain casually that it was premature. Now Freddie had been married less than a year, and yet they all knew that he was not happy. He had taken a flat on Twenty-third Street, and whenever he came to the restaurant, he was alone. With a woman's instinct, Sing Toy knew from the very first visit that the women in her husband's family were unfriendly to her, and she was too proud to come

235

to them. Besides, she was occupied with her two-months-old baby now.

Since Sing Toy was not going on the clamming party, Flora was eager to go and to take her baby out into the sun for a day. As the car would be too crowded, Loy stayed at home. By the time they had their lunch basket ready, it was already eleven o'clock. They borrowed a rake and took along some pails. Flora sat in front with the baby, and Tom with Elsie and Eva in the rear seat.

When the car started, Yiko heaved a sigh and said, "There's nothing like being back with the family. I'm glad to get away from Yisow for a day." His face was a little red. Eva poked Tom's shoulder, and Elsie looked at Eva.

"Did you ask her to come?" asked Eva.

"What's the use?" answered Freddie. "Tom, I advise you not to get married. When a girl marries you, she gets on your nerves. She don't want to go out with you, she don't want to dance. She just spends and spends."

"You are unfair," said Flora, looking up at Freddie as he sat straight above the wheel. "You don't expect a mother with a baby to go out dancing at night."

"Unfair! A fellow work all day and come home, and he hear nothing but whining. You hear the baby whining, and when the little baby stops, the big baby start whining. You call that fair?"

They said nothing, and Freddie drove on.

At Hampton Bays, on the road to Southampton, the car skirted Peconic Bay on the left and came to a deserted spot where the tide receded into a bay of shallow water. For miles the shore line, covered with brushwood and pines, curved to the north and jutted far out into the sea. The water was still as a lake on that May day. No human habitation could be seen except a few wooded estates on their left. The beach was a mixture of mud and sand, covered with clam shells and a few bloated blowfish here and there.

236

None of them but Tom had ever gone clamming before.

"Roll up your slacks," Tom said to Elsie, "but keep your shoes on. The bottom is full of broken shells."

"How do you do it?"

"Just reach down and feel for the clams with your fingers."

Tom took off his shoes. Flora picked a good spot on the beach for Marco and sat and watched. Eva and Elsie were hesitating on the beach when Tom, already in the water, shouted, "I've got one."

It was too exciting. Eva went slowly into the water, and Elsie followed.

Tom reached out his hand to Elsie, who was stepping into salt water for the first time in her life and walked very gingerly.

The party spread out in different directions. Small crabs darted about under the water to hide in seaweeds, and Elsie was a little afraid of them. After a while they reached a place where the bed was only clear sand. Elsie's hair hung down over her face as she bent to feel for the clams, and her sleeves got wet. After she had dug out a clam with her own hands, she was fascinated. At intervals, a clear metallic clang was heard as one of them threw a clam into a pail. Except for that, the place was so still they could talk back and forth without lifting their voices even when they were a dozen yards apart. Their voices had a special open-air quality when carried over the surface of the water. The whole bay was their own, and the sun shone and a breeze skimmed gently over the water.

Tom and Elsie went further and further out until they were seventy yards from shore and the water was up to their thighs, and it was impossible to reach the bottom with one's hands without getting the body wet. So Tom no longer felt with his hands but used his toes to feel for the clams and pick them up. Still further out the water was waist-deep and getting a clam from the bottom with his toes into his hands was quite a problem. But Tom's toes were expert; he would dig a clam and throw it up with a jump and if he was lucky, he would catch it in his hand.

"Tom, come back," said Elsie, standing ten yards away from him.

"There are big ones out here."

"You can't get them like that. Let's get back where it is shallower," she said.

Tom turned and they moved along the shore. Now they were alone and two hundred yards away from the others. Elsie stood knee-deep in water, her hair and her slacks and her sleeves all wet, holding before her Tom's jacket in which she put the clams.

"It is getting heavy," she said.

Tom straightened up and came close to her. "Lower it into the water. It will be lighter then."

"The jacket will get wet."

"It doesn't matter."

Tom reached for the jacket and lowered it for her and touched the back of her waist for the moment.

He stopped and looked at her. She stood with her face shining with happiness like a jewel in the sun.

"Elsie, I love you," he cried quickly. Then he added more softly, "Will you marry me?"

Elsie was taken by surprise; of all places that he should choose such a place to propose! She looked at his wet matted hair and his eager intense face.

"Tom," she said gently, "you know I love you. But you won't understand." She broke off. Her face was sincere, her words simple, yet once again she looked a little distant. This was the first time he heard that she loved him from her own lips though he had known it.

"What won't I understand? Elsie, you mean everything to me. I know I am not worthy of you."

"Hush, don't say that." She made a movement as if to comfort him and yet her hand stopped before it could touch him.

A fresh breeze coming over the water sent a rippling reflection across her face.

"What is the mystery? I lie awake thinking of you, of your face, your looks, all the things you say to me."

"There is no mystery." She turned her head to look back at the others far away along the shore.

"Then what is it? Is there someone in China? Does your mother have someone in mind for you?"

"No," she said gently.

"Is it because you are going back to China?"

"Perhaps. Tom, I have told you that I love you. I have never loved anybody else. Tom, don't be impatient. There is a whole world back in China that you don't understand."

"What don't I understand? I am Chinese!"

"Tom, I know you cannot go back to China. You are studying here, and your family is here."

"Elsie, I still don't understand. Perhaps your mother will say I am only a laundryman's son."

"How can you think that? My family is not that type. I've told you about my father. I'm thinking of going back, and you can't come with me. I know you want to finish college here. Who knows what may happen after a few years?"

"Elsie, please, we could be engaged now. I will wait forever for you. But why don't you stay? When I graduate from college and am good enough for you, we'll be married, and I will go wherever you want to go."

"Will you?"

Tom nodded.

"Tom! Tom!" Eva shouted from the distance.

Tom hulloed back.

"Come back!" cried Eva again.

"They're wondering what we are doing here," said Elsie. "Let's talk about it later. There are a number of things in the way."

As they drew near, Flora called, "Say, what were you two doing by yourselves? You were not picking clams!"

239

Tom showed them his jacket with its heavy load of almost fifty clams, which he poured into the pail.

2

It was still early in the afternoon. They opened their lunch basket and arranged themselves on the sand. Elsie looked a little flushed, and Flora saw a special light in her eyes. After lunch they lay in the sand sunning themselves or watching Marco tottering and squatting on the beach. For some reason Elsie kept playing with Marco and running about with him as if purposely to keep herself occupied.

"Elsie, come and sit down," said Tom at last.

She came and sat beside him, a little shy and silent. It was evident to everyone that Tom was very much in love. Elsie's red lips were like a cherry when she opened them. What was it in the sand and wind and sea that lent a certain dignity to a man and woman sitting or walking on the beach, a natural dignity that the drab dress and gray walls of civilization usually obliterate or conceal? Tom could have worshiped the sand that Elsie sat upon. Lying there with Elsie sitting beside him, he lifted and stroked the strands of her hair, ostensibly to help it dry more easily in the sun; but she knew that it was the touch of love. She turned her head and cast a tender look at him.

"Why don't you lie down?" he asked.

She shook her head. She would not, could not. Tom wondered why a girl so desirable should be so unattainable. She was near and yet very far from him.

He lay back with one arm across his forehead, letting his other hand rest on Elsie's back. High up a patch of white cloud was moving slowly across the sky, and it seemed to him as if the earth he was lying on were visibly turning in silent motion on a mysterious voyage.

After a while he said, "What do the clams do when they shut up and dig into the sand? It must be all dark. What do they do?"

Elsie laughed. She liked Tom for asking such impossible questions. "What do they do? They eat and sleep, like you and me."

"Yes, the salt sea water must taste delicious to them. And they reproduce. Who tells them to?"

"What's bothering you, Tom?"

"Who tells the clams to build shells out of the calcium in sea water and dig into the sand and eat and sleep and reproduce like men? Who cares? I ask these questions but there is no answer."

"What makes you think we are more important than the clams?" Elsie asked.

"Aren't we?"

"Not a bit."

Tom sat up. "You don't mean to say you have an answer for me?"

Now Tom brought up his favorite Problem of the Feathers to show how insoluble it was. "Look at the parrot's crest, the peacock's tail, the lark's eyebrow. Who painted them? Take a single feather out of the peacock's tail. It is black here, green there, and gold there, and then it turns black again. Now tell me who did it. Who cares?"

"The answer is that we don't know."

Tom relaxed. "I thought perhaps you had an answer."

"It *is* an answer. We don't know."

He drew his finger along the sand.

"Why won't you take that for an answer?" said Elsie.

"What?"

"To know that we don't know. Tom, why do you puzzle about things so? You'll wreck your brains and never know."

"That was what I thought." Tom looked disappointed. "We know that we don't know."

"Tom, if you know that you don't know, you know. If you don't know that you don't know, you really don't know. Isn't that something to begin with?"

Tom got up and walked about as he always did when he was impatient.

"Daisow, do you know why we live?" he asked Flora.

"No. God wants us to live, I suppose."

"Do you know, Eva?"

"Don't know."

"Do you know why we live, Yiko?"

"Tom, sit down and don't act crazy, asking silly questions like that. Who knows?"

"Yeah, who knows?" said Tom, and he lay down again.

"Didn't I tell you?" said Elsie with a little smile.

"All right, you win."

Elsie noticed that there were thin lines of bruises on her legs. She rubbed them cautiously.

"Did you cut yourself?" Tom asked.

"I thought I felt something sting me in the water."

"Oh, it must have been the jellyfish."

"Tom, if you stop wondering, things get simpler. Don't assume that you are more important than the peacock or the clam, and you won't be so surprised."

"Yeah, or the jellyfish from which you got that sting."

"Or the jellyfish. Tao is in the jellyfish as it is in you or me. You'll be happier if you know that."

"Oh, the Tao again. And one part of Tao stings another part of Tao. Tao must be unkind."

"That is exactly what Laotse said. Tao is impersonal. It does not care."

"I thought you said you didn't know."

"There are things we can know, and things we cannot know. We cannot know the Tao."

"That does not really answer my question. And it does not lessen the mystery."

242

"Why should you want to? It is more beautiful like that. Life is limited and knowledge is limitless, and it is dangerous to pit the limited against the limitless, as Chuangtse says."

"Who says that?"

"Chuangtse. He says Tao is in ourselves. It is a part of the clam, a part of the jellyfish. Chuangtse says, 'Tao is in the ants, it is in the bricks and tiles, it is even in the excrement.'"

"What kind of religion are you preaching?" Flora asked.

"No religion. It is just a way of understanding things, of understanding life and the universe. Tao is in life, in the universe, in everything."

"What is this Taoism?" Flora asked again.

"I don't know how to put it briefly. Let me see. It is a philosophy of polarization, reversion and cycles, of the unity of all things, the leveling of all differences, the relativity of all standards." Turning to Tom, she said, "You ought to read Chuangtse."

She opened her handbag and took out a comb and began to reset her hair.

"Did you say polarization?"

"Yes, polarization."

"Elsie," said Flora, "I don't see how you know so much."

"I really don't know so very much. It is like you. You were brought up a Catholic and naturally you know a great deal about the Catholic faith. I was brought up with Taoism."

"But you must have read a great number of books."

"No, I haven't. My father said one ought not to read many books. One should read a few, the really good ones, and know them well. Tom, do you want to comb your hair?"

She offered the comb, and Tom took it.

"Give me your hand cream," he said.

She gave it to him, and he began to rub it into his hair.

"What are you doing, Tom?"

"That is Tom. You don't know him," said Eva with a laugh.

"He cleans his shoes with Barbasol, shaves with it, and combs his hair with it."

Elsie broke into spasms of laughter. "Tom, you really are funny."

"Isn't it all one basic cream? They use different names to extort money from the ladies," said Tom.

"I bet you don't clean your teeth with it."

"I have tried, but it doesn't taste good. But Barbasol is a cleansing cream. If it cleans the skin, why shouldn't it clean the teeth?"

After a while Elsie asked, "Shall we go home?" But Flora did not want to leave. She was seldom able to leave the city, and she was enjoying herself, and Marco, tired of playing, was sleeping sweetly and very confidently in the sand.

"Let him sleep a while yet. It is his afternoon nap."

Freddie was enjoying the day too. He was no longer the man who had no problems but knew all the answers.

"Eva, you are going to graduate this spring, aren't you?"

"Yes."

"How old are you this year?"

"Shame on you. You ought to know. I am nineteen."

"Eva, you ought to get married."

"A few hours ago you were warning us not to get married, Yiko."

"But I was talking about men. Men have everything to lose and women have everything to gain by marriage."

"Don't talk nonsense. I don't want to get married now."

"Isn't it wonderful?" Yiko said. "She was just a child when she came to this country. And now she is a grown-up young lady."

Eva was always his favorite. Indeed Eva had grown up. It was truly wonderful, Yiko thought, how young girls grow up and mature every year to take their places in life as inevitably as the procession of the seasons. It was one of those miracles of nature, a transformation like the perennial clothing of the meadows and mountainsides in spring, not the less surprising because it comes every year.

"Eva, you look more and more like Mother as your face fills out like that," said Yiko. "I have noticed some more white hair on Mother's head."

"Mother works too hard," said Eva. "Sometimes I think she seems to be aging."

Suddenly Yiko said, "Father used to work too hard, too. I have been a scoundrel."

"No," cried Eva. "You have helped the family."

Tom and Flora looked at him sharply.

"I used to think I was smart. Do you think, Eva, that Yiko is smart?"

"Yes, you are."

"No, your Yiko was too smart, maybe."

"You love Yisow, don't you?"

"Yes, that is the trouble."

"What's the trouble?" Tom asked.

"Nothing. Nothing you will understand."

Marco woke, his big round eyes looking up at the blue sky. Flora said that Marco had been out a long time and they should get home. So they gathered up their things and the two pails of clams, which were almost full, and went back to the car.

As they drove home, Freddie asked how business was in the restaurant.

"We can just meet expenses now," Flora replied. "After June, we shall discharge the cook and save two hundred and fifty on the cook's salary. Loy has learned to cook."

"I thought we were doing quite well," said Freddie.

"Yes, but we make so little profit and there are so many expenses. You know Mother. She will not leave the buying of meat and poultry to the cook. She wants Loy to do it, and she insists that we buy fresh-killed poultry and live fish. She will not hear of frozen chicken; frozen broiler chicken costs forty-

245

five cents a pound, but fresh-killed costs sixty-four and live fish costs almost twice as much as fish on ice."

"Mother's policy is sound," said Eva. "She is building up a reputation for good food."

"Of course. Customers come back when the food is really good. Mother goes in for good meat and poultry. The secret of good food is fresh meat, and half the secret of cooking is in buying. The cook is a little angry because Mother will not allow the use of gourmet powder."

"Mother is right," said Eva. "If our customers always come back, we are sure to have more and more customers as time goes on. We are doing well already."

When they reached home, it was sunset. They asked Freddie to stay and have supper with them, but he said that he had to go back, though he seemed sorry to leave.

"Yiko is changed," said Tom. "He no longer gave me any advice, except not to get married."

"I feel sorry for him," said Eva.

They asked Elsie to stay since the restaurant was closed and they would be all by themselves. Elsie knew that this was a family dinner and said that she must go home and leave them alone. Everybody urged her, but she would not stay.

"All right, as you wish, then," said Tom. "But at least stay and taste the clams we caught. It will take only a few minutes to boil them."

"All right, if you insist."

The clams were boiled in the shells for only a few minutes so that the meat was still very tender. Elsie enjoyed them and then excused herself, thanked them for the party, and went home. Tom went with her to the school though it was only half a block away.

"What good manners that girl has!" said Mother Fong.

But she thought to herself that Elsie looked as if her heart were troubled.

Chapter 20

JUNE CAME, AND TOM WAS PREPARING to take summer courses in the daytime at the polytechnic school in Brooklyn. Mother Fong still had one thousand dollars saved for Tom's education, which she refused to touch for other purposes. When she asked Freddie if he could begin to pay back the thousand he had borrowed, he always answered that he had to spend four hundred dollars a month because of his wife and baby and was not able to save a cent.

"Ah-Tong, you are not happy with her," the mother said.

"Happy? Don't talk of it. If I only could be left alone."

"Ah-Tong, I'm afraid you are not doing right by your wife. When you wanted to marry her, I did not approve. But now that you are married I want you to do right by her. Why don't you bring her sometimes to see us? She is still my daughter-in-law, and I will have no one say that I don't try to have the family live peaceably with one another."

Freddie was silent. He did not repay the money, and he still did not bring his wife to the restaurant.

Except on week ends and holidays, there was not much business before four o'clock in the afternoon, but someone had to help serve during the lunch hour, and Tom and Eva took turns. Eva wanted to take courses at New York University.

"No," said the mother, "you wait until Tom's schedule is fixed. You go on days when Tom does not have classes."

"Mother! That is unfair," Eva protested.

"Eva! What does a girl want to know so much for? You've gone through school. Tom is the only one going to college. You go when we can spare you. And don't get silly notions into your head. I will be fair to you. What you save in college fees, I will put on your dowry."

The restaurant business was picking up as Mother Fong had planned. When the employed cook was dismissed, the two hundred and fifty dollars' salary saved was clear profit. Mother Fong spent most of the time in the kitchen. She wanted only genuine, wholesome food, cooked with selected fresh things available each day. She figured that if others could make a profit with forty per cent or even thirty per cent of the price of a meal put into the food itself, she ought to be able to put in fifty per cent because she had no paid employees.

Mother Fong was in Chinatown, and Chinatown was a society in itself. Pell Street was not like an uptown street; it was intimate, closely packed, and full of neighbors where everyone knew everyone else by sight at least. People knew through unofficial but intimate sources how each family was faring and almost how much business each transacted in a month. Mother Fong began to know her neighbors. All around her people talked her dialect, and it was as if she were back in Canton. She sat in the shop and watched and tried to remember to send gifts to this family and that when there were wedding presents or birthdays. Now that Freddie was out of control and Loy was doing well, she planned for Tom and Eva.

When her friends of the Women's Committee came, Mother Fong made it a point of honor to come out of the kitchen, suggest the menu, and attend to it herself. Sometimes she would present her friends with the *pat-po-fan,* which was her pride, and which as likely as not they might not be able to sell next day. Mrs. Yang brought her friends and a number of rich Chinese families from uptown to eat at Mother Fong's little restaurant, and all the people at the Chinese Consulate knew it. Not infrequently a meeting of the Women's Committee ended with a dinner at Mother Fong's place. The women said in the American way, "We go Dutch treat," but on these days Mother Fong added extra slices of pork and chicken to her dishes.

Mother Fong had other ways of making and saving money. She joined with some of her women friends a *tsung-hwei,* a mutual savings society run on a pari-mutuel basis. A group of housewives would get together and pledge a monthly saving of ten, twenty, or thirty dollars. At each meeting, each member would bring the pledged sum, and the one who bid the highest interest would get the whole amount for that month. The bids were written on slips of paper, folded, and turned in to be opened during the meeting. Those who did not need money that month did not bid. Sometimes the interest would be as high as ten per cent, and on rare occasions, when some member needed money badly, it would be even more. Thus a member who brought ten dollars to the meeting might get back a dollar in interest for that month. The members who did not join in competitive bids and waited until the end got the greatest advantage. The drawings might be once a month or once in two months, and the sums pledged varied. It was a system of co-operative savings to ensure the highest current interest.

Such a society always consists only of men and women known to each other or to the sponsors, the *tsung,* from which the name *tsung-hwei* is derived. It is the sponsors' moral responsibility that those who have already drawn continue to pay their monthly savings and do not abscond. Various forms of the system exist. Some do not go by bids of interest. The whole schedule of monthly drawings and graduated interest is fixed at the outset and calculated to exact terms in dollars and cents. Those who draw early pay more interest, and those who draw late pay less, the exact figure for each month being always specified. The drawing is then by throwing dice, and the monthly collection goes to the one throwing the highest numbers on the dice. The written contract always follows a known formula, and says:

"If two throw up the same number, the one who throws first gets it. If a cube rests at an angle, it must be tapped down. If a cube happens to rest on top of another cube, it must be moved down with the same face up. Transactions among members outside the society may not be settled through the society at the drawings."

2

Elsie Tsai was one of those strange girls who keep their heads while they are in love. On her desk stood a small leather frame in which were photographs of her parents. She sent money home whenever she could, but letters sometimes did not come for a whole month. Her happy days were when she got letters from her mother or from girl friends at home. She showed Tom a few selected letters from her mother, which she kept in a jewel box with a lock, her most precious possession. It was a beautiful box with characters on a label that in English could only be translated as "Words of a Mother."

The handwriting of Elsie's mother had the culture and stamp of a scholar's family. It seemed unfair to Tom that Elsie had been brought up in such a home and he had not. The letters were usually two or three pages long, touched here and there with succinct, effective, intimate phrases of description. "The frost has arrived and the leaves are falling from the pear trees in our western garden." In winter, "I sit alone in the long nights facing the dim oil lamp." In spring, "the colors of spring make me restless." Here and there, in every letter, there would be one or two classical phrases that Tom did not understand.

"Elsie, you love your mother very much, don't you?"

"I lie awake at night thinking of her," said Elsie.

"And not of me?"

"No confessions, Tom."

"If you love me, don't you think your mother will approve of me?"

"Will you write a letter to her in Chinese?"

"Don't make fun of me. You know I would be ashamed. I have a feeling it will spoil everything if your mother sees my handwriting."

"Tom, I was only joking. I have written to her about you and told her everything."

Tom felt encouraged by this.

"Tom, let's be serious. I have thought and thought. This war has come very close to my family. It has separated us, mother and daughter. My father has been killed, and my mother is very lonely. She is living with a Mrs. Li who was her friend when they were young girls."

"Does she want you to go back?"

"No, on the contrary, she asks me to stay here where it is safe. But you know I want to live with my mother as long as she lives. I won't do anything else. She cannot come to the United States. You will be studying here until you graduate, and you belong with your family here. If I can get the money, I may fly home soon."

"Elsie, I know what you mean. But you are doing much more for the war here. What can you do for China when you go back, just by suffering and wandering? And your English is not yet sure."

"I know I can't talk English like Eva," said Elsie humbly. "But, Tom, it looks bad. A European war may break out any moment. Who knows how long the war will last?"

"That's it. You may not be able to go back at all. And while you are here, the days will be so beautiful if you will promise to marry me."

"Tom, you still don't understand. Your family is with you,

but mine is not with me. We are so young. How long will it be before you graduate?"

"Three or four years. I only want you to wait until I am good enough to marry you."

"Can't we wait? We don't have to decide so quickly. Tom, don't be impatient."

"This is one time when I don't admire your patience. Your Laotse says, 'The sage rejects no man and no men are rejected.' "

"What would have happened if Laotse were a girl?" Elsie answered.

So they went round and round in a circle.

"Elsie, I have asked you and I am asking you again. Why won't you decide and make me happy?"

"I cannot decide."

"Elsie, will you answer me one question. Your mother comes first, is that it?"

Deliberately Elsie nodded her head.

When Tom went home that day, Eva said, "I can tell from your face that you have proposed again, and Elsie has said no."

"She did not say yes," Tom answered, "but she did not say no."

The mother, listening, said with a penetrating look at her son, "Tom, I do wish very much that you and Elsie could be engaged. I do not want you to think that I am opposed to the match. But if she cannot decide, there must be a reason. Perhaps we are not good enough for her. We are a laundryman's family, you know."

"Do you really think that?"

"I don't know. She comes from a scholar's family."

"But she denied that they would care that Father was a laundryman. I asked her."

"Would such a nice girl admit it to your face?"

But the thought grew in Tom's head. Elsie came from such a

cultured family. Was he really worthy of her? And Tom began to doubt himself and was tortured with uncertainty.

Elsie went to a summer camp of Chinese students for a week when her school was closed. After the camp many students came to New York to see the World's Fair. A number of Chinese students had discovered Elsie and often invited her out. Tom was jealous and worried. Then he would reread Laotse. "Do nothing and everything is done." He did not believe a word of it, yet he held himself back and did not press her again.

Chapter 21

I

IN SEPTEMBER HITLER INVADED POLAND, and Europe was at war. War had been threatening for a year, and when it happened nobody was surprised. The only shock was Stalin's pact with Hitler, which paved the way for the war, and the way the Soviet Army marched from the east and Hitler's army marched from the west to cut up Poland between them. There was not much enthusiasm, and there was plenty of cynicism. The statesmen accepted it; the common people accepted it. The world was sick. A generation of men eaten with cynicism was sick, mentally, intellectually, and morally. Common men were interested in a war with moral principles, a war with meaning. The politicians were interested in power and were themselves seized with fear, and fear led them to horse trading of the nakedest kind. No voice was heard to make this the war to end all wars. The men of this generation were too wise to believe that such a thing was possible. They had the physical courage to respond to danger, but they had not the courage to hope and plan for a better world. Politics was horse trading, a politics that was not horse trading could not even be imagined or believed in. There were a great many national leaders; there was not even one second-rate world leader. A political horse trader was acclaimed a hero of the mob, and the hero exulted in his power and the worship of the mob. American airplanes for China, loaded in New York, were taken off the ship at Los Angeles. Scrap iron was poured into Japan. No moral principles were involved. Tom was disgusted. Victory was necessary, but victory was not enough. Beyond the horizon of victory was silence. The people asked for a meaning. The politicians answered with an ingratiating smile and a gasp, and behind the gasp there was no voice. In time, the people who wanted to hope for a better world made themselves hope, despite the politicians, and gave the war meaning by the act of hoping.

Although the United States was not in the war, it lent an air of tenseness to the World's Fair at New York. The fair symbolized the nations' solidarity in a world at war. The nations of South America and Asia and Europe were represented by their respective pavilions, and the Court of Peace was the stage for colorful pageants and parades given by the different nations in turn, especially on their national holidays.

2

One day in September Tom was back from his classes and was washing dishes in the kitchen when Eva flashed the red, green, and blue lights above the sink. Tom thought it must mean that Elsie had come into the restaurant and rushed out. But it was not Elsie.

Yiko had come in with Sing Toy, carrying their baby in his arms. This was indeed a surprise. Mother Fong had often asked Yiko to bring Sing Toy to see them, but Yiko had never done so before. There were few customers in the early afternoon hour and the family all came out to welcome them as if they were receiving a rare visit from relatives.

"Hullo, everybody!" said Yiko, wearing a smile above his stiff collar and bow tie and dickey. He often wore a stiff collar, declaring that it was good for his morale, but the dickey was the sign of something special.

The family surrounded Sing Toy and the baby, and there was much excitement.

"What is the occasion?" they asked.

"Congratulate me!" said Yiko. "I have been promoted. I'm going out to Detroit and Cleveland and Cincinnati on an expense account, hotels and everything paid. Sandy has been a good friend, and the company has confidence in me. One day last week Sandy said to me, 'Freddie, you done a swell job. You got about all the policies from the Chinese community here we are likely to get. You want to make some real dough?' and I said, 'Sure, I want to make some real dough.' Sandy said he had spoken to the boss, and he gave me an increase of twenty-five dollars a week and appointed me to take care of Ohio, Michigan, Pennsylvania, and Maryland. He would have given me New Jersey, too, if it had not been given to some guy already. They usually appoint Americans for the other states, but they appointed Yiko. I'm going to make a few thousand dollars in commissions on this trip—and all expenses paid!"

"Aren't you proud of him?" said Sing Toy. She seemed very happy, and the family was very pleased to hear the news and congratulated him.

"I keep the New York downtown district up to Thirty-fourth. This is only a trip. I may be back in about a month. Sing may be lonely while I am away, and I want you to take care of her."

"I'll be all right," said Sing Toy. "Sandy will take care of me. I've wanted to come more often to see you folks, but you know how it is with a baby."

"Who is Sandy?" asked Flora.

"Sandy Bull," answered Yiko. "Remember you met him one day at a dinner? He is my direct superior. He gave me this job."

"I'm glad you give him credit for it," said his wife.

257

"Are you taking the car?" asked Tom.

"No, why should I? Sing will need it. I leave it here for her."

"May I come and learn to drive when she is not using it? I'm a good mechanic, you know. I don't think it will take me long to learn."

"Sure, you can. Sing will teach you."

"When are you leaving?"

"Tomorrow. Sing, you just come here when you are lonely. This is your own family. Boy, the Fongs are doing all right! And Eva, you go to New York University. And Tom, you'll be an engineer. I'm proud of my family."

Eva cried, with a wide gesture of her arms, "Yes, Frederick A. T. Fong is proud of his family!"

Everybody laughed and they all were happy.

3

The Women's Committee was very busy again. October tenth—Double Ten—was coming and that was to be China's day at the World's Fair. There was to be a gigantic parade and all Chinatown must turn out to make the best showing it could. The Benevolence Association was the central organization for raising war funds and all patriotic activities. The Women's Committee was responsible for the organization of all women and girls.

Elsie and Eva had been busy enough in their spare time. They were already sending Christmas cards for sale for the relief of Chinese war orphans to cities all over the United States and Canada, Cuba, Mexico, and South America. As usual, there were three or four in the organization who did all the work, while the rest appeared at the meetings and rallies. But now the work of calling up all the Chinese women in New York was not something that could be done in the office alone.

The war, had, in fact, brought about a social change in the life of the women in Chinatown. The Women's Committee, consisting mostly of English-speaking women and their daughters, combined with the non-English-speaking Chinese women in the Women's Patriotic Society, a rather quiescent organization that sprang into activity after the war began in 1937. This society had been formed in 1932 during the fighting with Japan at Shanghai, and became dormant when that war of six months was over. A Y.W.C.A. Chinatown branch had failed to arouse the women's interest. The housewives were too busy to attend the classes in English. What did they need English for anyway? Their life was entirely in their homes, with babies coming at the rate of one a year. Their only occasions for going out were weddings, funerals, birthday parties, and visiting sick relatives. Otherwise they were too busy with babies and cooking for their husbands. But now, with the war on, there had come a change.

Yes, the women of Chinatown were coming out. There were meetings and meetings. For the first time, the wives of Chinatown did not go home to cook supper for their husbands. "Let them cook it themselves or go out and eat at a restaurant."

There were over three hundred Chinese wives and mothers in the city of New York. The majority of the women could be reached by phone. The newspaper notice was not enough. The personal touch was the thing. But calling up the members for the parade required great personal technique. Face was involved. If you could call a woman up by telephone, uptown, midtown, or downtown, it was fine. But you couldn't always do that. There was no complete telephone list of the members; some did not have telephones, and many were listed as "Eddie Chan's mother," "Joy Far Lee's wife" or "Henry Ho's second aunt." Who was Henry Ho's second aunt? Yes, somebody knew. Did Henry Ho have a telephone? They could not insult Henry Ho's aunt by failing to notify her of the parade. If she should say after the parade that no one had notified her, who was willing to take the blame? So they went down the list, and the work was divided, and women and girls were assigned to call on Henry Ho's aunt and Eddie Chan's mother.

Henry Ho's aunt lived far uptown on Broadway in the hundred and eighties. It was a business call. But there was no such thing as a business call. Henry Ho's aunt was so touched by the visit that she would not let the delegates leave without staying for lunch. Then they had to excuse themselves and call on Eddie Chan's mother in the afternoon. Eddie Chan's mother was found, after due process of investigation, to be living on Thirty-eighth Street in Forest Hills.

Mother Fong rarely could give her time, but sometimes she did. She felt she had to go when Grandma Howe, a woman of her own generation, came to ask her to go with her on certain trips to solicit money for expenses. Grandma Howe, and that is the way her name was officially spelled, was known as "quite a character." She made the rounds of the restaurants, and it was such a rare thing to receive a visit from her—and it was such a good cause—that she seldom came out with less than a ten-dollar bill and a bowl of noodle soup.

Coming out of one restaurant with Grandma Howe, Mother Fong spat in the street. "They call that noodle soup! Dishwater and soya bean sauce! Pfui!"

And again, after visiting another restaurant, "Did you taste that sliced chicken? It tasted exactly like stewed cotton. Why, they had boiled all the juice out of that chicken to make soup for something else and put the dry slices of meat on the dish for show. Call that sliced chicken!"

"But Hong Far Restaurant is good," said Grandma Howe.

"Well, it is tolerable," Mother Fong admitted with ill-concealed reluctance.

Incidentally, as they went about, Mother Fong noted which restaurants were doing well and which were not doing so well.

And so everybody was given face, and nobody wanted to lose face by not doing the right thing. And so when the parade of more than a thousand men was ready, about two hundred and fifty women and girls were there to march.

4

Tom was learning to drive. He learned to drive and also learned why Yiko had not been anxious to bring Sing Toy to their house. How she talked!

"Why, your Yiko is a devil with women," she told Tom in the very first ten minutes of the first driving lesson. Sing Toy was sitting on his right. "Lift the clutch gently. Otherwise you would jerk everybody. I could not leave him alone for half an hour with a pretty girl. Keep to your lane, yes, that's better, we don't go to night clubs any more, or dancing, keep your hands firm on the wheel. Why, I wouldn't trust my best friend with him for ten minutes, did I tell you about Vicky? That is Vicky Lamore. She comes to see us sometimes, she is such a darling friend, living all alone, her parents are down in North Carolina, here's a sharp turn, you did it beautifully, why, I can't understand Yiko, look out, watch for that car coming! I tell you, once he told me he had to go to Boston and didn't come home all night, but he was right here in town. Sandy told me."

"Sandy?"

"Yeah, Sandy Bull. He's a most wonderful person. I don't know why I'm telling you all this. Don't tell a soul. I don't want to come to your family and complain."

This news was a shock to Tom.

"You can tell me everything. I'm his brother. Doesn't he love you very much?"

"Sure, he loves me. He would make a perfect lover if one were not married to him. We quarrel and make up and quarrel again. Tom, I tell you, I think when a man marries, he ought to stick to his home, don't you think? We are in love with each other. . . . I think we are." Her tone was pathetic.

"Yes, sure, he is madly in love with me," she resumed as if to reassure herself. "But when I sit at home all day looking after the baby, and he comes home and grouches, and when I snap at him, he bangs the door and goes out. But he loves me still, I know."

"How do you know?" asked Tom.

"From the way he kisses me."

Before long Tom learned to drive well and took the car out alone. One night, when he went to return the car, he pressed the bell at the door of Sing Toy's apartment house. The door buzzed, and he went inside and heard Sing Toy's voice upstairs.

"Who is it?"

"It's me," Tom said. "I've come to give you the car key."

"Is the car there?"

"Yes, it is parked outside."

"Never mind, then, slip the key under the mat below the driver's seat."

"Yisow, I have something to talk to you about. May I come up?"

"It's late. Why don't you come up in the morning?"

"It'll take only a few minutes."

"All right. Come up."

Sing Toy met Tom on the landing. She was in her house gown. Adjusting her hair, she said, "What is it?"

"The Benevolence Association wants you to act as majorette and lead the parade at the World's Fair on October tenth. They asked me to speak to you."

"But who will look after the baby?"

Tom said he was sure the committee would find some woman to sit with the baby. Sing Toy did not ask him in, and he gave her the car key.

As he turned down the stairs, he heard a man's cough behind her door. He darted down the stairs. He did not want to discover what could only be shocking to him, but he could not resist it. He stopped in the street and looked up at the lighted window. He had heard a man's voice, and he wanted to know. After some fifteen minutes, the light went out. Perhaps he had made a mistake.

He was starting away when he saw Sing Toy coming out, dressed in evening clothes, and a man was with her. Tom hid in a dark doorway. The two got into the car and drove away. The man, he thought, must be Sandy.

Chapter 22

I

OCTOBER TENTH WAS BRIGHT AND SHIN-
ing. All Chinatown shops were closed for the day. Almost all
the young Chinese girls appeared in their national costume.
Elsie, dressed in a splendid blue silk gown she had brought
from Shanghai, went with Tom's family. It was to be a full
and tiring day, and as the lantern parade was to be at night,
the party had packed a small basket of food including Marco's
milk bottles. Mother Fong went along as a point of honor.
Elsie carried a brief case and Eva a bundle.

They had to be at the gate at ten, to be sure that each
parader was provided with a button bearing the Chinese and
American flags. Chinese men and women, boys and girls, were
crowded about the gate. After they had their buttons, the
family moved about the vast area, went around the Federal
Building, the colonnade of columns, the Lagoon of Nations,
the Hall of Nations, where the walls were decorated with huge
photomurals, stopped at the Chinese Pavilion to deposit their
bundles, and went on to see more. After lunch, they went to
see the Perisphere, the Futurama, and other exhibits.

There was, they decided, too much to see in one day. Mother
Fong's legs were tired, and she found a bench and held the
baby, and Elsie sat with her while Tom, Eva, Flora, and Loy

went about looking at chromium-plated machines, miniature models, giant motors, and the humming, flashing, flickering signs of the progress of science and industry.

Elsie was playing with the baby when Tom returned.

"Let's go to the Amusement Area," he said with great enthusiasm.

"What's there?"

"Monstrosities!" said Tom. "And fire-eaters and sword swallowers. And we must see the parachute jump."

"Tom, are your legs never tired?"

"Come on. You should not have put on high-heeled shoes."

Elsie's ankles were sore. She had known well enough that the place was very big, but she could not resist putting on her best shoes.

"But we'll miss the meeting at three o'clock."

"Come on, forget about the meeting."

"How far are we from the Court of Peace?"

"Just about a mile."

Elsie gave in because the Amusement Area was nearer. After they had seen the parachute jump and came to the Court of Peace, they were just in time to see the show of Chinese jugglers. The new ambassador, Hu Shih, and Mayor La Guardia had already made their speeches and were seated on the platform with about two hundred people, watching the entertainment.

Mrs. Yang and her children were there, and Mrs. Yang saw Elsie and called out to her, "Oh, I've been looking for you. Where have you been? Come and sit with me."

From that moment, Mrs. Yang would not let Elsie leave her, and Tom and his family looked on from below. Tom saw that Elsie was happy when she was with Mrs. Yang.

They knew and recognized many people on the platform. Then suddenly they saw Sing Toy, sitting with an American man.

"Who is that?" asked Loy.

"That's Sandy Bull. Yiko's boss."

Tom said nothing more. He had been ashamed to speak to the family of what he had seen. He had not been sure, but now he was sure.

"Yiko's marriage will go bang one of these days!" he commented.

On the platform, Elsie asked Mrs. Yang, "You are going to stay for the parade with your children, aren't you?"

"Of course we are."

"Oh, that's wonderful," said Elsie. "We pick up our lanterns at suppertime and gather at the Lagoon of Nations at seven. There will be fireworks and a colored fountain display, beautiful to see at night. And there'll be a lion dance."

"What are you going to do?"

"I have nothing to do except join in the lantern procession, and I have to play the piano for the national anthem."

"Why, I never knew you played the piano," said Mrs. Yang.

"Only a little. I am out of practice, for a long time. There's no piano at the school."

"Why do you stay in that place?" asked Mrs. Yang. "Isn't it lonely for a girl in that building at night?"

"I stayed there when I came because that was the room they gave to me free. It is so hard to find a room, and rent is high and I'm trying to save."

"Elsie, you are my goddaughter, remember?"

Elsie smiled a happy "Yes."

A juggler was dashing about with a pile of twenty dishes on his head. He dashed in one direction for about ten steps, turned abruptly and dashed back. It was funny and spectacular at the same time, and everybody applauded and laughed.

"Elsie, why don't you come and stay with me?"

"Oh, I wouldn't dare."

"I wouldn't offer this to just anybody, but you are my goddaughter. We have a spare room, and we have a piano."

"I can't pay for rent."

267

"I'm not renting a room, Elsie. Why would I offer it to you unless I really wanted you to live with us? And I cook such good food!"

Elsie looked at Mrs. Yang, delighted inwardly, and accepted on the condition that she be allowed to help with the housework and pay a little for her food.

"How my mother will thank you when she knows! I've told her about meeting you."

What are those two talking about so much? Tom thought from below.

When the entertainment was over, Elsie came down and told Tom about Mrs. Yang's invitation. "Am I not lucky?" she said.

They went up on the platform and talked with Mrs. Yang.

"Tom, don't worry," said Mrs. Yang with a full smile. "I have only daughters at home. I'm not taking Elsie away from you."

But from that moment Elsie was wrenched away from the family.

Flora decided to go home early with Loy. As Tom watched Billy Rose's Aquacade, he kept wondering what would happen when Elsie moved uptown. But he remembered that her work was in Chinatown and he still should be able to see her almost every day.

By half past seven, everybody had forgotten his troubles. The rainbow-colored fountain display had started in the Lagoon of Nations where more than a thousand Chinese men and women had gathered, each holding a lantern. Tom met Elsie again at the huge national flag. A band led in front, playing the Chinese national anthem. The girls and women were gathered around the flag, and it began to move along. A Chinese woman with a rich contralto voice sang *"Cheelai,"* a marching song with a strong rhythm. Men, women and children lifted their voices as they marched to the martial music. There had never been anything like this in Chinatown's history, this marching and mass singing to the rhythm of war music, the feeling of a nascent nationhood, a nation born out of war. The gay lion dance brought up the rear.

When they reached the place of the meeting, the paraders stood around, some on the ground, some on the steps. An American star sang the Chinese national anthem, and Elsie was on the platform playing the accompaniment. Her head and hair moved to the music. A women's chorus sang the song of "The Lone Battalion" in honor of the eight hundred who had died rather than surrender in the first year of the war. There came a few speeches which closed the ceremony.

Nobody felt tired. Only the next day did men and women discover how stiff their legs were.

Going home, Tom said, "Elsie, I did not know you could play so well!"

"Anybody can play that song. I took up piano only for two years when I was in college."

"Why don't you take piano lessons?"

"I just can't afford it. Mrs. Yang says she has a piano at home, and if I stay with her, I can keep in practice."

"Are you really going to live uptown?"

Elsie told him that she was very lucky and that it would be convenient since she was working closely with Mrs. Yang on the committee.

"When are you going to move?"

"Oh, right away."

Chapter 23

I

FREDDIE CAME BACK FROM HIS BUSINESS
trip ten days later. Sing Toy was expecting him because he had
sent a triumphantly worded telegram, but she could not meet
him at the station on account of the baby. She was grateful for
his absence. She had never been happier than in the past
month.

"Darling, oh, darling, darling," she said as she held him in
her embrace and cooed like a dove. Freddie responded well
and covered her face with kisses. He, too, had been very happy.

"Did you enjoy yourself?" she asked.

"Enjoy myself? No, darling, what do you think I was
doing? I was tearing from city to city. You got my post cards.
But I made at least twenty-five hundred in commissions on dis
trip."

"Darling!" She gave him another passionate kiss.

"Wasn't Sandy grand to get you this job?"

"Oh, yes. How is Sandy? Did he come to see you?"

"Hm, hm," said his wife sweetly.

"And he took good care of you?"

"Hm, hm. Let me call him up. We ought to celebrate."

"No, let me do it."

So they had a wonderful celebration that evening at the

night club where Sing Toy used to work. They found Vicky Lamore there and asked her to join them, and they danced until two o'clock, and everybody was gay. Sandy complimented Freddie on his trip, which had made a lot of money for the company. With Vicky and Sandy, Sing Toy was entertaining and vivacious and quite unlike the whining wife at home. Freddie had not seen his wife so happy and relaxed in the past year, and the feeling came back to him of the good times when he was making love to her. Yes, that was the way it should be. Success was knocking at their door.

"I love my wife," Freddie reflected. "This looks like a good beginning—a wife, a kid, a good position." He had a hazy memory of the girl he had taken out in Cleveland and was conscious that he had not been strictly faithful, but he would not permit the thought to rise to the surface. "Yes, I love my wife and my kid."

Sandy went with them to their apartment, sat for a while, and then left them. Sing Toy threw herself on the couch and exclaimed, "This is wonderful."

Freddie sat down beside her and said, "It's not bad to be Mrs. Frederick A. T. Fong, is it? If I have luck, I shall soon be making eight thousand a year. Oh, boy!"

He came closer and touched her affectionately.

"Don't, please. I'm tired," she said.

He drew closer still and would not leave her alone, but Sing Toy held his hands down, and surveyed him from that strategic vantage point.

"Listen, darling, do you love me very much?"

"Of course."

"Very much?"

"Very much."

"Darling, there is one great wish in my life. Can you guess?"

"Don't you have everything already? A home, a kid, a husband who is earning seven or eight grand a year. You have a car. Is it a new car you want?"

272

Sing Toy shook her head.

"To be a movie star, I suppose."

She shook her head again. Her eyes looked closely at her husband's face, aware of the drama of the moment. "Freddie, now that we are coming up in society, you want your wife to appear like we belong, don't you?"

"Come on! Out with it. What do you want?"

"Freddie, what is it that gives class, true class, to a lady? What gives her attention at the best hotels, the best restaurants, and theaters?"

"Plenty of cash. As for entree to theaters, a theater ticket."

"Don't be so stupid. Tell me, what makes a lady?"

"Come on, don't talk in riddles. What are you talking about?"

"Oh, Freddie, you have no imagination. A mink coat! That is what makes a lady. I have looked at a coat on Madison Avenue. It's only fourteen hundred."

By this time, without his realizing it, Freddie's head was sunk on her shoulders so that he heard the last sentences spoken softly, close to his ears. "Only fourteen hundred. Freddie, you can afford a mink coat for your wife." When her hands moved over his face, he became acutely conscious of her tactics. "The devil, she is selling me something," he thought.

He considered for a while. The idea of going out with his wife in a mink coat suited him rather well. The last memory that he was a laundryman's son would be gone.

"What do you think of Vicky?" Sing said.

"Why, she's a nice girl. She's not a young chicken, but she has good hips. Why do you ask?"

"Don't you think Sandy was a little too sweet on her? Did you see the way he looked at her and talked to her?"

"What business is it of yours if he is sweet on her? He acted awfully familiar to you."

Sing Toy sat up quickly. "What do you mean? You aren't jealous, are you?"

"No, I am not jealous. I just thought you two were very close when you danced together."

"Why, Freddie, you are detestable. You like him yourself. He took me out a couple of times when you were away. You wanted him to keep me company, and I must say he does not dislike my company. But there was absolutely nothing between us."

"All right, all right. Why get so excited? I didn't mean anything. And he has been wonderful to us."

"I'll say he has. You wouldn't have had this chance if he did not give it to you."

Sing Toy appeared one day in her mink coat at Marco's Cathay. Flora looked until her eyes burned. And so life for a time was changed for Freddie and his wife. Sing Toy showed the coat to Vicky and her friends, and they had to go out at night because of the coat. The old life came back, and for weeks they stopped bickering.

"When are they going to send you out again?" asked Sing Toy. "You may make a couple of thousand more."

"I have a lot of work here at de office. But I would go on anoder trip any time dere was a chance."

"Shall I ask Sandy? He'll be glad to help you," said Sing Toy.

In November Freddie was sent on a trip to Florida, covering New Orleans besides.

2

Elsie's change of address had brought a difference in her relationship with Tom. Elsie had accepted Mrs. Yang's offer because she knew that Mrs. Yang's mind was essentially simple; she said what she meant, and she could not say what she did not mean.

It was a great change for Elsie to live in an uptown Fifth

Avenue apartment, not because it was uptown, but because of the people who lived there. She had a small room to herself and was treated as a member of the family. The great attraction was the piano in the sitting room. Mrs. Yang's children were taking piano lessons, and they could play a little. In the evenings, sometimes, they would gather for music, and the children would sing. Elsie felt the atmosphere of a well-ordered and secure home in which nothing could go wrong. Mrs. Yang was firm, active, strong, and yet very feminine. Her home was her job, though she was busy with committee work, and she carried both at the same time. Mr. Yang did not count because he accepted his wife's decisions and left all family matters to her.

Elsie dared not be late for supper. When her classes were over, Tom would be waiting outside the Chinatown school to catch a word with her.

"Tom, I musn't stop. As it is, I feel guilty about it. Mrs. Yang goes to the kitchen the moment she returns from her committee office."

Tom went away without saying anything. He had not expected it to be like this. When Elsie had announced that she was really going to live with Mrs. Yang, he had said, "I am glad for you. But you are coming here every day. I can still see you."

"Of course," she had said.

But it was getting more difficult to see her. Some days Elsie went to the uptown office with Mrs. Yang, and she had started a music course in Columbia. What with her classes and piano practice and the committee work, she was seldom able to come early to Chinatown, and she had to rush back for supper. Since Tom went to Brooklyn Technological Institute, his time was occupied, too. He was getting interested in radio, besides taking some courses in physics. When he was free and called up, Elsie was usually occupied. She had office work or she had to go to college. And on Saturdays and Sundays, he was usually busy at the restaurant.

He was often sad and felt that Elsie was slipping away from him. "Perhaps I am not good enough," he thought to himself.

But one afternoon he said, "Elsie, I am free Friday evenings. Can I come up to have you teach me again?" He said it without the keenness of an ardent lover, and Elsie felt it.

"Certainly," said Elsie.

So he began to go up on Friday evenings, and he never missed one. While he was with Elsie he felt very happy, but he no longer made love to her, and she did not ask why he seemed to drift apart from her. She played the part of the teacher and waited for him to play man's traditional part of the wooer. But he came only to study, chiefly to practice calligraphy under her guidance.

The great difficulty with Tom was that his written characters fell apart. Calligraphy was as important to an educated Chinese as a correct English accent to an educated American, or a good face to a girl, for one is judged by it. Ever since Elsie had joked about letting her mother see his writing, Tom had known what calligraphy meant. Elsie taught him all the short cuts, the traditional ways by which good writers solve the problems of writing characters that, without these eliminations, would get too crowded or lose cohesive form. She taught him the principles of composition and structure, of contour and axis, of lifting shoulders and establishing footholds, of pausing at corners and executing swift turns and graceful curves, and the principles of subordination, integration, contrast, balance, "embrace," alignment, tightening, spacing, irregularity, novelty, and finally spirit. Art is long, and the practice is a labor of years. But Tom was making progress; his characters were getting to be tolerable, and in places remarkably good.

But Elsie saw a change in him. When she looked at him, he avoided her eyes. Was he too busy with college work and tired? Was he merely growing older and more sober? Had he lost the first fervor of a youth in love? Elsie could not understand. She saw the change in him but she kept quiet.

3

"Elsie, why don't you two get engaged?" said Mrs. Yang in her usual abrupt manner, one Friday after Tom had left. Matchmaking was Mrs. Yang's favorite hobby. She often said that she had made seven or eight matches and all of them had proved to be successful.

Elsie blushed. She explained that Tom was still in college, and she was not sure how many years it would be before he could go back to China or whether he would go to China at all, and that she would marry only a man who could go back and live with her mother. "Lately, I have noticed that Tom seems depressed and withdraws more into himself. He still loves me, I think, but he isn't as he was before when he proposed to me."

"Did you discourage him?"

"I did not say yes, and I did not say no. He said he would wait, and now several times he has said he is not good enough for me. Mrs. Yang, my mother is far away and I have nobody to talk with about this."

"Elsie, I can help you. Has he asked you again lately?"

"No, lately he hasn't. He seems to be burning up inside. What do you think?"

"That depends on what he is burning up about."

"How do I know? He seems so tense."

"About what?"

"About his studies, perhaps. Sometimes I soften toward him when I see his face. Isn't he a little queer?"

"What is wrong or queer if he is tense about his studies? Perhaps he is all wrought up to make himself worthy of you.

Elsie, you are a young girl. You don't understand a young man's heart. It is perhaps a good sign. A young man usually gets a little afraid of the girl he really loves when in her presence, and you are a very unusual girl. He worships you silently, I am sure. I can see clearly enough what he is trying to do. Elsie, you are twenty-one. Don't make the mistake that young girls often make, when they are unable to decide. I can see he is very brilliant."

"Yes, he is."

"He is brilliant and serious and queer, and he is in love with you. What more do you want?"

Now Elsie's feeling toward Tom changed, too. Such is the human mind that the more Tom felt unsure of himself, the more Elsie felt sure she wanted him and was afraid of losing him. When she had been sure of him she had been unable to decide, but now his restraint made her realize by sheer instinct what a difference it would make if she had to live without him and how important he was to her, not in the cold light of reason but deep down in the unknown depths of her being as woman. She looked up. Mrs. Yang seemed so confident. She was glad to have some one decide for her.

"Why doesn't he take you out?" asked Mrs. Yang.

"Perhaps he is too busy, and his week ends are occupied. We used to have wonderful Sunday walks together."

"Why don't you suggest it to him?"

"That I won't do. It is not for the girl to ask. He has to ask me."

Right now, if Tom should ask her to go out in the rain with him, as they used to, or go on one of those airily happy trips, she would drop everything and go out with him. But Tom had not asked her.

"Do you mind his coming from a laundryman's family?" asked Mrs. Yang.

"No."

"And your mother?"

278

"I know she won't. Mrs. Yang, my mother is a little like you."

"If I were your mother, I would advise you to accept him."

"I will write her again and tell her what you say. Let me show you my mother's letters."

Elsie showed Mrs. Yang letters that she had not shown Tom. The mother and daughter wrote like friends, with the exception of the address.

My child, from the snapshot you sent me, that young man has got good ears and a good chin. I am truly worried about your affair. I do not know whether you are silly to love him or silly to refuse him—it may well be the latter. It is good to be silly. Every young girl, I think, ought to get silly notions at times. I was once silly about your father when I was a young girl. I married him and have never regretted it. If you feel very happy when you are silly, tell him you'll marry him. Forget about me. Can I live with you all your life?

Mrs. Yang was amused, while Elsie said, "There you see. That's my mother. Don't you love her for saying things like that?" Elsie told her with a laugh that when her parents came to the boat to see her off, the mother and daughter cried together for about half an hour. They were so fond of each other.

In another letter, her mother wrote:

In your letter you asked me if there is a difference between *silly* and *crazy*. There is. Silliness is a pleasureable sensation, like being half drunk; craziness is like being quite drunk. It is a warm feeling that makes you feel happier than usual. My child, don't lose your head. You said he was "so wonderful"—that makes me suspicious. You might be on the crazy border line. Sip the wine slowly and if it has not bad effect on you but only makes you warm and comfortable, keep on. That is the mark of a good wine, and the token of a beautiful love that will last. And don't be influenced by the movies and bad novels where the hero and the heroine fall violently in love. I hope that your man isn't that sort of a lover. I liked it when I heard that he proposed to you in the water in broad daylight and not in the moonlight. That shows that his head was clear when he proposed to you and that you were beautiful even in the sunshine.

Elsie folded the letters carefully as she finished showing them, and as she took them away to her room, Mrs. Yang saw a sweetness on her face that she had not seen before. She could well understand why Elsie wanted to live with such a mother.

4

One evening Mrs. Yang had thoughtfully invited Tom to come to supper, and for once he was able to leave the restaurant.

"Come sing for us, Elsie," Mrs. Yang said after supper.

At Mrs. Yang's home no one knew jazz. Elsie herself could not understand it, and she knew that Tom disliked it. She knew a few old popular songs, songs that belonged to another age, that were written when men's souls did not crave the hot rhythms of modern days and were foreign to them, when ears were attuned to subtler tones and nuances of melody, when music did not require the grimacing of drummers, the getting up and sitting down of saxophone players, the shaking of the conductor's knees to overcome the callous lumps of insensibility and inform the listener that he was having a wonderful time in case he did not know it. Music is always the expression of an age and reflects the emotions that a generation craves. Jazz grew out of the modern man's need for it. It came with the motor car and Hemingway's *The Killers* and the "lost generation" of the twenties. It was not that men began to love jazz but rather to live jazz. To ears attuned to the raw rhythms of jazz, rhythm that was not obvious, not staccato, was not enough and could not produce any response. Jazz was one of the things that Tom, though brought up in America, could not understand. He had once gone to a Broadway movie theater with Elsie and had to sit through a performance by a famous jazz band. The audience went wild over it and gave thunderous applause.

"They really enjoy it," said Elsie in great surprise.

"You can see they do. Suppose you want to make a three-year-old child listen to music, what do you do? The child does not pay attention. What do you do to get and hold the child's attention? First, you've got to make a lot of noise. You blare something into his ears. Now the child takes notice. You make the high notes very shrill and the low notes very low. The trombone is the thing. Then you bang and clang and click your tongue and pull your cheeks and pop your mouth and trill your lips and make as dramatic squeaks as you can. That is, you make it obvious to the child. Then you shake your knees and make yourself funny and you squat on your toes and put your hands to your ears and imitate a donkey, and the child laughs at last and is entirely with you. He claps and he laughs because he is having a good time. You see, what that jazz band does on the stage is exactly to reproduce what it would have to do if the audience were all three-year-olds."

Elsie had had no training, but she could sing in a delightfully soft voice in this small room. Her favorites were the world's old favorites, music that was sweet and sad and sentimental and low, "Carry Me Back to Old Virginny" and "Whispering Hope" and "Solvejg's Song," which last she sang most successfully after a few trials:

> The winter may go and the spring may die,
> The spring may die,
> The summer may fade and the year may fly
> The year may fly;
> But thou art surely coming, I know thou'lt be mine!
> My troth I have plighted, I'm waiting ever thine,
> I'm waiting ever thine!

When she sang "A Resolve," she gave a half-serious and half-playful expression to the words, "I can die, I can die." It was when she hummed to herself, when she forgot herself, that she was best.

She was not singing for the company or for Tom; she was singing for herself, and thoroughly enjoying it. Tom sat quietly and puckered his brow as if he were listening and yet not listening. His appreciation of Elsie's music made him even more conscious of her cultured background and a little ashamed that he was a laundryman's son.

Mrs. Yang suggested that Elsie sing some Chinese folk songs. Now, to the amusement of everybody, somehow her whole manner of singing changed. She sat down, turning half away from her listeners and dangling her handkerchief before her face, ready to cover it at any moment, bashful and coquettish in the truly Chinese manner, and the sound of her voice was thin and small, more like humming than singing, reminding Tom of the time when she was learning English words from him. The melody and the words were playfully sad, typical of Chinese folk songs:

> Little cabbage grows, pale in the ground.
> Seven was I and my mother was gone,
> All alone with father at home,
>   *Yi-ko-ya-erl-yao.*
> I saw father marry Mrs. Wong,
>   *Yi-ko-ya-erl-yao.*
>
> And she brought her boy along,
> He is always right and I am always **wrong,**
>   *Yi-ko-ya-erl-yao.*
> My tears are falling all day long,
>   *Yi-ko-ya-erl-yao.*

"What do you think?" said Elsie after Tom had left. "Tom

282

didn't seem to hear. He seemed occupied, or unhappy about something. He wasn't natural at all."

"Don't worry. Leave it to me. He has a very bad case. It's written all over his face."

"What do you mean?"

"Tom is very unhappy because you refused him."

"Are you sure?"

"I'm quite sure."

Elsie was grateful to have Mrs. Yang help her to think, but after she went to bed, she lay for a long time confused and at last cried herself to sleep.

Chapter 24

THE NEXT WEEK TOM TELEPHONED TO say that he could not come up on Friday. Something had happened in his family, he said.

"What is the matter?" Mrs. Yang asked Elsie.

"He said he didn't want to talk about it over the phone," Elsie said. "His voice was cold and distant and sad. I don't understand."

In the morning Elsie told Mrs. Yang not to expect her at dinner, and when her classes in Chinatown were over, Elsie walked into Marco's Cathay.

Eva flashed the signal, and Tom came out.

"Tom, what has happened?"

Tom looked at Elsie, his face red. "There's trouble in the family," he said after he had come close. "I didn't want to talk about it. Yiko has gone away, and Mother is terribly upset. Yiko and Yisow are separated, and Yiko has lost his job. He has gone out of town."

Tom did not want to tell Elsie everything. Freddie had come in a week ago and announced coldly that he had resigned and was going away.

"I made a mistake," he said. "She made a sucker out of me. Yes, I was a sucker. Frederick A. T. Fong, the great sucker!

I went away to make money for her so she could make love to someone else."

"No, it isn't true!" cried Flora, although she really believed it.

"Why, she confessed it herself. She even threw it at me. At first she denied it and said I was falsely accusing her. Well, I said I was through with her. Then she threw it all at me and admitted and boasted about it and said she was thinking of leaving me anyway. Well, that's that!"

"What about the baby?"

"I let her have the baby and everything. I'm staying at a hotel. I'm going out of town." Suddenly he dropped into a chair and put his face into his hands and burst into tears.

Mother Fong stood over her son.

"If the marriage isn't going to work, it is better it has happened now than later. It is good that you found her out in time. Ah-Tong," she said firmly, "I knew that girl would not be a help to you, but you would not listen. Listen to me, if you have better sense in your head now, you will forget her. She is not worth your crying over."

"Leave me alone," was all Freddie said.

The next day he left town.

Elsie learned only the bare facts from Tom, because he was ashamed of the whole affair.

"Elsie," he said, "I am very busy now with my college work. I don't think I shall have time to come up for my Chinese lessons."

When Elsie returned to her apartment, Mrs. Yang saw in her face that something was wrong and asked her kindly about it.

"He's not coming any more."

"Now Elsie, you are really very stupid."

"What do you expect me to do? Go up to him and say I want to marry him? No, Tom has changed."

"You do want him very much, don't you?"

Elsie blushed. She had not realized how much she wanted

him, in spite of everything, until she felt that perhaps she was losing him.

The next morning her mother's letter arrived. In it was enclosed a formal letter to Mrs. Yang, thanking her profusely for giving Elsie a home in a foreign land.

I am troubled about my daughter's marriage [the letter continued]. She is of age and if you see any worthy young man, I would appreciate your help. Treat her like your own daughter and you will earn a mother's undying gratitude. From what Elsie tells me, I seem to know you already. I leave it all to you and what you do will satisfy me.

Elsie read the letter and handed it to Mrs. Yang.

Mrs. Yang read it and said with a broad smile, "Now I shall get busy."

2

The Women's Committee was planning a three-day collection in the week before Christmas. The preparations for this collection brought Tom and Elsie together again for a few days. Elsie cut her classes and came to Chinatown early, and soon they were happily chatting about the work, although it took some time for Tom to come out of his shell of shyness and become quite natural with her once more. He saw her now and then steal a look at him, a look of reproach and yet of tenderness, and he wondered if he had not been wrong in staying away from her.

Elsie took part in the street collection in an exalted state of patriotism and romance. The collection covered most sections of midtown with the center at Fifty-seventh Street and Fifth Avenue. All the Chinese restaurants co-operated and opened their doors as resting places for the girls working on their assigned streets. The people on the streets were generous before

Christmas and it was easy to fill a can with coins and bills in one or two hours.

The days were damp and bitterly cold, and it looked as if it was going to snow. As Elsie stood at the subway entrance, a north wind blew and cut into her bones. She was not shy like the other girls. Shaking her can vigorously, she cried, "Give, give to China!" and her voice and her hair blowing in the wind attracted attention, and people stopped to look at her. The girls had discovered that Fifth Avenue, outside the smart stores, was the worst district, that money was seldom to be expected from a lady carrying a fashionable handbag, and that the less well-dressed people at the subway entrances were the best givers.

But Elsie did not stay at any one place. She dashed across street corners, in hope of catching likely givers. The air grew more frosty, and her fingers were numb, but she was happy and inspired, and she did not care.

On the last night of the collection hundreds of cans had been filled with money. When Elsie returned with Eva to the office on Fifty-seventh Street, Mrs. Yang and other women were sitting there chatting happily about the results. Elsie came in shaking a full can and proud of it. Tom was waiting for Eva.

"Well, we have filled almost three hundred cans," said Mrs. Yang. "If a can holds five dollars, we shall have raised fifteen hundred dollars. That is not bad. We had only about forty girls at work."

Elsie went over the cans stacked on the table and shook them. Some were only half full, and she discovered that there were ten cans that had not been used.

"Come now, we'll go home for supper," said Mrs. Yang.

"You go home," Elsie cried. "I am not hungry. The restaurants fed us every few hours. We can fill three or four cans yet. Eva, let's take these empty cans and go to Forty-fifth and Forty-sixth and catch the people going to the theater."

"Elsie, you'd better come home. Your lips looked blue when you came in. You mustn't tire yourself out," said Mrs. Yang.

"I'll be all right. You go home. I'll be responsible for closing up. Tom, how about you?"

"I'll come with you if Eva will."

And the three of them went out again at eight o'clock to the theater district.

When Elsie came home at half past ten, Mrs. Yang said, "You are coughing."

"I don't think I want any dinner," Elsie said.

"You're all tired out. Come, eat something, have a hot bath and go to bed."

3

The next day Elsie could not get up. She felt weak and unwell, she coughed incessantly and she had a slight temperature.

"I guess I caught cold," she said. "I can't sleep it out."

In the evening her temperature went up further, and the next morning she was worse. Mrs. Yang called in the doctor.

"I'm afraid it's pneumonia," he whispered to Mrs. Yang in the sitting room. "She must go to the hospital immediately."

"Is it very bad?"

"I don't want to frighten you. But it is serious. The hospital is the place for her."

When Elsie was taken away in the ambulance, Mrs. Yang went with her. Elsie was conscious but so ill that she could not speak. Secretly Mrs. Yang was blaming herself. "Poor girl, I shouldn't have let her go out again that night."

Mrs. Yang sat by Elsie's bedside all that afternoon as her temperature went higher and higher. She did not know what she would say to Elsie's mother if anything should happen. She was so worried as she sat and watched Elsie breathing hard that she could not think. The girl was all alone, and she had registered at the hospital as her guardian.

Late that evening when she went home, one of her daughters suggested that she should inform Tom.

"Perhaps I should. He is not really engaged to her. Yes, but I should," Mrs. Yang repeated.

The next morning Mrs. Yang called the hospital and found that Elsie was no better. She called the restaurant and asked for Tom.

"Tom, come up immediately," she said. "Elsie is sick, and I want to talk to you."

When Tom appeared at her door, he cried at once, "Where is she?"

"In the hospital."

"I must go to see her. How sick is she?"

"Sit down, Tom. The doctor doesn't know yet. We go in the afternoon." Mrs. Yang looked at him with compassion.

Tom would not sit down but paced the floor restlessly.

"Tom, you love Elsie, don't you?"

Tom did not reply.

"Why did you stop coming to see her?"

"Well, I thought— I didn't want to—"

"Tom, I want to tell you something. Elsie really loves you."

The words shot across Tom's brain, and he lost all control of himself.

"Oh, Mrs. Yang, you don't know."

"No, I'm telling you the truth. Why did you stop coming to see her?"

"I thought I was not good enough for her—not good enough yet. I just could not be sure of myself. My father was a laundry-man, and she comes from a scholar's family."

"Don't be ridiculous," said Mrs. Yang.

"If she loves me, why did she keep me in doubt?"

"Tom, a nice girl doesn't go out and tell a man to come to her. You should have gone to her. Tom, I have something to tell you. Her mother has put her marriage in my hands. Elsie and you love each other. You shouldn't keep each other guess-

290

ing. Your visit to her in the hospital will really do her good. That is why I've asked you to come."

At two o'clock Tom and Mrs. Yang went to see Elsie. As they walked into her room they saw that her eyes were closed.

"She is asleep," the nurse whispered. "She was in delirium."

"Has her temperature come down?"

"No, but we're giving her the best treatment. The doctor says she has a fighting chance."

Tom stood by the bedside, his legs feeling like wood.

"Elsie," he called lightly.

"Let her sleep," said the nurse. "Sleep is best for her."

They waited an hour. Tom went out to smoke a cigarette and came back and found her singing a song in her delirium, the song that Tom knew so well from the time when they went walking in the forest in Van Cortlandt Park. *"There's a long, long trail a-winding, Into the land of my dreams . . ."*

As the memory of their happy walks together came back to his mind, tears formed in Tom's eyes.

He bent down and whispered to her. "Elsie, it's me, Tom," but she did not hear.

Mrs. Yang saw him sobbing silently. Elsie's words were no longer clear, but she was humming the lines, and on her lips there was a happy smile.

Tom and Mrs. Yang had to leave at four o'clock. When they returned at eight o'clock, Tom called Elsie's name, and her eyes opened and she smiled. She saw the tears in his eyes as he bent down and kissed her.

She coughed and stretched out her hand, and Tom quickly gave her a tissue.

"I feel drowsy, Tom . . . and all hot inside."

She said nothing more and dropped her hand to hold his, happy that he had come. Then the nurse walked into the room and said, "You have to go now."

On Christmas Eve Tom brought Elsie a dozen red roses. On

Christmas Day she felt better, and the fever was gone. She was able to ask, "Tom, why did you leave me?"

"I never left you, and you never left my heart. When you get well I shall never let you get away from me."

"Am I getting well?"

"Yes, your temperature is going down, and all the rest is just good care. Elsie, you'll never leave me again, will you? Elsie, I've been a fool. Mrs. Yang told me. I was afraid to ask you to love me."

Their eyes met in love.

"Tom, I want you above all the world. We have to thank Mrs. Yang. She is my godmother. You'd better speak to her."

After a week she was able to sit up when Mrs. Yang and Tom came in, with broad smiles on their faces.

"Elsie, my calligraphy has improved," said Tom. He held out an envelope.

"What is this?"

"It's the letter I have long wanted to write, in Chinese. It's to your mother."

Elsie took the envelope and opened the letter and read:

DEAR AUNTIE TSAI:

I am an unworthy son from a poor family and your daughter is a bright gem from a scholar's home. Her virtue is as distinguished as her learning, and her conduct is a glory to her clan name. I have had the good luck to be her pupil, and admiring her talent from the distance, I have trembled at the thought of asking for her hand, and hope alternated with despair. Your daughter has deigned to look on me without disfavor, and I now make bold to aspire to the position of a son-in-law. Your daughter is a filial child, and I promise to go with her wherever she goes. The very fact that I can write this letter, uncouth as it is, is due entirely to her excellent teaching.

Yours Humbly
TOM FONG

Elsie let the letter rest in her hand where it lay on the blanket. Looking up at Tom with a bright smile, she said, "Tom, I think your calligraphy has improved."

He bent and kissed her again. She turned to look at Mrs. Yang. "Mrs. Yang, we both ought to thank you."

Mrs. Yang stood up. "Congratulations! That's right. You two should thank me. A young boy and a young girl can be so confused about themselves."

"Would my mother think I am being silly now?"

"Yes, but it is the wisest thing you'll ever do in your life. That is true for both of you. I think I ought to go and write a letter to your mother right now."

Mrs. Yang went out and closed the door behind her.

Chapter 25

THE SNOW WAS STILL DEEP IN THE streets. Mother Fong, Tom, and Eva got down from the Fifth Avenue bus, Tom carrying a can wrapped in a cotton handkerchief, and splashed to the curb through the slush. On the pavement the bright afternoon sun printed clear wriggling shadows of the sparse trees. Tom's face was shining and Eva giggled; Mother Fong felt important and deeply happy underneath. As they went into the circular entrance of the hospital, Tom said to his sister, "Now, Eva, behave yourself." Eva did not reply.

The door of Elsie's room on the fifth floor was ajar. Tom knocked and walked in.

Elsie was sitting up in bed. "My mother has come to see you," said Tom. Mother Fong and Eva tiptoed in after him.

"Oh, Mrs. Fong, you shouldn't come yourself," exclaimed Elsie.

"Who says I shouldn't?" said Mother Fong gaily. "Eva, give the soup to the nurse, and tell her to heat it and bring it in."

Elsie adjusted her hair and patted her pillow as Tom and his mother sat down. As Eva went out, she gave Elsie a long silent look as if she had never seen her before, one of those woman's looks that take in another woman's whole being. In a moment she returned, and she came close to the bed and stood looking at Elsie. Their eyes met and for a moment they did not say a word. The hardly perceptible smiles on the lips of both showed that they understood one another. Words were quite unnecessary.

"Soon you'll be calling her Samsow," said the mother, looking at them proudly. "Elsie, I want you to know how happy our family is about you."

Elsie blushed. "Mother Fong, you are very kind. I don't know what your son sees in me."

"Never mind that. This makes me very happy. My Tom is a good boy. I am sixty-one now, and I already have one foot in the grave," said Mother Fong heartily.

"Oh, Mother, you mustn't say that," protested Tom.

"When I go to join Tom's father, I shall feel good to know that you are taking care of him. I know his spirit will be happy in the other world when he learns this news. He always thought a great deal of you."

Mother Fong's eyes filled a little at this moment of her happiness.

"Why, Mother, this is a happy occasion!" said Eva.

"I just want you not to forget. Where would we all be if it had not been for your father? At times like this, I don't know why . . ."

"Mother," said Eva, "I know you are going to cry at the wedding."

When the nurse came in with a tray holding the chicken soup, Mother Fong stood up and helped serve it to Elsie.

"This is fairy chicken. I chose it myself and prepared it specially for you."

"Oh, Mother Fong, you shouldn't!"

When Elsie tasted the first mouthful, she felt a sensation that put her spirit at ease. There are moments in life when the spirit is uplifted because of a sense of perfection. Whether that perfection is in color or sound or form or taste, the effect of supreme fitness and spiritual uplift is the same.

"Mother Fong, that chicken has not died in vain," said Elsie.

"What do you mean?"

"I can imagine the spirit of the chicken saying to herself, 'I never realized I was that good until Mother Fong cooked me.'" They laughed as she went on, "I have read that the duty of a cook is to bring out the particular talent of a meat or vegetable. If he fails, it is plain murder to kill a cow or a chicken. If he succeeds, then even the spirit of the animal will be satisfied, because the best in him has been brought out. The poet says that is the only way we can justify killing an animal for food and atone for the sin."

"Who said that?" asked Tom.

"Yuan Mei. I suppose you would call him Yun Moy."

"You are a wise girl," said Mother Fong.

"Tom, you must taste this. See if it is not chicken at its best."

"Well, that comes of your marrying into a restaurant keeper's family," said Tom.

"What did you do to the chicken?" Elsie asked Mother Fong. "Twice in my life I have tasted chicken like that. Once in Soochow and the second time today."

"What did I do?" the mother replied. "It was nothing. All I did was to choose the right chicken and time the cooking. When a chicken is very young, just the right age, properly fed and freshly killed, it is good by itself. All a cook needs to do is to attend to the timing. Perfect timing, that is the whole secret. You must marry right away, and I'll teach you myself."

"No, Mother," said Tom quickly. "We're both at college. I won't marry until I can support her."

"Tom, what are you talking about?" The mother's voice suddenly hardened. "You are twenty-one, and you should be married."

"I am only twenty, Mother."

"No, you are twenty-one. I say you are twenty-one this year. The New Year has just passed."

"My birthday is still several months away."

"You are following the Americans. They get one all confused. One member of the family increases his age in May, another in June, another in July. How can one ever keep track of it? I say you are twenty-one and Elsie is twenty-two."

Mother Fong's tone made it very final. When she mentioned Elsie's age, she looked at her and Elsie understood what she meant. The look seemed to say that Mother Fong had never heard of a girl reaching the age of twenty-two without being married, unless she were pock-marked or hare-lipped.

2

Elsie went back to Mrs. Yang and continued her course at college. She and Tom were both busy, and time flew very quickly.

"Elsie, you don't have to hurry back for supper," said Mrs. Yang. "Just give me a ring, and we'll not wait for you."

But Mother Fong did not let them alone. Tom's idea that he should not marry before he was graduated and could support himself was a kind of heresy to Mother Fong. But besides that, perhaps there was also the fact that Mother Fong was getting old and, like all aged parents, lived for the day when all her children should be married and responsibility could be passed on to them to begin their lives and build their own families. Mother Fong was becoming impatient even about Eva, and on this subject she spoke with unusual heat. Tom saw she was not to be denied the pleasure of his wedding in the immediate future.

"When you and Eva are well married, I shall close my eyes in peace."

It was a flat statement of a psychological fact.

"But, Mother, it isn't right!" said Tom.

"What isn't right?"

"To marry before I can support myself."

Mother Fong flared up again. "Fine, fine! So you want to be independent! Go and support yourself at college! Who is supporting you now? I feed you. Can't I feed my own daughter-in-law? You have no sense of obligation to your family. A young one trying to fly away from its nest before its feathers are dry!"

"Mother, I really don't mean that."

"What do you mean? Are you too proud to let your wife become a part of the family?"

"No, Mother, but—"

She would not let him finish. "You are an American! That's what you are."

"Mother, I mean she is studying, and I am studying."

"And who says a man and a woman cannot study when they are married?"

"She is living up there with Mrs. Yang where she is comfortable. If I marry, we'll have to rent a room."

"Can't she come back to Chinatown and you two live together in her old room? A girl should marry when she is twenty-two. No girl of twenty-two is really interested in books. They study to occupy themselves until they can get a husband and a home. Tom, listen to your old mother. I have lived old enough to know. Don't try to fool nature. I have to think of Eva, too. You have no idea how quickly a girl grows up."

3

Two months later, Tom received his first letter from Elsie's mother, and in it she formally accepted the proposal for his marriage with her daughter. Mrs. Yang, as **the** go-between, came to see Tom's mother, and the formalities of an engagement were completed.

"Elsie, what are we going to do?" asked Tom. "I can't argue with my mother. She wants us to get married as soon as we can get ready. Do you mind?"

Elsie thought a little while. Her whole woman's instinct told her that she was ready, that she would be happy to have a home and a man to look after and to look after her.

"Perhaps your mother is right," she said. "We can take the room here. That's simple enough. I shall earn my upkeep by teaching, and you can go on with your studies. You know, Tom, your mother is a very wise woman. She is thinking of Eva's marriage now. I think that is as it should be. My own mother always told me that she believes in early marriage. And when we are married, you must let me take care of you from then on."

Tom had a sudden feeling that his world was being run by women; one woman was passing on the responsibility to another. Through all his childhood and his growing years, his mother had decided what he was to do, and now here was Elsie, ready to guide him through the rest of his life.

"Elsie, I ought to be grateful to my father and mother," he said gravely.

"We both ought to be grateful to our parents," she replied.

4

Some time later, Eva wrote to Freddie, who was working in the office of an agent for steamships and marine insurance in Chicago's Chinatown:

Dear Yiko:

Many things are happening to our family now, and it makes me sad to feel that you alone are living away from us. Tom and

Elsie are going to get married this summer. It was Mother's idea. Mother is growing old and her hair is showing more white, but she is still the same and in good health. Tom didn't really want to get married while he is still at college, but Mother would not hear of it. She was actually sore at Tom when he refused at first. Well, you know Mother. She got quite mad at me and Flora and called us *fankwei* when we said it is the modern idea that a man should not marry till he can support his wife. The idea seemed outrageous to her. That is why, she says, so many men and women in America are unmarried.

Yiko, what do you think? I am perhaps too young to understand, but Mother is sure she is doing the right thing. It is all wrong in this country, she says. The men don't live with their parents in old age, and their parents don't want to live with them. The children don't support their parents, and the parents don't want their children to support them. That is why you see so many old men and women still working as elevatormen and washwomen when their sons are already earning money. Mother calls it silly and criminal. I am in between, and I can see both sides.

Well, we all had to yield to Mother. Tom will wait till the end of the term when they will have more time to fix up a new home. I can just see their room full of wires!

What I am writing you about is a secret which we are keeping from Mother. Her sixty-first birthday is coming on April 29th. Yiko, you must come. We are going to celebrate, and the party will be incomplete without you. Don't tell Mother, but when you appear, it will make her so happy to see the family reunited. Daiko and Tom and I are all planning. If you can come a few days ahead, you can be of great help. Daiko and Tom and Mother wish me to tell you that we all miss you.

Love from

Eva

Freddie returned a week before the birthday. There was great excitement in the family. Somehow his separation from Sing Toy and his few months' absence made him seem closer to them. Their welcome was hearty and genuine.

"My son, you are looking a little thinner and darker," said the mother.

"How are you doing?" asked Loy.

"I'm doing fine. Never felt better in my life. There is a lot of money in marine insurance."

Still the same Yiko, Tom thought, expansive once more, and in fairness to him, it must be said that he truly loved his family.

"Yiko, you never answered my letter," said Eva reproachfully.

"Didn't I?"

"Nothing except a short note to say you were coming."

"Well, I've come, haven't I? I will get two tables of guests myself. We must make it big."

"What tables? Make what big?" asked Mother Fong, puzzled.

"Your birthday! It is your sixty-first," they all burst out, looking fondly at their mother.

"It is good of you, my children, to remember it," she said, "but you shouldn't spend too much."

"When will a sixty-first birthday come again?" replied Eva. By all established tradition, the sixty-first, marking a new decade, was a "great birthday," overshadowed only by the seventy-first, and the eighty-first, which are rare.

"All expenses mine," said Freddie.

"No, we will all share," said Loy.

That night Flora said to her husband, "Freddie is a big-hearted fellow after all. But we should all share the expenses. I am thinking of setting aside one hundred and fifty dollars for the party. We can well afford it. But I'm glad, Loy, that you didn't tell him the truth about how much we have made, when he asked you."

"We just couldn't afford to," replied Loy. "If he knew how much we have saved—how much have we saved?"

302

"We have nearly five thousand dollars." There were pride and exultation in Flora's voice.

"You must go out and get yourself a new dress for the party, and get Eva one too. And, Flora, there is that ring you have been thinking about all these years."

"Oh, Loy!" Flora cried. "Do you really mean it? Do you think I should ask Mother first?"

"No. It is our money. Buy it first and tell Mother afterward. She knows you deserve it."

Flora gave her husband an ardent hug and kiss.

The next day she went out in the morning with Eva and got for herself a new rayon dress in black and peach, while Eva chose a blue dress. Then they went to a jeweler's shop, and Flora bought a diamond ring for five hundred dollars. As they left the shop with the little box in her bag, she gave a happy sigh.

As soon as they returned to the restaurant, Eva exclaimed, "Mother, we bought a ring for Flora! It's a beauty."

Hesitantly Flora opened the box and showed it to Mother Fong. "I have waited for it so long, Mother," she said. "I hope you approve."

"How much did it cost?"

"Five hundred dollars. It is more than a carat," Flora said, looking anxiously at the mother. "It was from our savings."

"Put it on, put it on," said Mother Fong.

As Flora slipped the ring on, her smile told of endless satisfaction.

"It is becoming on you," said Mother Fong, looking kindly at her daughter-in-law. "You deserve it, my dear."

5

The invitations went out, and a few days before the birthday presents began to pour in. Freddie had rounded up the leaders of Chinatown, which gave the family much face.

The day arrived, and Mother Fong felt truly happy with all her children by her side. The dinner was given at the Pacific because their own restaurant was too small. All the members of the family appeared in their best clothes. The restaurant shone with the red and gold of silk festoons and ceremonial scrolls. On such an occasion, hearts were gay and everybody wore a smile. The sons and daughters of a parent were supposed to be dashing about in their joy, grateful that their parent had arrived at this venerable age. Marco, a little child of two, was dressed like a China doll, trotting about in a "tiger hat" that they had been able to find in a neighboring store. It would have been jollier if there had been a half dozen or a dozen grandchildren. But Mother Fong was satisfied. She had three sons and a daughter, all doing well. The occasion was proof that she had raised a successful family, which was as much happiness as one dared to hope for in a world full of tricky pitfalls and sad failures. Toasts were drunk to her, and since it would have been discourteous to leave any of the China-town leaders out of the speechmaking, there were more than a dozen eulogies of her virtue as a mother.

The most important speech, as usual, was that of Old Tuck. After the polite preliminaries, he said, "My friends, we all want to live long on this earth. I have been doing some thinking in these last twelve years and want to tell you some of the results of my thinking. But let me first tell you a story.

"Twenty-five hundred years ago, there was a very old man. He was a contemporary of Confucius and of Laotse. He was over ninety when Laotse, then a young man, went to see him. The old man had white hair and rosy cheeks, and Laotse was greatly impressed. Laotse asked him what was the secret of his long life, and he opened his mouth wide and told Laotse to look into it. 'Are my teeth gone?' he asked.

"Laotse looked and said, 'They are pretty nearly gone.'

" 'How about my tongue?'

" 'It is still perfect,' answered Laotse.

" 'Remember this,' the old man said. 'The hard and brittle breaks, but the gentle survives. That is the secret of my long life.'

"Life is a wonderful gift, and none of us is quite willing to relinquish it. All of us want to live long, and some of us want to live forever. There is the immortality of the spirit, there is the immortality of work, and there is the immortality of the race. Chuangtse calls death the 'great journey home'; that is immortality of the spirit. Laotse says, 'A man lives long when he dies and yet remains with us'; that is immortality of work. Confucius says, 'Keep the ancestral altar fire burning'; that is immortality of the race.

"I know we all want to live long, to live forever. But Nature takes care of that, except that we don't know it. Every oak tree is immortal, so is every apple tree. It dies but its kind goes on forever. When the old tree dies, the sapling grows up. I used to wonder why Nature does not just provide for a tree, or an elephant, or a man who never grows old and dies. I think I understand now. Laotse says, 'When a baby is born, he is soft and pliant; when a man dies, his body is stiff.' And it is not his body only, but his spirit grows stiff also as he gets along in years. Nature does not want that. For even as a child grows into maturity, he becomes fit for certain things, but in becoming fit for certain things he becomes unfit for others. A man forms certain habits of mind; he is no longer fresh and pliable and adaptable to change. Stiffness means incapacity for growth and change and progress and adventure. If you tell me today to lead a band of compatriots across the Wyoming wilds, I can't do it. Not only can't I do it, but my spirit refuses to do it. And so Nature provides for immortality of the race by providing for eternal youth in the young who come after us. When the old dog's bones grow stiff and he loses his freshness, the young puppy takes his place. That is how Nature keeps herself forever young. That is Nature's provision against hardening and stiffness and Nature's secret of eternal youth. I must say it is a pretty good scheme.

"I drink to Mother Fong and her children and her grandchild, Marco, and to the immortality of Tom Fong, my friend."

At the end of the dinner, Mother Fong was slightly drunk. Several of the speakers also referred to the Italian daughter-in-law as one who knew how to "help her husband and run the affairs of the family." All Chinatown knew that she was a good wife and a good daughter-in-law. "That is what keeps society in order," said Old Tuck solemnly.

The next day, at Mother Fong's order, the family went to visit the father's grave in Brooklyn. Mother Fong had insisted that, since Freddie was usually away, they should take this occasion to go together. It was only four or five days before the second anniversary of Father Fong's death. How much had happened since then!

During the dinner Mother Fong had said, "Elsie, you had better come along." So for the first time Elsie took her station as a member of the family. She wore a cotton print dress in white and black, cut in the Chinese style.

The restaurant was closed for the day and Uncle Chan left his shop and went with them. They took along a pewter pot of rice wine, a basket of fruit and nuts, and a great bouquet of fresh flowers. Freddie brought his camera.

They hired taxicabs, crossed the Brooklyn Bridge, and turned north until they came to a large cemetery situated in bare country.

The family filed in and came to the Western-style grave, lying close to many others with very little space between them. They laid the fruit and nuts and flowers before the tombstone, and Daiko, as the eldest son, poured the rice wine on the grave as a libation. Mother Fong knelt down and wept bitterly. The others knelt too, including Flora, but only Eva wept aloud. Elsie, who did not quite know what she should do, remained standing, holding Marco by the hand, and watched. After a few minutes, Mother Fong stood up, breathing hard and keeping silent, and then the others rose.

The tombstone was a square slab, with Chinese characters in vertical columns. In the center were the words, "Here rests our deceased father, Tom Fong of Sunwei." The names of the sons and daughter and grandchild of Tom Fong were listed in the left column. Pointing to them, Mother Fong said, "We ought soon to have more grandchildren's names there. At this age, I have only Marco. Elsie, I depend on you."

Elsie blushed.

Flora stood trying to read the hieroglyphics.

"Where is Marco's name?" she asked.

"It is down there at the bottom."

As they stood about the tombstone, Freddie took out a light-meter and held it before their faces.

"Let's take a photograph for a souvenir," he said.

He set up his tripod while the group arranged themselves around the stone, the mother and Uncle Chan in the center, Loy and Flora and Eva and Marco on one side, and Tom standing with Elsie on the other.

"Eva, you come over to stand beside me," said Freddie. "Remember the picture we took on the dock when you arrived? You and Tom were just kids then."

"Yes, and you put your arms around us. It seems such a long time ago."

When the camera was focused and the exposure set, Freddie set the self-timer and dashed back to his place. The camera clicked. A spring breeze blew softly across the grass, and it seemed at that moment that the spirit of their father was with them.

As they turned away, Tom and Elsie walked behind Mother Fong. Eva was assisting her. When they reached the gate, Mother Fong turned and said to Tom and Elsie, "And now I have to think of Eva."